DELIA'S *Song*

Lucha Corpi

Arte Publico Press

Houston, Texas

This volume is made possible by a grant from the National Endowment for the Arts, a federal agency.

Arte Publico Press
University of Houston
Houston, Texas 77004

Corpi, Lucha. 1945-
    Delia's song: a novel / by Lucha Corpi.
        p.   cm.
    ISBN 0-934770-82-4
    I. Title.
PS3553.0693D4   1989
813'.54—dc19   88-9401
                                        CIP

This work is dedicated to all the Chicano students who participated in the Third World Strike, at the University of California at Berkeley, with my deepest gratitude. Without their courage and determination my son, Arturo, most likely would not now be a senior and a Regents' Scholar at U. C. Berkeley.

I would also like to thank the staff of the Chicano Studies Library on the Berkeley Campus for allowing me to pry into their archives; Norma Alarcón, Yvonne Yarbro-Bejarano, Barbara Brinson-Curiel, Martaivón Galindo, Francisco Alarcón, Chuff Aflerbach, James Opiat and Mark Greenside for their invaluable feedback and support.

I

Faithful to the essence of the name given me at birth
through the meandering creeks of feelings
and the hard winding roads of reason
I seek the elusive pair—love
and truth—for I was also meant to hunt light
blue and red and sometimes blinding yellow

Chapter 1

*Yellow fire   Yellow fire   Endless fire   Walls
of fire   Darkness   Campanile   one   You
killed him two Who are you   three   You killed him
four   I didn't I didn't   five   He was coming at
me and I hit him but I didn't kill him   six   Tell them
father tell them seven Blades shining in the dark   Run
Run   Ruuuuuun   eight Can't you see him   Look
He's there   Fernando Fernando Tell them you're alive
nine   She tried to kill me Get her ten Your time is UP
GET HER   RIP HER OPEN   NO-O-O-O-O-O-O-O
WAKE UP   WAKE UP   Wake up   It's only a
dream   No No They're coming   Dwinelle Hall is
burning   Walls of yellow fire Fire   Fire   They're
coming Samuel   Samuel   Don't hit back   Get
arrested   Where's Jeff   Mattie   I Can't breeeathe
Yellow   Fire   Fire   M o th e r Pray Delia Ask
for forgiveness   Our Father   Yellow fire Our Father
who   art   Fire   In   Heaven   No   escape
Burning Burning AAAAaaaayyyy*

Delia sat up in bed, her body shaking, perspiration and tears
mingling on her face. Her eyes were wide open, yet she was unable
to see anything but the darkness around her. Little by little, the
darkness became populated by the shape of familiar objects in her
room. She leaned back on the pillow and took a deep breath, held it
in as long as she could, then got up and turned the light on.

She went over her dream, piecing it together in an effort to get
at its meaning. *No point in writing it down   It's just like all
the others   Meaningless   Just the same old nightmare*
Her legs and arms ached, but her heart had slowed its pace. She
looked at the clock; it was ten past ten. *No wonder it's already*

dark   Been asleep four hours   That tenuous line between dream and awakening   Danger zone   Maybe that's what insomniacs fear She went into the shower, stayed under the warm water for a long time, and emerged from it somewhat calmer.

She applied a bit of rouge and mascara, and reached into the cosmetic basket for a lipstick, but withdrew her hand immediately. *I keep forgetting nuns don't wear lipstick*

She pulled the carmelite habit out of the closet and put it on. Securing her hair in a bun on the back of her head, she put the headdress on, pushing in a few rebellious strands. She pinned on the long black rosary, looked in her purse for her key ring, some money and her driver's license, and put them into her skirt pocket.

She stepped out onto the porch, put the key in and turned twice to lock the door, then went down the few steps to the sidewalk. *I better call Aunt Marta tomorrow*

She walked leisurely down College Avenue to Derby Street where her car was parked. It was a mid-autumn evening, and she welcomed the cool air on her face.

Her entire day had gone into filling out job applications, and writing her vitae, a tedious task she intended to complete the next afternoon only because the idea of leaving something unfinished bothered her more than monotony.

We're lost Paula We're going to be late   Relax We're almost there Yes I think There's the Arco station No Wait It was a Shell station I'm sure It's somewhere around here Look there's the bus Let's get on We can ask the driver   We don't even know where it's going   Oh Delia Com'on It'll be fun It's Saturday We don't have to be back home until four   I don't know Com'on So what if we don't make it to the party No Don't tell me You told Candy you would be there   That's right   You can call her later   It was fun all right   It was always fun with Paula   Knowing where we started from but never where we would end up   I envy her   Pack a few things and go Leave everything as it is   The applications on the desk The hairbrush still full of hair on the dresser   Mother The tiny cactus that blooms in February   Father   The spider plant They would die without someone watering them She vanished No trace of Delia   Someone saw her in Morocco a month ago   It can't be Daniel and Lydia were honeymooning in Quito only last week They say they saw a woman who looked like her I got a letter from Paula She says Delia went to visit her in Pakistan Paula Will she ever come back   Our last summer in Monterey Monterey   Should really go home   I don't want to go home Better stay in Monterey for a couple of weeks   The cypress towers blue in the mist   Its twisted roots probe the rocky soil for nourishment   Trade beauty for survival

Delia was not even sure she would mail some of the applications. Other than teaching—and she had no desire to become a teacher—there was little else to do with a degree in literature. She had been a part-time secretary on campus for many years and knew she could always find a job in an office, but that prospect did not seem very attractive either.

Berkeley   Mournful blues of a guitar   Black man on   the   steps   of   Sproul   Hall On the steps of Sproul Hall   Sproul Hall   Nine years of my life like graffiti scribbled with invisible ink on the walls   I was there   We were there but no one knew us

Delia had come to Berkeley in the fall of 1968 as a freshman, full of plans—finish her degree, support her parents, do something for people in the barrio, marry and have a family. Nine years later, at age 28, she had achieved only one of her goals, a degree that seemed as useless as it had been hard to obtain.

Second day of November   1977   I can hardly support myself   What am I going to do   Professor Ruvalcaba You don't have to be creative Just finish the damned dissertation   People will treat you with respect   What people   Who   The same professors who witnessed the beatings and the gassing and went on with their daily lives as if nothing was happening What do I care   Shapeless entities That's what we were for them No history   No destiny   Is that who Professor Ruvalcaba How can two letters placed before my name suddenly validate my existence Erase the pain Do away with betrayal Mend the broken dreams   You Chicanos are so afraid of succcess I thought you were different

9

You   Chicanos   What   is   he   Success   Success
Success   Dreams built on shifting sand   Dr Delia
Treviño   Delia   Treviño   comma   Ph   D   I   hate
it   Hate it   I have to get out of Berkeley

Delia turned the corner slowly onto Derby Street. Her car was parked a few feet away. The solitary rosebush on the lawn across the street caught her eye. She crossed over to look closely at it. Despite the fury of the wind and the rain the night before, one rose still clung to a naked branch. *The solitary rose in November Collective memory of spring on a bare limb* Except for the ghost-like presence of the rose, the night seemed empty of images or sounds. The semi-darkness around her held neither horrors nor dreams.

Delia let her hand slide toward her skirt pocket. She touched the rosary. Its beads were cold and smooth. She played with them and almost automatically began to pray.

Our   Father   Our   Father   who   wh
Yellow fire   Fire Burning   Burning   Blades
shining in the dark   They're coming!

She closed her eyes and the darkness in her mind burst into lights—red, then green, then yellow. All the yellow lights converged into one that turned faster and faster until it became a whirl darkening with every spin to total blackness. She felt empty inside, a carcass floating in a dark space. Only her legs and her stomach tingled in expectation of the fall she knew would follow.

On   strike   Shut   it   down   On   strike   Jeff
Morones is an FBI plant   Bring in the Brown Berets   I
know how to shoot Go back to your cactus and sombrairos fucking
bastards   What are you doing with that gun   Get out
of my way   Listen we're not in Korea Viet Nam vato We don't
shoot anyone cabrón   Give me the gun   Be careful
He's going to do something crazy   No he's not You're not
going to shoot anyone   Take him home I'll take him home A
few toques of the yerba santa   That's what he needs Here
carnal   Will you be all right Julio   Sure man Don't
worry We lived through the hell in Korea This ain't nothing man
nothing I'll take him home   Are you okay Delia   Yeah
I'm okay   You sure   Just shook up That's all I'd never
seen a gun before Do you think he'll use it   No It was just a

flashback I think What's a flashback   The war you know It happens You mean he thought he was back in Korea Something like that   No   one   needs   to   know   No one   Flashback   Is that what's happening Where am I then   No No   They're coming   Why Why Yellow fire   Yellow fire   It's burning   It's burning Yellow fire   Walls of fire My God   Our Father who Our Father You'll pay for this   All of you   Get her Get her

Loud whispers muffled her prayers until she could no longer hear herself. She began to raise her tone to drown out the other voices. *Our Father who art Our Father In Heaven* She couldn't go beyond the first few words. She shouted them over and over, tried to hang onto them and to the beads and the crucifix, but the gravitational force of a bottomless abyss was pulling her, and she was turning, falling endlessly. *Mother Mother*

A moment later, the thump of her body hitting the ground told her the pit wasn't bottomless. *Papá hold me   Hold me* She was lying on the cold ground of a November night; she felt no pain, had no desire to move. The whispers were dying down. Then there was total silence and coldness.

"Sister, are you all right?" she heard someone saying and she opened her eyes. "Let me help you up." A man was kneeling in front of her, shaking her lightly as if to bring her back to her senses from a nightmare or a bout of hysteria.

Delia felt the warmth of the man's hands on her arms. She shivered. In that short time, she had grown accustomed to the coldness of her own flesh and blood, and his warmth shocked her into an undesired acknowledgment of pain. She pulled away from his grip and extended her hands as a signal for him to help her up.

"I'm all right," she said and repeated the phrase louder in an effort to convince herself that she was in control again.

She couldn't see his face well in the dim street light, but she made out the outlines of a hat, glasses and a moustache. *I know him   No I don't   Get away   Where are my keys* The palms of his hands felt somewhat rough, but their backs were smooth. *Interesting* She liked touching his hands as much as she had feared their warmth a moment ago.

"Are you feeling better now?" the man asked, and she nodded. "What happened?" His tone was pleasant but there was a trace of clinical concern in it. He had turned and was facing the light more directly. A similar face but from a different angle flashed in her memory and quickly disappeared. *I know him*

"I don't know." She was annoyed at his questioning. "I don't," she repeated in a gentler manner, "but I'm grateful." *No I don't know him*

"I don't mean to intrude but . . . "*Here it comes* He made no effort to continue. *What's he waiting for   My God he could be a rapist   No he isn't* He seemed to be sizing up the situation, asking himself whether he should press her for an answer. Delia thought he might be someone who dealt with delicate situations often. He inspired trust and she had to make an effort not to guess the rest of his question and offer an explanation. *A priest-Maybe   A psychiatrist   Am I going mad   For madwomen only   Dropping to my knees   Praying Was I praying   I can't even remember   What time is it*

That other familiar face flashed before her eyes again. *A photograph   Newspaper*   "Has your photo appeared in a magazine or newspaper recently?"

He was puzzled at her question for a second, but then seemed to remember something and began to laugh.

"I see." He pushed his glasses up. "You think you've seen me before . . . Yes, many people have seen my photo all over the world." He laughed again, took his hat off and placed it on his chest in a polite gesture. "I am James Joyce . . . At least for tonight I am Joyce."   *He's nuts   Where are my keys The car Did he say James Joyce   "And first I put my arms around him yes and drew him down to me so he could feel my breasts all perfume yes and his heart was going like mad and yes I said yes I will yes"   No   Yes   No I didn't hear right   Did he say James Joyce   No   Yes he said James Joyce   I'm sure*

Either his laughter was contagious or Delia needed a release from her previous state of mind, for soon she was laughing along with him.

"You don't mean . . . You can't mean the writer . . . *The*

James Joyce Don't you know you're dead? Dead!" She was laughing uncontrollably; her stomach felt weak; her cheeks were moist. She realized she had stopped laughing and perspiration and tears were running down her cheeks. She felt embarrassed and searched in her pocket for a handkerchief but couldn't find one. He offered his.

"Does this happen to you often?" *He thinks I'm crazy Don't laugh   You might upset him   Don't   What else could he thinks   We're both crazy   Mad   He* was now looking intently at her, pressing for an answer. She felt uneasy and avoided answering him.

"You mean meeting James Joyce?" She asked teasingly. *Why did I say that*

He smiled. "May I take you home?" He put his hat back on. "No, thank you. I have a car." *Don't go please   Don't go*

"Good night, then." He said as he turned around to leave.

Delia did not answer him. Somehow she had expected or perhaps wanted him to inquire further, but he was already walking away from her. She stood there watching the man who called himself James Joyce turn the corner two blocks down and disappear. She began to look for her car keys, found them and walked over to where her car was parked.

Disconcerted, she sat inside retracing the events of the last half hour. Meeting a man who dressed like Joyce was odd, but anyone who had lived in Berkeley for a few years was always ready for the unexpected. *Berkeley a King of Heart's delight or a town of collective loneliness depending on one's degree of mad sophistication* She laughed nervously at the thought but felt no relief.

For many years, as a child, she had experienced the same sensation of falling into an abyss just before sleep overtook her. She would start and wake up instantly, reassure herself she was still in her room, and go to sleep. But this time it was different; she had been wide-awake and she had prayed, or tried to, as if she had been in danger of being possessed by an awesome power and prayer had meant salvation.

I'm losing my mind She sucked in breath and exhaled it slowly to calm herself. *Now I'm living my nightmares* She felt flustered and lowered the window to let the cool air in. "This is silly," she told herself after a while, wiping her brow with the handkerchief Joyce had lent her. She examined it carefully, unfolded it and held it up with both hands against the light, as if she did not believe it was real, then smelled it. _In the odor of my skin at night I look for you_ She laughed.

In a way it had been a funny experience. She knew Joyce was dead, and the man she had just met was an impostor. Did he know she was an impostor, too, that Santa Teresa was also dead? Would he go home and tell his friends or his wife he had just met a nun who was going mad? Wasn't it just like Berkeley? Perhaps he did not even know where he was or thought he was still in Dublin.

She was laughing again, but this time she knew what she was laughing about, and the thought comforted her.

A young couple walking past her car looked at her, shrugged, and went indifferently on their way. She started the car. Mattie and her other friends would already be wondering why she was so late getting to the party.

Chapter 2

"You must restore the ban on grapes."

"You must understand the university is a public institution. It cannot take positions on public issues other than those directly related to its own welfare."

"The grape issue transcends political and even religious considerations. It's a human issue. We won't move until the ban on grapes is restored and UC increases the number of special admissions to reflect the ethnic make-up of California and sets up a Mexican-American study center. We won't move.   We can't."

"You leave me no choice."

"Since the students involved have a good history of working through channels and in a law abiding way, since they were not destructive in their conduct, and since they have already spent several days in custody, I have directed members of my staff to bring these facts to the attention of the Court, and urge the Court to give them due weight, as I am sure it will do. Chancellor Heyns and I agree that it would not be in the best interest of the University or the students concerned to have University disciplinary proceedings on this matter."

Mattie Johnson gave two parties a year, one for her Marxist-Leninist friends, and another, a costume party every second of November, for her academic colleagues and students. The convention this year was to dress as the writer or literary character each guest most admired. Attentive to detail, she had designed what she called "literary scapularies" where her guests would pin a picture of their chosen character on one side and the name on the flip side. From the moment they stepped in the door, they would be required to address one another by their assumed names.

Mattie was a vibrant woman who, contrary to the austere principles of the Socialist Alliance for Progress, indulged quite frequently in bourgeois pleasures. Her socialist friends frowned at her pleasure-seeking extravagance, and her academic friends were not totally pleased with her socialist practices, but no one questioned her dedication to either of her endeavors.

Everything Mattie did became special: helping to organize a workers' strike, coordinating an academic conference or staging a first meeting for two prospective lovers.

Mattie and Delia had met a few days after Delia had entered the university as a freshman.

"There's no Heaven and no Hell for us," Mattie told Delia the first time they talked. "Philosophers and psychiatrists have taken care of both. We can count only on our environment and economics. And we must carefully protect both."

"What about love?" Delia ventured to ask in that irritating student-addressing-teacher tone, meek yet arrogant, Mattie told Delia later.

Mattie simply looked at her. "Are we talking about anything else?"

Delia wanted to explain what she meant, but refrained. She had never been able to talk back to anyone, even when anger made her head throb. Her parents had taught her that keeping still in the face of argument was better.

She still remembered that afternoon her father had come home early. He had been unjustly fired from the factory, and when he had complained to his boss about it, the man had threatened to give him bad references and had thrown his severance check on the floor. *You shouldn't have said anything Te lo dije José Guadlupe Maybe they would have let you go on working*

The image of a broken man, walking with his head bowed, rushed through Delia's mind. Mattie was her professor. What if Delia questioned her authority? She couldn't risk a bad grade, so she kept quiet and listened to Mattie.

"When we talk about a better world for our children and their children, and all the people we love, we usually mean a good and safe environment, and the money to pursue their interests. However materialistic that may be, it is the way we express our love and concern." Mattie was going to continue but she saw the pained look in Delia's eyes. She wished Delia would open up to her. At the first class meeting, she had told her students they could speak frankly to her without fear of reprisal. Delia stood before her reserved, poised and inaccessible. Mattie wondered how long Delia would be able to resist confrontation.

"What do you think?" Mattie asked. Delia wanted to respond with an intelligent argument, but could not bring herself to do it. She had always managed to avoid discussing any issue that would require a strong position on her part. *We take everything they dish out and look what it's got us   Sebastian don't talk like that Lies   They're all lies   Why do I expect her to be different   Sister Marguerite   Delia Delia you got the scholarship You're going to Berkeley To Berkeley Why are you crying   You should be happy You've worked so hard for this   What if they take it away   They won't   I don't want to go   But you must You must prove to them that you can You owe it to your parents Sebastian God be merciful is gone You must go to Berkeley Prove*

"I don't know," Delia said and felt angry at herself for not saying what she thought, and at Mattie for forcing the issue.

"Don't you think that everyone has a right to a safe environment and to an equal share in the benefits of his labor?" Mattie insisted.

There was ineluctable logic in Mattie's words—platitudes, Delia thought. She had heard them all her life, but was it really so? Did all people in the U.S. share alike? She and her family had had few choices. She was at Berkeley because an Anglo nun in high school had managed to open some doors for her.

Her brother, Sebastián, had not been so lucky and had died of a drug overdose in a damp, putrid-smelling shooting gallery. Her second brother, Ricardo, had gone into the Army because he was afraid he would suffer the same fate as Sebastián.

"What a choice," she had told Ricardo when they kissed for the last time. "You either die like Sebastián or you die on a battlefield."

Ricardo smiled and tried to be hopeful. "There won't be a war, *hermanita*, and I might just come back with a career." A year later, he was lying dead in a swamp in Southeast Asia.

Delia felt a pang of anger. *What does she know about me and my people   Does she really care* "For the Mexican-American there are no choices," she uttered in anger and her tone surprised and scared her; yet she felt exhilarated.

"Good. You're angry." Mattie smiled. "But you are a part of this system, and you have to fight back, if it's telling you that you're not."

Delia was surprised at Mattie's attitude. She had expected, even wanted, a rebuttal so that she could vent her anger. Instead, she heard herself asking, "How does anyone deal with it?"

Mattie looked at the clock on the wall, scribbled something on a piece of paper, and handed it to Delia. "Begin by studying the problem, then write a paper on the socio-economic status of the Mexican-American in the United States. Here, see Samuel Corona at Eshleman Hall. He's a graduate student in the Sociology Department. He can help you." And she rushed out.

Delia stayed in Mattie's office for a while. Her anger and fear were giving way to a feeling of dissatisfaction. For the first time she had dared to confront authority, but still had to be led to the answers instead of actively pursuing them. She felt better when she could just observe and judge things without having to become involved in them, but also disliked herself for her lack of assurance. None of that had any bearing on her discussion with Mattie, she told herself.

She went home that day wanting to believe that Professor Mattie N. Johnson was just another *gringa* with exclusive, personalized ideas neatly embroidered on her academic sleeve to show her professed devotion to mankind. But she did write the paper for Mattie's class, although it proved to be the most frustrating task she would ever encounter during her student years.

She spent countless hours searching through the library to find only one book and a journal article that dealt with the history or sociology of the Mexican-American in the United States, neither one by a Mexican-American author.

Not wanting to accept defeat, Delia decided not to seek Mattie's help, but went to see Samuel Corona, as Mattie had suggested.

"Now you know where it's at," Samuel said after Delia explained her problem, his small eyes narrowing almost to lines below his thick brows. "It isn't the Afro-American who's invisible; it's the Mexican-American people, a curtain of air the white man cuts through on his way to his Manifest Destiny."

"More like cockroaches," said another student, wearing a cowboy hat with a red button that said *Boycott Grapes* in black letters. He was standing a short distance from them. "Turn on the light and they disappear. Now you see them, now you don't, but they're there, waiting." He laughed. "I'm Jeff Morones," he added, moving closer to Delia.

"Delia Treviño. Nice to meet you," she said and looked around the room. She noticed Jeff looking intently at her and lowered her eyes. *Is my zipper down   My period   No He's looking   at   me   Good-looking   Boycott   Grapes Cowboy hats and boots   Aunt Marta Jeff is coming with me Yeah I'm happy How stupid can you be   Already making plans   Turn   around   a   little   Move   your   hand— Don't let him see you Now   It's not my zipper*

Samuel went into a cubicle that served as his office in Eshleman Hall, a building where most of the student organizations were housed, and came back a few minutes later with a two-page bibliography of books and journals about *Chicanos*. Delia had heard the term Chicano before, but wasn't sure about its meaning. *Chicanos Chicanery   No   Mexican   Mechicas   The Aztecs   That's what Sister Marguerite said they called themselves   That   must   be   it Me-chicanos   Maybe Not an elegant word   What's this about Chicanos I'm not a Chicano We're Mexican American   Ricardo   Was so upset   Mr Martinez was just teasing him   Mexican American   That's worse Chicanos   Yes   Chicano   Brown Dark sun*

Delia looked briefly at the two sheets of paper, then inquisitively at Samuel.

"Yes. That's all they have in the libraries here," Samuel said, answering Delia's unspoken question. "If you find any others, give

Jeff the titles, authors and publishers." He looked at Jeff. "You can pass them on to Mattie Johnson. She'll request them for reference."

"I'm taking a class from her. I could give them to her if you like," Delia offered.

"Are you going to major in history?" Samuel asked.

"Maybe . . . I don't know yet." Delia paused, then added, "I'm more interested in literature."

"That sounds great." Samuel was enthusiastic.

"Bullshit!" someone said behind her and Delia turned around to look at the newcomer. "Bullshit! We need lawyers and social workers."

"Just because they wouldn't publish your 'Conga Songs.' " Jeff laughed, turned to Delia and pointed at the other student. "Meet Julio, our *Chicano Bard*."

"*Wátchate, vato*. One of these days, *cabrón*." Ignoring Delia, Julio turned around and stormed out of the office.

"Julio is okay," Samuel told Delia. "I'm afraid his poems are not."

"Maybe they're the best he can do." The words poured out of Delia, much to her surprise, but she was pleased with herself at having said them. *Whatever they think   I said what I think*

Samuel and Jeff looked at each other, lowered their heads, raised their eyebrows and nodded, turned toward her and smiled.

"It's a pleasure to meet you, Delia Treviño." Samuel began to walk back to his cubicle.

Jeff was disappointed and trying desperately to find a pretext to see her again. "Maybe Delia would be interested in joining MASC," he suggested to Samuel.

"What's MASK? M-A-S-K?"

"The Mexican-American Student Confederation," Jeff added in haste.

"Mexican-American, not Chicano?" Delia asked, looking at Samuel, then at Jeff.

Samuel's eyes lit up; obviously pleased at Delia's comment he said, "You have to join. We need you."

"We've been trying to convince the others to say Chicano instead of Mexican-American, but some don't like it," Jeff explained to Delia, who nodded, but couldn't quite figure out the implications of all that was being said.

"I . . ." Delia hesitated. "What does MASC do?"

Jeff was going to explain, but Samuel cut him off. "Come to the next meeting and find out."

Delia was taken aback by Samuel's commanding tone, but was not annoyed. There was no trace of condescension or defiance in his reply. She liked not being treated as a youngster who couldn't decide what to do, as had been the case with the graduate students who were teaching assistants in two of her classes. She found Samuel's attitude toward her flattering.

"Are you the president of MASC?" she asked Samuel.

Jeff laughed. "No. He's our intellectual flunkie," he said. "Our 'boy genius.' "

"I'm Nobody," Samuel said laughing, too.

"Ulysses Chicano himself." They laughed.

Ulysses   Odysseus   Intellectual   flunkie
They're good friends   Ricardo and Sebastián used to do that
Tease each other   More like brothers

"I'm not the president of MASC. We have no president, but we have a chairman and that's Manuel Delgado," Samuel explained.

"Will you come to the next meeting?" Jeff asked Delia, handing her a slip where he had noted the date, time and place for the meeting.

"Yes, I'll go." Delia put the slip into her purse. "Thanks for the bibliography," she said to Samuel.

Samuel was pleased. In his characteristic manner, he quickly reviewed Delia's qualities—quiet-mannered and soft-spoken but aware of her own mind, compassionate, unaffected, disciplined, quick-minded, thirsty for knowledge, interested in literature, beauty. Yes, he told himself, she would be an excellent addition to the group and they would be good for her. He had plans for her. There was only one thing that disturbed him about her, a sadness in her eyes that, no matter how much she tried to hide it, was there even when she smiled.

Unaware of Samuel's thoughts but sharing some of his concern, Jeff watched Delia put the bibliography into her binder, and he found himself almost wishing that she would drop it so that he could pick it up and stand very close to her. He wanted to look into her eyes and perhaps discover for himself the story he sensed she was afraid to tell. But Delia tucked the sheets neatly into the pocket of the binder and shut it. She turned around, looked over her shoulders to say goodbye to him, then walked out of the room.

It would be a week before the next MASC meeting and that already seemed so long to Jeff. The next day, he paid a visit to Mattie Johnson on the pretext of checking on the status of the books they had ordered, but he hoped to find out more about Delia from her. He was disappointed when he realized that, although Delia had made a good impression on her, Mattie knew very little about Delia's background.

"A very bright girl, very mature. Perhaps too mature . . . Beautiful, too." Mattie winked at Jeff.

Jeff pretended not to notice Mattie's gesture. "*El compadre* Samuel and I invited her to the next MASC meeting."

"Good idea. I hope it helps," Mattie said. "She seems to be looking for something other than making the grades and then the money," she added. "I just wish she would open up. I don't know what her story is, but it must be a heavy one and she's been carrying it for a long time."

Jeff nodded and a while later left Mattie's office as intrigued as he had been when he came. Mattie smiled and told him she would keep him posted about the books and other pressing "affairs." Jeff rightly interpreted her last comment as news about Delia, but his instinct told him that it would take a long time before either one of them was able to break through Delia's defenses. No matter how long it took, he would find a way to get closer to Delia, he promised himself.

Mattie's curiosity had been piqued from that first time she had talked to Delia, and that was reason enough to try to establish closer contact with her. More than that, it was Mattie's intuition that told her Delia was walking an emotional tightrope, a condition that could be aggravated by all the pressures students normally faced at Berkeley, pressures that had driven some of them to mental breakdown or physical collapse.

Mattie was also concerned about Delia's possible involvement in the potentially explosive and almost inevitable confrontation between MASC students and the administration. MASC had recently asked for the removal of grapes from the dining commons, in support of the United Farmworkers' boycott of agricultural products, and the establishment of a Mexican-American Studies Center on campus. The university administration was reluctant to grant either one of the students' demands.

Unaware of the feelings of protectiveness she had aroused in Mattie, Samuel's plans for her or Jeff's interest in her, Delia was walking to the one-bedroom apartment she shared with Sara González. They had met while standing in line at the Registrar's Office two weeks after Delia's arrival on campus.

Sister Marguerite had arranged for Delia to live in the house of a woman on Piedmont Avenue in exchange for housekeeping, but Delia wasn't happy there because the woman drank too much and often burst into her room in the middle of the night, demanding that Delia clean this or that mess.

Not having any other friends on campus, she had told Sara about her problem. Sara had just rented a one-bedroom apartment and was looking for someone to share it with her, so she suggested that Delia move in immediately and Delia accepted.

Delia was afraid of confronting her landlady and had to wait until that evening to sneak her things out of the house. She handed Sara her two suitcases, a box, her coat and jacket through the open window, then climbed out one leg at a time. They made their way quickly to the street where Jim, Sara's boyfriend, waited in his car.

They laughed all the way home, and Sara made dinner and a cake to welcome Delia and celebrate the success of her escape from "San Quentin," as she put it. Things had worked out and Delia devoted all of her energy to her school work, and was now looking forward to the MASC meeting and to seeing Jeff and Samuel again.

Jeff Morones   I like him   I think he likes me too
Wouldn't it be nice   No   He probably has a girlfriend

She delighted on the turnings of liquid amber leaves twirling in the wind. Feeling a sudden burst of happiness, she made a few turns herself, and ran the rest of the way home.

She wrote a cheerful letter to her parents, then called collect to her aunt Marta in Monterey to tell her how wonderful life in Berkeley was going to be.

She looked at herself in the bathroom mirror and smiled, pleased for the first time with the face of the woman staring back at her, happy and self-assured, ready to begin the journey that would take her to that place where there were no dreams, because reality was better than any dream her imagination could design.

"They were exhilarating times, weren't they? All of you were amazing," Mattie would comment to Delia many years later. "Ah, *le temps perdu.*"

Through her friendship with Samuel and Jeff, Delia became involved in the Mexican-American Student Confederation, whose small membership seemed to represent the entire Mexican-American population on campus.

"What do you think, Delia? Should we become MECHA, Movimiento Estudiantil Chicano de Aztlán?" Julio asked Delia after one of the meetings. "No more MASC. No more masks. We are who we are."

"I'd vote for that," Delia answered. "MECHA. Yes, that sounds good. But, what about the others? Do you think they'll vote it down?"

"Guillermo, Sal, Manuel, Sid, Fernando, Jaime, Richard, Thelma, Frank, Estela—they're all in favor." Julio was pleased. "We're going to write history, *vatita*. No. We're going to re-write it."

History   There was so much to learn   Sara and I did everything Samuel and the others told us   Follow orders We didn't know enough   We're going to re-write history I didn't even know enough of the wrong history to learn the right one Has that changed   Students now   Do they know the right history   Can they tell we were the first MECHA Wick Flint   Powder keg   Trigger   Bullet   Mortal wound All in one   There I go again   Such a romantic Heroes and heroines of our own lives   I wasn't the only one All of us were such romantics   I was nineteen and knew nothing Would I have done anything if I had known   Samuel must have known the answer to that

"Okay," Delia told Samuel after the meeting where the name of MASC was changed to MECHA. "I understand now that U.C. is involved in agricultural research, which benefits the growers, but not the farmworkers."

"That's right. And the farmworkers are mostly Mexican-Americans," Samuel explained. "It's the power elite. The University has no trouble justifying doing research for agri-business, but don't talk to the administration about the the pyramid. U. C. is definitely not on our side. Beyond the political ramifications, there's a human issue involved in all this. This institution may deny it all it wants, but they're afraid of us. The administration will fight us all the way." Delia rubbed her forehead and Samuel smiled. "It's confusing, I know."

"I understand some of it. My father and my aunt Marta, his sister, were farmworkers. I agree we have to support the grape boycott." Delia sighed. "So much I don't know; I don't understand. And then all those other things about the Afro-Americans and the Asians."

A few days later, Samuel handed Delia a stack of papers. "Read these. They may help you understand better what MASC is doing and why it is important that we join the Blacks and the Asians." He also gave her a chronology of events he had begun.

April 1968: Afro-American Student Union submits proposal for a Black Studies Department to the chancellor.

August: In support of striking farmworkers, MASC representatives meet with the vice-chancellor to ask that table grapes not be purchased anymore by the University of California. He verbally agrees to stop grapes if the agreement is kept confidential. The Business Manager for Housing and Food Services gives his word that grapes will be removed immediately.

The chancellor appoints A. Billingsley as his assistant to develop a proposal for a Black Studies Department.

October 1: Earl Coke, State Agricultural Secretary, joins Reagan and Rafferty in their efforts to stop the grape boycott. MASC students find out that grapes are still being served at all campus dorms.

October 11: President Hitch claims a position of neutrality. He instructs the purchasing department to continue buying grapes in accordance with established U.C. policies.

For October 14, the day after Samuel had given Delia his chronology, there was only a statement that read, "MASC representatives meet with President Hitch for a half hour to discuss the issues further."

That day, Delia and Samuel were walking to the Doe Library, a gray stone building in the center of the campus. As they went through Sather Gate, the south entrance to the campus, Samuel stopped. "You see any bars here?" He asked Delia, then walked on. Delia followed, puzzled. When they were at the door of the library, he said, "There are bars all around us, not to keep us in but to keep us out. We have to bring them down."

The next day, October 14, President Hitch refused to discuss the issues with MECHA students and left his office. The Chicano students and representatives from other student groups decided to stay until he returned. Twelve students were arrested and taken to jail, Samuel Corona among them. Those in jail would fast and refuse bail until their demands were met. Those left on campus were in charge of delivering carefully-drafted letters to university officials and holding press conferences to make the campus and city communities aware of the students' plight.

Despite minor incidents, everything worked out as planned and the President agreed to establish a Center for Mexican American Studies; he also asked for leniency toward the students in jail, who were subsequently released on their own recognizance.

We're in jail and we already know President Hitch and Chancellor Heyns are asking for leniency One of the guards has the radio on and the news is on I hear Julio talking to a reporter and he's saying that if we are kept in jail there will be violence We know we have to get out quickly   I wish   I know you wish you had been there with us It's too soon   Too soon for what   He was right   I wasn't ready I read and read Suddenly it all made sense   I had felt it before   Then I knew I was a Chicana   We were no longer Mexicans or Mexican American   Chicanos   A thorn in the system A threat

The day after Samuel was released, he and Delia walked through Sather Gate. Samuel stopped and looked back on Sproul Plaza on the south side of campus. The plaza faced Telegraph Avenue—The Avenue, as it was called by the street people who flocked to the campus every day. It was flanked by Sproul Hall—the

Admissions and Registrar's Offices—on the east and the dining commons and the Student Union Building on the west. A fountain the students called Ludwig's—named after a dog fond of dipping in it—stood between those two buildings in front of the steps leading to a lower plaza. Two rows of trees, their naked branches rising against the gray sky like raised fists, lined up the main walkway toward Telegrah Avenue and Bancroft Way, the cross street. *The guardians   Of what*

There was nothing unusual going on. As always, Hubert The Preacher and a black man were arguing about sin and hell, surrounded by a hollering crowd under the steady autumn rain; Hare Krishna followers chanted, oblivious to the howling of dozens of dogs loose on the campus; an emaciated man played his violin for nickels; students played chess under the protection of their umbrellas at Ludwig's Fountain; dazed-eyed hippies sprawled on the Student Union steps next to their knapsacks. Beyond, on The Avenue, street merchants peddled their wares; people walked in and out of stores, and drug pushers checked their stock, making ready for noon customers.

"Business as usual, eh?" Delia said to Samuel, whose fist was so tight that the skin was turning purple.

"We'll see about that, *cabrones*," he said and raised his fist up in the air in defiance.

Delia had taken some steps back and from where she stood, it seemed as if Samuel was saluting the trees. Although she smiled at the irony of the picture, immediately after she was overwhelmed by fear that changed into anger then anguish. She looked around at the stone buildings, then at the campanile rising above all, and listened to the first bell of the noon hour. *El Señor es mi pastor No me falta nada   He looks like a kid Such a waste   Y bien parecido el muchacho   Qué pena   Qué pena Sebastián Sebastián   Mami don't cry Don't cry You're dead Dead   Dead* Samuel's fingers on her elbow brought Delia back to reality.

"I don't know why we're beating around the bush," Julio said during one of the newly-named MECHA meetings. "Let's call for a strike. The administration is just playing with us. They think we should be happy just because they've admitted a few more *vatitos y vatitas* for the spring quarter. And they're just giving us the run around about the study center."

"We're not ready yet," Samuel protested. "Let's call for the strike when we're ready. Let's continue talking with the Afro-Americans and the Asians. We have to unite under one organization. That's where it's at."

"Okay, man. I'll go along with that, but something better happen soon. I'm tired of waiting." In his characteristic manner, Julio stormed out of the meeting.

Delia, who had taken over the task of writing the chronology that Samuel had started, followed the events closely until the end of the quarter. She had also begun to keep a journal where she wrote down everything that had happened to her since her arrival in Berkeley. Somehow, writing about it relieved her feelings of anguish and uncertainty, and made her loneliness more bearable.

Writing the chronology was different. She was an observer, noting down facts, dates, names and events, "documenting," as Samuel had told her and Jeff. "One day someone will come looking for all that information. Historians, maybe a writer." *But who would look for us   Ants   Vermin   Invisible Remember*

Delia and Jeff looked at each other and smiled. Samuel saw himself as the preserver of history, and went around saving papers that to Delia and the others seemed insignificant. But she admired in him that ability to look into the future, particularly on political issues, so lucidly that it even scared her for, on many occasions, it wasn't long before his predictions came true.

The fall quarter came to an end and Delia got ready to go to Los Angeles to spend the holidays with her family. Although not much was expected to happen during the winter break, she asked Jeff, who was staying in Berkeley, to make notes of anything that happened while she was away. Jeff took her to the Greyhound Depot.

"What are you going to do here by yourself?" she asked him.

"I have an incomplete. I might as well make it up," he answered trying to sound casual, not wanting to explain that he didn't get along with his stepmother, and felt abandoned by his father. "I might go riding with John in Hayward."

"Who's he?" *He seems so lonely   First time I see him like   this   Maybe   that's   why   he's   always   laughing Does   he   have   anyone   We   don't   know   each   other Any of us No I won't ask him about it   He would tell me if he wanted   I   wish   I   could   invite   him   to   come   home   with   me   No My   mother   would   have   a   heart   attack   Dice tu mamáque te portes bien Father's last letter   She won't even write me Probably thinks we have orgies every night   Political orgies*

"He's a campus cop." Jeff stopped when he saw Delia looking inquisitively at him. She was trying to remember John; she'd seen them talking one time, on Sproul Plaza.

Jeff thought she was showing her disapproval and added, "He's not 'fuzz.' Actually, he thinks we're right on in what we're doing. Anyway, he lives in Hayward and he's invited me to his house. His wife's brother lives nearby and has horses."

"Do you like riding?" Delia felt at ease talking with Jeff. It was a quiet moment and Jeff seemed so different from the one she knew, the one who always gave a humorous twist to everything happening around him, his sonorous laughter breaking the solemnity or monotony of a moment. She liked that side of his personality, but was fascinated by this other quiet, melancholic self.

"Next to having sex," he whispered. He regretted saying that almost immediately after. He wanted to provoke a reaction in Delia, shock her into showing her feelings, negative or positive, but she sat next to him as poised and distant as always.

Is   that   an   invitation   What   would   it   be   like Hmmm I better stop thinking about that   But if he wanted Yes It would be him   No   What would he do with someone like me He would probably get tired of me very soon Poor Sara She thought Jim lived just for her   God He was making it with every girl in town   Estrenando verga she said   Crying and laughing   That won't happen to me   It won't   I'm glad her period finally came What a mess

He interpreted her silence as displeasure, but was surprised when she kissed him on the cheek before boarding the bus. "Happy holidays," she said to him as she stopped to wave at him. "Don't work too hard."

"We'll go riding when you come back," he shouted and she nodded. "Maybe make love," he said to himself.

During the next three weeks, riding on the hills in Hayward, Jeff asked himself why he wouldn't simply take Delia in his arms and kiss her. What if she rejected him? That would hurt him badly. He'd have to risk it, he told John, seeking the advice of the older man who was more a father figure than a friend to him. John thought it was a good idea and Jeff decided he would kiss her next time he and Delia were alone.

That opportunity would come only once again during their student life, on a cold January night, in the midst of a moment filled with anxiety. A quick encounter of mouths, a slight touch of tongues, a moan breaking the stillness of a winter night, then silence and distance.

Chapter 3

Nine years ago   A lifetime   A flickering on the screen of this night   Jeff   Samuel   An instant quickly gone Nine years   "Sprawled I watch the towns" How does it go   Mattie and I used to recite it together Now I remember only lines   The Heart   That was the title No moon tonight   Yes   "In the waiting dark I loose Like marbles spinning from a child The crazed and hooded creatures of the heart"   Where's the moon   The crazed and hooded creatures of my heart   Why have they come out of hiding Where's the moon   Ricardo   Sebastián   Jeff Samuel Sara   Mattie and I   Only survivors God   Total recall   Is that what's happening to me   Am I about to die Madness   Maybe that's it Uncle Simon   Will I die with fireflies in my mouth too James Joyce   Am I already dead At least I'm in good company   No   he was real   What am I saying Real real   The man has been dead almost 40 years But I saw him   Touched his hands   He tried to help me   Someone is always trying to help me   Protect me From what   From myself maybe   Don't start crying again I cried tonight   I cried   Nine dry years They won't take us in They have mace Tear gas Clubs This is it This is it Death to the ants   Samuel's down   Stop Stop You're killing him   Stop   Stop   Stop Almost went through the stop sign   Better watch it Get to the party Dance your sorrow away   Sweat the pain out like a fever Cry the memories out   Then wait for the morning to come For the morning to come   Write it down Then forget it Forget If I could only forget

Delia touched her forehead, then her cheeks with her cold hands; they felt warm but there was no fever. She almost wished there were, so the fever would take over her mind and body; the pain and the urgency to remember what couldn't be helped anymore, drawn out of her with every drop of sweat. Instead she was

31

on her way to a Day of the Dead party at Mattie's house, thinking
that it would have been much better to have stayed in bed, but
changing her mind an instant later at the memory of her nightmare
earlier that evening.

She tried to concentrate on her driving, watching out for stop
signs and for cars, sparse at that time of night in the Berkeley hills.
She lowered the window and breathed in the cool night air, stopped
for a moment at an intersection to see the city below. She looked
for the silhouette of buildings in downtown Oakland, and the
stream of car lights on the Oakland-San Francisco Bay Bridge,
quivering in the mist of the November night.

*Seven in the morning   It all looked so peaceful from up
there   But below they waited   Dark glasses Helmets at
hand   Clubs   Gas canisters   Armed and ready
They waited   For us   The damned   The damned
who dared   Twisted faces of people in pain   The pungent smell of blood and gas   The sound of clubs against
skulls arms legs   Glass shattering   Screams then cold
silence Paralysis   Anger that has nowhere to go but back into
your mouth   Down   Cutting through the hard knots in
your throat to form a shield around your heart   February
19   The inevitable   Police attack in full force Mace is
used for the first time on campus   I was writing the
words   I felt nothing   Nothing   Thinking of Jeff
We never went riding   Never another kiss   In a few
hours   How short the time it takes to shatter a dream So
long to pull its splinters out   I wish I was stupid Not know
Not think Not hurt   God   Think of the good things
All the things you'll do when you leave Berkeley   I've been
leaving Berkeley for so long   I tried   Don't go
Please don't go   I wanted to say that to Jeff   I didn't
How could I   I wanted to leave myself   Like everybody else   Pack up and go So stupid   Someone had
to stay Go on with the work we had begun   I'll be leaving
now Spend Christmas in Monterey   Then on home*

Delia started the car up again. She felt calmer, finding comfort in the thought that she would leave Berkeley soon, to spend
Christmas with her parents and her aunt and uncle in Monterey.

Her degree finished, there was nothing left for her to do in Berkeley.

It would be a joyous holiday, unlike the ones she had spent at home through the years, sitting at the dinner table after midnight mass, between the two empty chairs her mother insisted on placing next to her, the three glasses of sparkling cider lined up in front of her as if waiting for Sebastián and Ricardo to materialize and drink them, and listening to her mother's sobbing for her two dead sons in the next room. Delia would bite her tongue not to shout at the top of her lungs, "Look at me, Mother. I am not Sebastián or Ricardo, but I'm ALIVE!"

Why don't you love me Mother   What must I do   What can I do   I wished I had died instead of them   I live I live   I love you Mother   It isn't enough   It'll never be enough for you   Fill the emptiness   Why did you abandon me   What did I ever do to you   I was a girl Was that it   I wasn't a boy   We never talk   We don't even fight   Silence between us   Dark web you've crocheted to hold me there   Speechless   Why can't you love me Mother   Why   I'm not much but I'm all you've got All you've got

Delia could remember only one Christmas, in 1968, when she didn't mind the necromantic rituals and smiled through them, thinking about going back to Berkeley, riding with Jeff on the hills in Hayward, doing her schoolwork and the chronology Samuel had entrusted to her.

She searched in newspapers for news about Berkeley, but found none. She clipped a few articles that would be of interest to Sara, who had started a "historical trivia" scrapbook.

"You have your diary and your chronology; Samuel has his historical documentation. Now I have my trivia chronicles. We are now equal." Sara displayed her scrapbook for Delia to see.

"The Hong Kong flu epidemic has claimed the lives of 5ll7 people in the United States"   The virus Those Asians You see Del There's method in my madness Look at this one "Visiting students from Venezuela and Argentina in their native costumes were featured at the American Field Service Committee breakfast" Were

featured The poor bastards Bet you they were happy to read this shit And this one "Negroes making progress in TV" Negroes This is Berkeley California mind you   The Black Beauty Boom In Fashion   The model says "Why stress the word black Black is political It's a forced term Especially of late it's been an advantage for me to be a Negro It's the Oriental models that are having a harder time of it I'm really sorry for them"   Sara will enjoy this one   Perfect   This one too   Pope Paul VI "This generation"   Meaning us of course "Intoxicated with the spirit of change is ready to forget the past interrupt tradition and abandon custom Extreme student movements"   Really Yeah this one too   I can't wait to get back

Delia had hardly had time to unpack and give Sara the clippings she had brought for her when Jeff was already knocking at their door.

"What's happened?" Sara asked Jeff, handing him a cup of coffee. "You look terrible."

"Samuel and I have been working all night. The Committee deadlocked. They can't make up their minds on whether Black Studies should be a department or a program," Jeff explained.

"That's not unusual, is it?" Delia asked, thinking that there was something Jeff was not saying. "Did they reject it?"

"No, they haven't, but they haven't let the student representatives attend meetings." Jeff gulped down the remaining coffee and wiped his mouth with the back of his hand. "They're keeping their mouths shut. No one knows what's happening."

He paused to look for Delia who had walked out of the kitchen the minute he finished his last sentence. She was putting on her jacket and struggling to refold and strap her umbrella. He looked at her long hair hanging free on the side opposite him. He fought back the urgent need to go to her. He caught Sara's gesturing hands out of the corner of his eye.

"Twenty-one years old, a graduate student in anthropology and you can't tell her how you feel about her," Sara whispered in Jeff's ear. "I have more guts than you, I swear."

He put his fingers over her mouth to hush her. "You don't understand."

"Oh, but I do." Sara chuckled. "This is the real stuff. Listen.

I can arrange it if you want," she offered.

"No!" Jeff said with such emphasis that Sara moved her head back and raised her eyebrows.

"Okay. Okay. Then you do it." She was quiet for an instant, then laughed softly. "I've got it! Yesterday, Samuel was talking about getting cans of paint to write something or other on the walls." She smiled pleased with herself. "I'm smart, *no hay duda*. You and Delia—you know?"

"You, conniving . . ." Jeff chuckled, moving quickly away from the kitchen door, when he saw Delia coming to join them. "Don't say anything."

Sara shook her head and shrugged her shoulders. "Do you think we'll go on strike after all?" she asked Jeff in a casual way.

"It looks that way. It's really difficult to tell at this point." He turned to Delia. "Are you going to campus?"

"Yeah. I'm going to Eshleman Hall."

Jeff offered to take her, but she refused. "You better go home and get some sleep."

"Yes, Ma'am," he answered and left.

A few days later, on January 10, 1969, Delia recorded the joining of the Afro-American Student Union, the Mexican-American Student Confederation and the Asian-American Political Alliance to form the Third World Liberation Front.

Late on the night of the 21st of January, armed with cans of red spray paint and working in pairs, Third World students wrote the acronym TWLF on the walls of several campus buildings, to inform the campus community about the possibility of a strike.

Samuel had picked up Jeff, Delia and Sara, parked his car on Bancroft Avenue, three blocks away, and instructed them to meet him back there in an hour.

Sara picked up a can of paint and handed it to Jeff. He did not waste any time and was happy when he took Delia's hand and she did not withdraw it.

Delia and Jeff made their way to the flagpoles a few feet away from Sproul Hall. She crouched behind the bushes around the poles while Jeff lowered the California flag, then handed it to her. She spread it on the ground and painted the words "Third World Power" on it, and helped him raise it up again.

They heard a door close nearby and hurried around the back of the building to the parking lot on the other side of Sproul Hall to Dwinelle Plaza.

They heard the clinking of keys and two campus policemen talking. Jeff deposited the can of spray in a litter basket after wiping it clean with the lining of his jacket.

"Let's stop here and just walk down normally." Jeff held Delia's hand.

She was panting, partly because of their sprint, but mostly out of fear. She had to breath in deeply a few times.

Jeff stopped and looked at the two policemen approaching. "Whatever I do, don't fight me. Okay?"

Delia squeezed his hand. Jeff unbuttoned her jacket, raised the hood over her head, and put one arm around her waist. He leaned forward and kissed her.

"What . . . are you . . . doing?" Delia whispered, her eyes opening wide, a tingling sensation running from her neck to her nipples, zigzagging across her belly, then nestling between her thighs. She trembled. *No   Yes   Don't   stop Don't* She closed her eyes and kissed him.

"Delia. I . . ." Jeff couldn't finish the sentence. The two policemen had stopped a short distance from them and were watching them. "Let's get out of here." He buttoned her jacket.

"Move it along, kids. Time to go home," one of the policemen said.

They walked fast toward Telegraph Avenue and Bancroft Way. They stopped briefly by the flagpoles and smiled at each other. Jeff brushed her lips with his and passed his arm around her shoulders. They walked across the street and headed for the car parked on Bancroft Way, where Samuel and Sara anxiously waited for them. Jeff was going to get into the back seat with Delia, but Samuel handed him the keys. "You drive," he told him and walked around to get in. Jeff was puzzled but didn't say anything.

Jeff was very surprised when Samuel got out of the car, saw Delia and Sara to the door and, without saying a word to him, began to walk in the opposite direction. He drove the car to Samuel's house, left the keys in the ashtray and walked home.

The next day, Samuel greeted him as usual, leaving Jeff more confused, but there was no time to ask for an explanation because the strike was imminent, pending only the final vote of the membership at a general assembly.

They had been so sure the vote was going to be favorable that there were already piles of picket signs and stacks of information leaflets. Students walked in and out of the office all morning long, and later joined the first informational picket line at Sather Gate.

Delia sat down to write the entry for that day.

January 22, 1969: TWLF students vote in favor of a strike, and informational picket lines are set up. Demands: That a Third World College with four departments be established and controlled by Third World people; that Third World people be appointed to positions of power, including faculty in every department and proportionate employment at all levels, from regents, chancellors and administrative levels to clerical and custodial personnel, throughout the university system.

"No disciplinary actions against students or employees participating in the strike, during or after the strike. You forgot that." Samuel was looking over Delia's shoulder. "Here. You can copy the specific demands from the abstract."

When Delia finished, she joined Sara, Mattie and other students who were addressing information packets to professors and teaching assistants of the College of Letters and Sciences, asking them to show support for the strike by taking their classes off campus or giving striking students incompletes instead of failing grades.

Delia thought about Jeff all day long, but saw him again for a brief moment the next day, since Samuel had asked him to monitor the picket lines at another building.

Jeff suspected Samuel was doing that to keep him away from Delia, because Samuel was in love with her. He confided in Sara who didn't agree with him.

"No. He isn't in love with her," she reassured him. "It's more like he feels responsible for her." She paused. "Like big brother, you know?" She patted his shoulder. "Com'on. She loves *you*, I'm sure."

"Has she said that?" Jeff's eyes lit up.

"Are you kidding? Delia? She would never tell me that. She

wouldn't tell anyone." Sara shook her head. "I like her, you know? But sometimes—Augh! She irks me. Someone did her wrong, very wrong."

"Someone?"

"I don't mean a man. I mean something bad happened to her sometime." Sara stopped, seeing Jeff's frowning face. "What the hell! I'll tell you. I think her brothers died not too long ago. Her father writes her and calls her, but she hardly gets letters from her mother. They don't get along. Anyway, Del has bad nightmares. Tosses and turns at night. Then, in the morning, she's her old self again."

"Do you think Samuel knows?"

"If she's told anyone, it's him, for sure. They've become very close. Very close." Sara looked at Jeff. "Ask him."

"That's going to be difficult." Jeff shook his head. "We're in for hard times. Samuel is already predicting beatings, gassing and the National Guard. And that *vato* is always right. *Maldita boca que tiene el cabrón.*" He laughed.

"But that's never happened on campus." Sara wasn't laughing. "Never. They wouldn't, would they?"

"That racist Reagan? He'll come down on us with everything he's got. This is his little *Mein Kempf.* He has to show us who's boss. White male supremacy."

"Yeah, but . . . the other students will join us. And he won't be able to get 10,000 people arrested." Sara sighed.

"I'm not too sure they will join us. See? If we were holding demonstrations against the draft . . . They can't see that it's all related. Blacks, Chicanos and Native Americans have been fighting that fucking war, too. No. They don't see that. We're in this alone." Jeff smiled at Sara, who looked distraught, and patted her hand in reassurance. "Who needs them, anyway?"

That night, Sara told Delia about Jeff's comments and Delia confided she'd had a similar talk with Samuel about the events to come. The phone rang at the same time that they heard fire sirens. Delia ran to the phone and Sara to the window. "There's a fire at Wheeler Auditorium. Jeff is coming by to pick you up." Samuel spoke fast and Delia wasn't sure about the cause of his agitation. "You and Sara call Sid, Sal, Guillermo, Manuel, Lenni, Thelma and Fernando. I already called Mattie and Julio."

They had barely finished dressing when Jeff knocked at their door. "They'll blame it on us," he explained. "Shit! We better be ready. This is war."

Mattie joined them in Eshleman Hall. She hadn't had time to get dressed and was wearing only a coat over her nightgown and slippers. She and Jeff went into Samuel's cubicle and began to draft a news release while Sara and Delia called everyone on the rosters. Delia made coffee and served a cup for Sara and another for herself.

"Why would they think that?" Sara asked Delia when they finished calling. Delia rubbed her forehead and sipped her coffee, but didn't answer.

No   We've been so careful   No guns   No violence That's not our way   It's getting away from us Jeff's right   We'll be blamed for it   Oh God Our Father who art in Heaven   I need air   Open a window   I'm going to be sick

"Hey, Del, are you okay?" Sara asked her. Delia didn't answer. She stood by the half-opened window looking into the night. She thought of her parents placidly asleep in Los Angeles, and of her aunt Marta in Monterey. *If this was only another bad dream   If I were in my bed in Monterey   No It isn't a dream   A living nightmare   A nightmare*

"I'm okay." The words came out slowly. "I'm all right. I'll be all right."

"Are you scared?" Jeff was standing next to Delia at the window.

"Aren't you?" Delia asked him, turning to look at him.

"Yeah. We're all scared. But we'll make it." He passed his arm around her shoulders. "We'll have our college. The cockroaches will have their college." What was happening had at least given him an opportunity to be close to her once again, he thought and smiled at the irony. From then on, it would be only moments, stolen moments, because as far as he could see into the future, the struggle would be a hard and bitter one. Their personal lives, feelings, dreams would be suspended until victory day, and perhaps even beyond then.

Delia smiled and relaxed a little. It was only two weeks since she and Jeff kissed. *It will never happen again now Maybe it wouldn't have happened anyway   I don't know I'm so tired It's better this way   Maybe one day When this is over If it's over*

Samuel and some other students came in and Delia read in their faces that what they dreaded most was about to happen. The next day, the *Daily Cal*, the campus newspaper, would report Chancellor Heyns' comments which implied that the strike had precipitated acts of violence. Four weeks later, the fire chief would report that all tests failed to show any evidence of arson. But by that time, rumors about undercover agents infiltrating all student organizations, even those remotely connected with the strike, circulated freely.

"Careful with what you say on the phone," Samuel told Delia and Sara. "Any phone."

"Hey, Del, they're going to find out all about my boyfriends," Sara chortled, but stopped when she saw that neither Delia, Samuel nor Julio were laughing. "You're serious, aren't you?"

"Dead serious," Julio said. "This ain't no fucking picnic, *vatita*. No more MASC—MECHA—picnics at Lake de Anza. This is war. And this is the time to get out if you have any doubts, 'cause I'm sure they've now begun dossiers on all of us."

Sara looked at Samuel, hoping he would reassure her that Julio's assessment of the situation was an exaggeration, but he nodded, and she shuddered amidst sighs. "War it is, then. What are my orders, *Comandante*?"

The horror was yet to come   An unlit pyre   In the moonlight   Children playing hide and go seek around it Under it   Everyone at risk   Everyone risking   It was that kind of time   Not only students   Professors Romano and Asturias   Wives   Secretaries   The unsung heroines

Chicana, Black and white secretaries on campus, some of them married to striking students, passed information about covert activities, at the risk of losing their jobs. Copies of memos outlining strike strategies and proposed repressive actions would come into the students' hands even before they reached the administration. But those documents also made them suspect that either the administration or the F.B.I. had been successful in penetrating their defenses. And all of them began to look over their shoulders, to watch what they said and to whom. Suspicions were cast even on those who had been with the strike from the beginning. Jeff was under suspicion, in particular because of his friendship with John, the campus officer.

On strike   Shut it down   Hey the Black brothers are up there having coffee and donuts and we're down here getting the chingazos   Hey man we're going to lose our G.I. Bill   Mira bato we survived Korea and a tour of duty in Viet Nam Fuck What's Berkeley   Don't trust Jeff man He's not one of us

Hour after hour, under the rain and the watchful eyes of the police, chanting, they walked the picket line held peaceable rallies. They drove themselves to the point of exhaustion in strategy meetings, leafletting, seeking support from an apathetic campus community, keeping the peace in the picket lines when white students would cross it on purpose with fists ready. *We are in the belly of the monster   We can't quit* The price each would have to pay seemed small compared to the vision of a bright future for many Third World students to follow, to have a Third World College to call their own.

During the few moments of respite, robbing themselves of sleep, Sara and Delia studied and prepared papers. They were lucky to have enrolled in classes where the teaching assistants, who would later join the strike, allowed them to do their work and still honor the strike.

Mattie was holding her classes at home. She and the few Chicano professors on campus spent countless hours talking with other members of the Berkeley Faculty Alliance. Finally, on January 27, the Alliance announced its support at a noon rally, at the same time that Governor Reagan declared a state of *extreme* emergency on the campus and adjacent areas to allow the mobilization of the Highway Patrol.

The Academic Senate tabled resolutions concerning the autonomy of the Third World College, Delia noted down, and the Third World Progress Committee continued to meet with the chancellor, reaching a tentative agreement. *Repudiated* *Make us squirm* *They won't give us what we want* *No Stop it* *Don't think that way* *They have to* *It's taking so long* *San Francisco State* *Months They've had it bad* *Hayakawa He's third world* *No he isn't* *Give us Hitch anytime Both are bad but Hayakawa is worse* *At least we always knew Hitch was the enemy No mistakes*

Those teaching assistants who favored the strike formed an informational picket line and were completely surrounded, then dragged to the Campus Police Office, in the basement of Sproul Hall. Although many times altercations had ensued when someone defiantly crossed the picket line, that particular day had been quite uneventful up to that time.

Jeff was walking from Eshleman Hall to join the teaching assistants, when the police charged against them. He rushed to the spot, then went quickly to the basement of Sproul Hall, trying to find his friend John, the campus policeman, to ask for his help.

"I found him all right," he told Mattie, Delia and Samuel later. "Damned bastard! He had Dan Salter spread eagle against the wall." Jeff paused to gain composure. "Dan couldn't do anything to him. That fucking bastard turned Dan around and clubbed him." He looked straight at Delia. "I stood there. I didn't do a damned thing."

Although he didn't say it, Delia knew what hurt Jeff most was feeling that John had betrayed him, while Jeff had protected their friendship even at the risk of being tagged a traitor because of it.

"Integrity means shit to these gabachos," he said under his breath. He, together with other witnesses, filed an affidavit accusing the campus policemen of use of undue force on those arrested. From that moment on, he supported every motion raised in meetings to retaliate physically against the abuses of the police, which were becoming more frequent. His insistence on the issue made some of the other students more suspicious of him. Suddenly, they did not return his greetings and hushed when he walked into a room, especially Julio who was always trying to pick fights with him.

Samuel, who had tried to keep the peace, finally gave up.

"Sorry, *carnal*, I can't battle all fronts. *Vas a tener que vértelas solo.*"

" '*Ta bien, ése*; don't worry. I understand." Jeff joined the picket line of the teaching assistants and Delia hardly saw him during the next week until that afternoon, one of the few bright days in February, when she, Sara and Samuel were picketing at the entrance of Sproul Plaza.

Sara was pointing at Mattie who was walking toward them and Delia had just raised her hand to wave at her, when she heard Samuel say, "Here they come. They have mace. This is it! This is it! GET ARRESTED! DON'T FIGHT BACK!"

Delia and Sara looked around in confusion, then saw the police coming at them, helmets and heavy jackets, clubs and mace containers. Instinctively, the students began to retreat. She felt someone pulling her sleeve, turned her head slightly and saw Jeff standing behind her. He handed her a blue handkerchief to protect her face from the mace. She took it, unfolded it, and held it in her hand. Jeff put his hands on her arms and began to push her gently toward the side. Sara who was hanging on to Delia's hand, began to move with them, too.

People passed newspapers around to use as shields against the mace. Then suddenly, as if someone had given the cue to a chorus, they all began to chant. "ON STRIKE. SHUT IT DOWN. ON STRIKE."

The policemen began to run toward them, indiscriminately beating and macing anyone in their path. This time there would be no arrests; their aim was to intimidate the crowd into dispersing.

Delia resisted Jeff's efforts to take her away from there, and began to look around for Samuel and Mattie. She saw Samuel on the floor, a big patrolman kneeling on his back and clubbing him, then saw Mattie hitting the officer with her umbrella and briefcase. The policeman raised his arm and pushed her away with such force that Mattie fell backward and hit her head on the ground, but got up the next instant.

A bottle flew through the air from the direction of the Student Union and hit the policeman who was still on Samuel's back. He and other patrolmen ran toward the Student Union. Another bottle followed the first one, then cans, books, umbrellas. Delia got free of Jeff's grip and began to push people out of her way to get to Mattie and to Samuel, who had by then gotten up, his shirt ripped and his face and shoulder bloody.

The police charged into the Student Union several times, slamming the doors open, breaking the glass. People ran in all directions, some blindly because of the mace, rubbing their eyes, or trying to get splinters of glass off their hands and faces, shouting, screaming in pain, angrily retaliating against the police.

Delia couldn't move. She watched it all as in a dream, tears rolling down her cheeks. From far away, it seemed to her, she heard Samuel tell Jeff to get her, Mattie and Sara out of there, then felt a hand grabbing her arm and pulling her. Later, she would find out it hadn't been Jeff but Mattie who had literally dragged her out and taken her and Sara.

Delia had a hard time falling asleep and sat in bed in the dark looking at the long blades of shadow moving rhythmically on the ceiling. Every time that sleep began to overtake her, making her close her eyes, she would see the helmeted head of a policeman staring at her, then a bloody face. Despite the burning sensation in her eyes from crying for hours, she kept herself awake all night, finally getting up at five to make coffee and write the entry for the day before in the chronology.

February 19th: The inevitable confrontation. Police attack in full force and gear. Mace is used for the first time on campus. *Las cucarachas   Exterminate them   Kill them Beat them to death   Death   Death   First time   We have no rights   They won't even take us in*   Police charge into the Student Union several times, beating people and using mace. Students choose to defend themselves.

She put down the paper and pen, and stared at the words she had just written. *This says nothing   Blood   Tears Pain How   Tell   This says nothing* She felt a lump in her throat but tears didn't come. *I won't cry   I won't I won't Never again   Never* "Never. If I'm beaten I will get up again, and again, and again. I will. I will."

She hit the table with her fist, then went into the bedroom and took out some clothes, which she carried with her into the bathroom. She let the warm shower run freely over her body for a long time, then shut off the warm water faucet and felt the jolt of the cold water hitting her face, shoulders and breasts at once.

Delia emerged from the bathroom, fully dressed and calm. Sara was already up and dressed, waiting for her with a cup of coffee in her hand. She drank it quickly when she saw Delia ready to leave, even though it was only seven o'clock.

They walked to Eshleman Hall, but didn't talk much on the way. They approached the campus from Telegraph Avenue and saw several county and city patrols already lined up on both sides of the street. Berkeley policemen and Sheriff's officers were talking and drinking coffee. Sara took Delia's hand thinking that they would have to make a run for their lives, but the policemen looked at them only briefly from behind their dark glasses.

They found Samuel in his cubicle typing away, red-eyed and puffy-faced, a gash in his right shoulder still bleeding. There were abrasions on his forehead and left cheek, and he still wore the same bloody shirt he had on the day before.

"There are a lot of . . . " Sara began to say, but stopped when Samuel waved his hand indicating he already knew about the policemen.

"It's called the mutual aid policy. They can call as many cops as they think they need from any city around, even the National Guard, if they so please." Samuel was still typing away.

"Would they?" Sara repeated the question over and over, until Delia squeezed her hand as a signal to stop.

Samuel stopped typing for an instant. "They're really scared this time. They're coming at us with everything they've got." He went back to his typing. Delia knew it was useless to ask him to stop, so she got the first-aid kit and told Sara to sit at the typewriter for Samuel to dictate whatever it was he was writing.

"No. I can't dictate. I have to do it myself," he said and stretched his arm trying to reach back, making the shoulder wound bleed more.

"Let me get your shirt off," she said. Instead, she thought about it and decided to tear the sleeve off, and getting the scissors from the desk, she cut off the material around the wound. "Sara, wash the coffee pot, and bring some warm water and a bit of soap from the bathroom." *Delia get some water and soap What hap-*

pened to him What happened to Sebastián   *Sssh Vas a des-*
pertar a tu papa Bring me the scissors

"You're pretty good at this," Samuel said, trying to smile but
managing only a grimace.

"We had a cat at home who was always getting into fights.
Ricardo and I used to doctor him 'cause we didn't have any money
to take him to the vet." Delia opened the kit and began taking out
tubes, reading the labels, then looking through the boxes of gauze
and band-aids. *Antibac*   *teri*   *al cream*   *Si Esa*
Tráemela Hold still Ay m'ijo Mañana don't take off your shirt He'll
see you

"What happened to the cat?" Samuel pulled himself closer to
the desk and reached for a pack of cigarettes. Delia looked at him
and frowned. "Yeah, I started again this morning." He lit one up.
"What happened to the *gato*? I want to know before you start doc-
toring me."

"He fell into the washing machine and drowned." *Yes he's my*
son   *Sebastián*   *Treviño*   *Rosa*   *Qué*   *pasa*
Quién es   *Delia*   *Ricardo*   *Vean a su mamá*
Yes Officer I come right now Delia reached for a white sheet of
paper, took out several cotton balls and arranged them on it, then
looked at Samuel out of the corner of her eye. He was laughing.
"Really. He did!" Delia began to laugh, too. *Sebastián*
Mira nomás lo que fuiste a hacer   *M'ijo*   *M'ijo*
Don't cry mamá Don't cry I'm here I'll never go away   *I*
won't I promise I promise

Sara walked in with the coffe pot and a bottle cap full of soap.
Delia and Samuel were laughing so hard that, without knowing the
cause, she joined them as well and started hiccuping which made
them laugh even harder.

Sweaty and teary, they finally stopped and Delia began to
clean and dress Samuel's wound. "You should really go to Cowell
Hospital. This isn't enough."

"What for? They'll just open it up again today." He went back
to his typing until he finished. "Do me a favor, Sara. Take this
memo to the chancellor's office when they open. Make sure to hand
it directly to his secretary." He turned to Delia. "As soon as Julio
and the others get here, tell them they have tear gas." Delia nod-

ded. "Call Mattie and Jeff, too, if they haven't got here by eight. Don't say much on the phone, just ask them to get here pronto."

"Where are you going?" Sara asked.

"I'm going to Manuel Delgado's house. We have to meet the Blacks and the Asians off campus. I'll be back soon." He stormed out as Jeff and Mattie were walking in. They turned around and followed him.

Delia and Sara followed Samuel's instructions, delivered the letter to the chancellor's office, and went back to Eshleman Hall. Julio had two boxes of old rags and handkerchiefs, and plastic jugs of water. They took the boxes and jugs to the picket lines to be distributed.

Policemen were everywhere, and a large crowd gathered in the center of Sproul Plaza. People were walking in from all directions, some joining the picket lines, others quietly standing to keep watch from the steps of the Student Union, the dining commons, Sproul Hall and those connecting to the lower plaza behind the Student Union. Soon, a carpet of people extended all the way past Sather Gate into Dwinelle Plaza.

Delia and Sara looked for Mattie and Jeff, finally found them near Sather Gate, handed them wet rags and stood next to them. People began to push aside to make room for a line of people coming through from Dwinelle Plaza. "The leaders of the strike," Sara whispered in Delia's ear. "Manuel Delgado is so handsome. Ysidro Macías *también*. I might go after him." Sara chuckled, and Delia shook her head but smiled.

Seven Chicanos—Samuel and two Chicano faculty members among them—ten Blacks and five Asians walked on, followed by Julio beating a small conga hung from his neck, heading a second line of Brown Berets.

Sara hiccuped trying not to laugh, and Jeff snorted next to Delia.

"*Cabrón!*" Julio said, moving closer to where they were, so that Jeff could hear him, but both his defiance and the beating of his conga were soon swallowed by the roar coming from the crowd, as people began their chanting. The police, their faces hidden behind their gas masks, began to move on them. Clouds of gas rose from everywhere; people gasped for breath and held the wet rags to their faces, taking them away only to join the chorus. They pushed on toward Telegraph Avenue.

Delia was caught in the mass of people and lost sight of Sara and Mattie, but felt Jeff's hand clutching her arm. When she didn't feel it anymore, she began to push on, harder and harder, putting the wet handkerchief against her nose and mouth, holding her elbows out to avoid being crushed by people around her.

For a moment, she didn't know exactly where she was. A curtain of gas and her own tears kept buildings from view and people made her sway from one side to another. Then she felt herself being carried down steps and quickly realized they were moving down to the lower plaza. The pressure of the crowd against her eased all of a sudden and people began to run in all directions.

Once down, she felt her way along the walls to the left, knowing that Eshleman Hall was in that direction. She wiped her tears with the handkerchief only to see two city police clubbing a man on the ground, and a third walking toward her. She stood there, frozen, looking at him, waiting. He raised his gas mask and Delia saw that it was John. He lowered the mask once again, turned around and signaled with his hand for her to be on her way. *Trying to make it up to Jeff* She heard someone call her name and began to look around.

Julio was coming toward her. "They arrested Manuel Delgado and beat up Sid Macías! He's unconscious. Got to find Matttie!"

"*Y* Samuel?" She ran after him.

"I don't know. I think he was arrested, too. Find Mattie. We have to call Fay." He was running faster and Delia couldn't keep up with him.

"Who?" she asked, wiping her eyes and forehead.

"The lawyer. Find Mattie or Jeff!" Julio disappeared.

Delia ran up the staircase outside the Student Union, thinking that she could get a better view of the plaza from the balcony on the second floor, but the building was locked. She ran downstairs again. By that time, the crowd had moved to Telegraph Avenue and Bancroft Way and Delia ran in that direction. She saw two police vans overturned where the two streets met.

Oakland and Albany police were running in from Telegraph Avenue, throwing tear gas canisters in all directions. One of the canisters hit her on the leg and Delia felt a sharp pain that made her scream. She reached down for the canister but someone else took it away from her and threw it back at the police. She was blinded by the gas and a chill ran down her spine when she felt someone grabbing her. She raised her arms to cover her face from the blows that she thought would follow, but felt instead someone pulling her away and heard Jeff's voice prompting her to get out of there.

"Manuel's been arrested," she tried to tell him amidst fits of cough.

"I know," Jeff said. "We have to get to Mattie's office."

They quickly made their way through to the back of Dwinelle Hall where Mattie was already waiting for them. "I haven't been able to find out where they've taken Manuel and Sid. Fay is on her way to the station right now."

"What about Samuel?" Delia asked.

"He's at Cowell Hospital, which is where you should be, young lady," Mattie told Delia.

"No. I'm all right." Delia stood erect even though her leg was hurting a great deal.

"At least go home," Mattie suggested. "Com'n, my car is parked over there. Jeff and I will drop you off. We have to meet Fay at the station."

Jeff passed his arm around Delia's waist and picked her up to carry her to the car. She felt blood rushing to her cheeks and buried her face on his shoulder. She could still hear the screams and the noise of the crowd battling the police, but they seemed to her to be coming from far away.

Jeff, who was as close to collapse as everybody else, stumbled going down the few steps to the parking lot and nearly fell with his cargo, were it not for Mattie's intervention.

"Don't kill her," Mattie said. "We're trying to save her." She began to laugh.

Picking up on Mattie's humor and thinking that Jeff was feeling embarrassed, Delia said, "You're dangerous, you know? You better put me down." She thought she had said it with a straight face but in a humorous way and Jeff would catch on. She was surprised and hurt when he put her down, with only a sad smile on his face. *Why   Why   I hurt his feelings   Stupid*

Stupid No　　He's the stupid one　　Always laughing at everything What about now　　Why not now　　I was wrong　　He's just like all the others　　I'll walk I'll drag myself Don't cry Up Up

Delia glared at him. Jeff lowered his eyes and muttered, "Don't *you* laugh at me."

She turned to Mattie. "You go ahead. It's important. I'll be all right."

Delia had hardly finished her last sentence when Mattie was already walking to the car, followed by Jeff, who didn't turn once to see how she was doing. *I will not cry　　I won't Ever again　　Ever* "Never again. I'll be beaten and I'll get up again, and again, and again." Limping and repeating those words over and over, Delia headed toward the east gate, past the Doe Library, and up the steps leading to the plaza in front of the campanile. She stood there for an instant, looking down the path she had just walked, then at South Hall, the first building erected on campus with its commemorative plaque and legend and ivy covering its brick walls. "I'm here to stay. Do you hear me? I'M HERE TO STAY!" she shouted, startling the pigeons and doves nesting in the magnolia trees, and making the passers-by hurry away from her, afraid of what she might do next.

Rallies, riots, the arrival of the National Guard for the first time on campus, the chancellor's constant refusal to meet with any of them, the support for the strike vote by the American Federation of Teachers and the American Federation of State, County and Municipal Employees, the Regents' vote for immediate suspension of all students who violated rules, the 150 people arrested, 38 students placed on interim suspension, 18 of them falling under the Regents' ruling. With a steady hand, Delia entered all events and dates in the chronology during the weeks to follow, but she stopped writing in her journal.

As often as possible, exhausted, Sara and Delia wrote cheerful letters to their parents, who had already called a couple of times after finding out about the trouble in Berkeley. They read their respective letters to each other to make sure there were no slips. Delia had watched the pigeons and doves fly on a sunny afternoon; Sara had bought a pair of cute red sandals she would wear to the next dance on campus. They both were looking forward to going home in the summer.

Despite Sara's prodding and Mattie's discreet inquiries, Delia refused to discuss why she would quietly slip out of a room when Jeff entered. It wasn't even that she was still angry at him, although at least to herself she admitted she felt hurt. Jeff hadn't approached her either, except on a couple of occasions and only to relate a message from Samuel. She avoided looking at him and answered with monosyllables. *I haven't done anything wrong He'll have to apologize   He won't What a fool Then I won't talk to him either   Go to hell*

"I don't know what to tell her, except that I am a *pendejo*," Jeff told Sara. "She won't give me a chance. We're never alone." He looked around the room, full of boxes and people going in and out. "Look at this room. *Un pedo* and everyone knows about it." He laughed and Sara shook her head. The joy was gone out of his laughter, she thought. "And out there . . ." He stopped in mid-sentence. "It's almost over. This phase, anyway."

"Do you think so?" Sara asked, with obvious enthusiasm.

"Yeah. It'll be over soon." He looked at a beaming Sara. Not wanting to disappoint her, he didn't tell her about Samuel's predictions. Before it was over, at least another hundred students would face disciplinary action. Judging by the case being built against him, it was going to be a long time before Sid Macías was released; he was facing nine months in jail without bail, a victim of one of the most severe sentences imposed on any student.

"We'll celebrate. Then I'll be gone." Jeff pinched Sara's cheek. "You've been a good friend. Thanks," he said and left the room before she could ask him what he meant. It seemed to her as if he were saying goodbye.

Sara wasn't wrong. Jeff had asked for a transfer to the Riverside campus, even though it meant three more years of coursework, since he had also decided to switch to another major. Nothing seemed to matter any more; the only one who could keep him there was Delia, and he had lost hope that she would ask him to stay.

Chapter 4

*March 21 1969   I didn't write anything after that Si-
lence   Fog   When the wind becomes a whisper
Fog rolls in   The first day of spring   Silence
The blank pages   The walls empty   TWLF
Washed away Samuel   Julio   The Marines Yeah Your
brother and I musta' been there at the same time He was in the
Army You say Ricardo Treviño   How was it over there Julio I
Suena callous But maybe your brother was one of the lucky ones
You know To have died right away Look at Güero That vato is in
bad shape Vivo pero muerto It was hell It was hell all right Those
of us who came back alive We'll never be the same again You loved
him very much He was my brother He was my best friend too
Know what you mean Mi carnala y yo We're good friends too
If my mom had asked him not to go But she didn't   Nothing
she could do He wanted to go Somos cabrones Men Warlords
Creemos que somos lo mas chingón This time the gun backfired on
us   I   Com'n Del No llores vatita Tu carnal ya está en
paz Now you have to find peace Forget and forgive   Julio
Forget Forgive Funny Even when he talked   Sounded like his
conga Forget Forgive   No militant talk   You were
okay Julio He's okay His poetry is not   Maybe that's the
best he can do   Jeff He thought there was something between Julio and me   Such a silly quarrel   Guess I'll
never be able to tell him   He must have known   The
victory dance   Hey compadre Want to buy my Harley Davidson   So casual   Dancing with that girl How much do
you want for it   Peanuts man Peanuts   Don't go
Please don't go   Why couldn't I say it   Hurt Anger
Silence between us It's a good horse It still has all its teeth Sneak-
ing a look at me   The first one to go then Samuel Sara on
probation then gone too   Silence   Distance
Painful memories Broken dreams Unanswered questions
Nightmares Too many things between us   Silence was the
only answer Silence   My old enemy   My only friend*

Nineteen In love   Love Wild flower in the ruins   A
single marigold next to an old grave   Flor de muertos
My love for you Jeff I did love you then   He's probably
married by now We never even said goodbye   Mattie One
minute you feel too much Next minute You think too much Maybe
she's right   No Feel nothing   Don't know how to love
anymore   Forgot how Maybe never knew Poor Daniel I was
so cruel He loved me Maybe no one will love me as much   I
was already saying good bye that first time we made love   A
virgin at 23   A rose   His rose   Untouched
No The solitary rose in November   Good looking   In-
telligent   And I couldn't love him Collective memory of
spring   Maybe you will in time   No Mattie On a bare
limb   Beautiful image   Look at it closely
Look at the petals Creased   Dying Slow and painful death
Cut it   Rip open the seed pod   Plant it Watch it grow
Bloom Watch it die at someone's hands   No Cut it
Crush it   This is morbid Morbid What's happening to me
What's happening to me Have to talk to Mattie   The party
How am I going to get through the night   Go back home
No   Have to talk to her This empty feeling in my stomach
Cold sweat I can't breathe   Breathe hard   Again
Again I will not die I won't I won't   Not here Not now No
No

Delia stepped on the gas pedal. The old engine heaved under
the pressure, but the car continued moving at the same speed, and
she gave up trying to go faster. She concentrated on her breathing,
and began to figure out how much money she had in the bank to
have the car tuned up before starting for Monterey.

During the time she was writing her dissertation, she had
worked only part-time. Through her student years, she had learned
to live frugally, and had managed to save some money which she
usually spent visiting her parents. Perhaps she would call Judy at
the student placement office to see if they had any temporary jobs
on campus, although that might prove difficult since she was no
longer a student. But Judy had always helped her, ever since Delia
lost her scholarship after the strike and had to earn a living, something she didn't tell her parents until many years later.

In time, Delia had been able to get waivers through the Educational Opportunity Program to help pay for her fees. She actually liked the feeling of freedom that being able to take care of herself gave her.

We didn't care about the price   We were young Naive None of that mattered   We'd have our Third World College So many years   We had nothing

For a time after the strike ended, there was an illusion of well-being and progress. Victory celebrations and dances followed one another at the closing of the spring quarter, to raise funds for the staggering litigation costs in defense of all students arrested, and in particular for Sid Macías. Sara and Delia went to every party, then to the victory dance at Pauley Ballroom on campus.

Julio brought his conga, joined the band during the salsa numbers, and played until his hands were hurting. He put it away then and asked Delia to dance. Afterwards they went out to the balcony and talked for a long time. Julio had been in Viet Nam and Delia found herself talking to him about her brother Ricardo, something she had only talked about with Samuel. She listened to Julio's somber retelling of his years there, a tale of betrayal and death, despair, blood and guilt. She fought back the tears, but could not hold them in. She closed her eyes until they stopped. *No more crying No more   You hear me*

"*Tu carnal ya está en paz.* Now you have to do the same," Julio said and hugged her. "Forget and forgive. Forgive. Forget. Forget. Forgive," he said, repeatedly striking the guardrail, as if it were a drum.

Julio went back in, but Delia decided to stay outside until she felt calmer. Sara joined her a while later.

"He saw you. We both saw you." Sara looked for Delia's eyes.

"Who saw me?" Delia turned around and leaned on the rail.

"Jeff, *pendeja.* Jeff saw Julio hugging you. He was *pretty* upset." Sara shook her head.

"Please, not again. Let's drop it." Delia was annoyed. *So what   What do I care what he thinks   I don't care I don't   I   I do care   Julio and I   He should know better*

"Okay. Okay. But I'm telling you, this might be your last chance," Sara said. She turned around and went back in. Delia followed her.

Samuel, who had just arrived, greeted them, a silly smile on his face. It was obvious to them that he'd been drinking for a while. He didn't say a word about politics, and even managed to dance a few numbers with Delia.

It was while she and Samuel were dancing to a potpourri of nortern Mexican music that she caught sight of Jeff shaking hands with Julio, who then introduced him to a girl Delia didn't know. Jeff invited her to dance and Delia, her hands sweating and her legs shaking, watched him pull the girl closer to him with every turn until his chin was resting against her temple.

Sara, who had been watching both Delia and Jeff, asked her to let her dance with Samuel, and whispered in Delia's ear, "*No seas pendeja*. Go there and cut in." She then put her arms around Samuel and began to turn him around to get him as far away from Delia as possible.

Delia began to walk around the dance floor slowly, trying to make up her mind to approach Jeff, but turned around immediately, her heart beating wildly in her chest, when she saw him say something to the girl who laughed and pressed closer to him.

She went into the restroom but had to wait in line. She leaned against the cold marble wall. She shivered, but she did not cry. There was nothing to cry about, she told herself many times, until she felt her hands warming up and her heart slowing its pace again.

She entered the ballroom again, and upon seeing her, Samuel and Sara joined her. Delia didn't want to look around, not afraid that she would see Jeff, but scared to find out that he and the girl were gone.

"Hey, *compadre*." Delia heard Jeff say behind them. "Want to buy my Harley Davidson?" *Oh God   I hope she's not with him Please   Please*

Samuel staggered when trying to turn back to face Jeff.

"Ho-o-o. Steady." Jeff put his arm around Samuel to keep him from falling.

"How much do you want for it, *cabrón*?"

"Peanuts, *carnal*. Peanuts. I'll let you have it for fifty bucks."

Jeff laughed. "It still has all its teeth. A good horse." He avoided looking at Delia. There was no point, he told himself. She would not even talk to him, and in a few days he would be gone from Berkeley, never to return.

"I know what you're doing, *cabrón*, but you're not going to leave." Samuel's speech was becoming slurried and he was swaying.

Delia gasped and looked at Jeff, then down at the floor. *Leave Leave   He's going away   Don't go Please don't go* Delia felt Sara's fingers tap her arm twice, as if saying, "I've been trying to tell you."

Jeff's eyes met Delia's for an instant. *Hurt   Anger Regret* What was it that Jeff was trying to tell her? If he indeed had anything to say to her . . . Delia thought. Jeff believed that the coldness in her eyes meant she felt nothing for him.

Samuel was about to get sick, and Sara and Jeff rushed him out. Jeff turned to see Delia only once before the door closed after him. She stood there for an instant, numb. Then, she walked slowly out of the room, the building, stepped up her pace until she was running home as fast she could to fight the tears, to ease the heaviness in her chest.

Covered with sweat, exhausted, she reached home, went into the kitchen, found the half-empty bottle of whiskey Samuel had bought a few days before to celebrate, poured a generous amount into a glass and took it to the living room. She gulped down half of the contents, put it down on the coffee table and lay down on the sofa. "You, too," she murmured. "Why is everybody always leaving me? Leave if you want to. I don't need you. I don't want you." The room seemed to be turning and she closed her eyes, not opening them again until the next afternoon.

"Hey, Del, wake up," Delia heard Sara saying. "The meeting is at four. You're going to miss it. Com'on. Get up." Sara shook her lightly. "It's the last before the summer. Get up."

"I don't want to go anywhere," Delia protested. *I just want to sleep   Never wake up   Never   Never*

After prodding and coaxing for a while, Sara gave up and left without Delia. That evening she went back home to find a note from Delia pinned to the door. "See you in three weeks. They called me from Student Placement and I start at the beginning of July. I'll be working at the library. Sorry I couldn't wait for you. I just want to go home and see my parents. Not going to be able to do that often now. Love. Del."

Delia spent only a week in Los Angeles. She had tried to talk to her parents about how wonderful it was going to be to have an Ethnic Studies Department that would grow into a college one day, but they hadn't seemed interested.

"*Sí, m'ija*," her mother said, not paying much attention. "You haven't been eating well."

"*Trajiste tu* report card?" her father asked Delia, who was thankful to Sara for suggesting that she change her address at the Registrar's Office during the fall quarter, so that her papers from school would not be sent to her home address.

"No. I won't get it until September." *Lies One year and I've gotten so good at lying Straight face There's nothing to do here One year in Berkeley I don't want to stay here I don't want to go back there He won't be there He's gone I'll never see him again*

Her father was on vacation, so Delia suggested that they drive to Monterey to see her aunt. Her parents were delighted at the idea and they left the next day.

In Monterey, Delia spent most of her time reading, taking long walks, helping her aunt and mother make skirts and blouses for her to take to Berkeley, while listening to her aunt's lively stories about their family in Mexico.

Little by little, Delia began to feel good again and even gained a few pounds. From Monterey, both Berkeley and Los Angeles seemed far away. Nothing could hurt her there, not the harrowing experiences of the last six months, not even the memory of Jeff, who would be gone by the time she got back to Berkeley. *There's so much we still have to do But we'll do it now Now we have time All the time in the world*

Soon after she got back to Berkeley, she realized that the real struggle had begun. As days went by, she grew more and more afraid that they had in fact gained very little. They had envisioned a college with four separate departments, and they had been granted

57

only one department with a meager budget to be divided among the ethnic groups. They were forced to fight one another for crumbs.

> *Black against Brown   Asian against Native American*
> *Asians and Blacks together   Brown and Native American*
> *commiserating   Blacks against Asians   Endless com-*
> *binations Fellowship   Brotherhood   Gone to hell*
> *Animosity Betrayal   Rumor   Conflict Day after day*
> *Week after week   Why are we fighting each other   We*
> *haven't got a thing*

Samuel and a few other students paid periodic visits to the chancellor's office to demand more services and funds for recruitment, and to remind the administrators that the department was set up only as a temporary program. The issue of the Third World College had not been settled.

Some of the other students began setting up health and child-care programs in the Spanish-speaking community in Oakland, but the rest of the students were beginning to settle back into passivity.

There were times when Delia felt it was better to be gassed and beaten up by the police. At least in those circumstances there was no doubt who the enemy was, she told Mattie once, but Mattie did not agree.

"This is just a normal process. The day after the revolution is always the hardest," Mattie said and Delia felt hopeful again.

But Samuel's predictions were turning bleaker. "Every opportunist is coming out for a piece of the pie. We're fighting each other and we should be fighting the administration," he told Delia one day. "Wait and see, they'll get us to destroy ourselves. They know how to do it. They've been doing it to us and the Blacks for centuries. And we will destroy ourselves." Delia tried to tell herself that Samuel was confused and tired, but doubt was already nagging at her.

Time confirmed Samuel's suspicions. Faced with the difficult task of screening and hiring faculty members who truly represented the interests of Chicanos on campus, the students who had fought hard during the strike believed they had the right to question the political and ethnic credentials of anyone asking for employment. Meetings turned into cannibalistic rituals where an applicant was asked to prove his Chicanismo, the outcome being either a sacrificial victim or an ally.

But man he's Luis Valdez You can't be more Chicano than that Yeah but he still has to prove that he's really interested in doing good for us He just wants to come in and teach his class and leave again   What's wrong with that   We need our people to be committed to our cause on campus   And he is but his work with the teatro is also important I'm tired of this bullshit We have so much to do on all fronts We're not separate from the farmworkers or the teatro We're all part of the same movement

Samuel began to lose interest in the events around him and to drink heavily. Although he was one of those who had been suspended, he had managed to convince the Dean to reinstate him, and after three months he had won his case. He would have to repeat courses and get good grades, but that had never been a problem for him, Delia thought.

None of that made any difference because Samuel had lost hope that things would change. Two quarters short of completing his M.A., he left town. Delia went with him to the Greyhound Depot. She understood why he had to go. Both of them had wanted to be part of a dream and found themselves instead unwilling participants in a departmental conflict that was tearing all of them apart. The results had not warranted the price exacted from all of them.

Divorce   Madness   Alcoholism   Despair The inventory of the damned who dare   For what Nine years A dusty document   A crumbled dream

"Please write me and tell me how you're doing," Delia begged him and Samuel promised he would.

As the bus rolled off she shouted, "I'll make it for both of us. I promise . . ." That promise kept her in Berkeley even when she would gladly have quit school.

The day Samuel left, she mourned him like she had her brothers. Samuel had joined the list of casualties, even if there were no tombstone with his name engraved on it.

Sara failed to make up her incompletes and was put on probation, then left Berkeley in the spring of 1970. Through the following months, she wrote Delia many letters promising to visit, and a year later, she stopped writing. Then, Delia's letters were returned, marked "No forwarding address."

Out of habit, Delia kept writing a chronology of events she considered important to send to Samuel when she heard from him again. La Raza Studies changes to Chicano Studies. Manuel Delgado establishes Frente. Students split into two groups: one headed by Manuel Delgado, the other by Sid Macías. Another co-ordinator (the third one) is appointed by faculty and students to head Chicano Studies

Out of a sense of loyalty, though she could never explain it to Mattie when they talked about it, she kept going back to the Ethnic Studies Department and involving herself in its affairs. For months she sat through countless committee meetings, joined task forces whose recommendations carried as much weight with the campus administrators as a sackful of feathers, and tried, together with other students, to bring members of the Spanish-speaking community in to participate in departmental policy; but a deep, insuperable chasm separated the communities.

After endless discussions each group would go its own way, with only a vague notion of what the other wanted, expected or needed. Faculty members would shake their heads disapprovingly at her and the other students, like parents mildly annoyed with their children, and clearing their throats and their consciences, would say condescendingly, "Maybe next time." Eventually, next time turned into never.

Nameless and faceless clusters of brown bodies   Like chocolate chips sprinkled on a sheet of angel cake   A barrio world   An alien world   Unretrievable   The world we auction off when age advances   And long for on quiet nights when winter comes   Who the enemy is does not seem clear It is the white man one of them says   No says the other It's the power structure that is white That's the enemy And the dream Brown brother against brown brother   What happened to the dream Maybe Montoya is right   Is it that the them are us

"Last night I woke up in the middle of the night," Delia told Mattie, one September afternoon in 1974. "I was repeating over and over, 'The dream's dead. There will never be a Third World College. Never.' I guess I've lost hope. It scared me."

"It's painful, but I'm glad you've accepted it." Mattie had watched Delia hold onto that dream until it had become an obssession. She was glad it was over and Delia could go on with her life, but she failed to realize that for Delia, the end of that dream was a loss greater than any other in her life.

From that moment on, Delia shunned the company of anyone connected with Chicano affairs on campus, and she stopped talking about Samuel, Jeff, Sara or the strike even to Mattie. She began to date, but after two or three times of going out with the same man, she would announce to Mattie, "He's boring. I'm not interested."

Mattie was happy when Delia met Daniel Spencer, a third-year law student, and began to go out with him, and happier when Delia announced they were going up to the mountains to spend the weekend. Delia was going to be twenty-three years old and was still a virgin. Daniel was intelligent, good-looking, quite sweet, and was obviously in love with Delia, the best ingredients for a first lover, Mattie thought.

Delia seemed quite happy with him, and Mattie was surprised when Delia turned down Daniel's marriage proposal.

"I don't love him," Delia explained in a casual tone. "I like him, but I don't love him." *God   If I could only love him I would   I tried   It was fun at the beginning I don't know   I don't know what happened   I've been so cruel to him   I can't Daniel Forgive me We can still be friends   I want a wife not a friend   You said you didn't want to get married I told you I didn't want to get married I lied   I didn't I don't want to be a wife I don't want to get married Simple as that   Simple as that*

A few months later, Mattie met Mario Konstantyn, a graduate student who was taking one of her courses and would be getting his doctorate soon. She liked him and invited him and Delia to lunch at her house in hopes of starting a romance, and she was pleased with herself when Delia and Mario began to go out. Delia again seemed happy for a while, but her interest in him subsided after a few months.

"He was showing me off at one of his friend's parties," Delia told Mattie. "Talking about his *exotic* girlfriend like one talks about a tiger in the zoo. No, thanks. Sara was always talking about Chicanos being a bunch of machos. Men like Mario are more danger-ous."

"Quite a liberated female you've become." Mattie laughed. "Good for you. Don't despair. There's just the right guy for you out there."

Delia shrugged. "I'm not sure I want to get involved with anyone. I just want to have fun." *Forget that every night for a week Coming after me   I don't know who or what   Blades shining in the dark   Their eyes   Yellow Bright Watch-ing me   Coming closer and closer   Screaming In a cold sweat   Maybe I should tell Mattie   No Bad dreams That's all   I wish I could go Leave this place Never come back*

Delia thought then about quitting school and taking her chances in the outside world, but when she tried to broach the subject to her parents on her next visit home, the pained look in their faces was too much to bear. After promising them to finish her degree, she went back to Berkeley.

It was then that her bad dreams not only increased in fre-quency but became more and more terrifying, to the point that she would lie in bed awake for hours, walk, clean the house, read, drink coffee, anything but go to sleep. Sometimes, the nightmares stopped for a while, and she was able to get some rest, knowing, however, that they would come back. One afternoon, when she and Mattie were having a cup of coffee at Larry Blake's, she told Mattie about them.

Mattie listened carefully to Delia, but didn't worry too much about it. Delia had been pushing herself a little too hard, she thought. Delia was set on finishing her degree as quickly as possi-ble and devoted herself to it with the tenacity and single-mindedness with which she approached everything she did, qualities Mattie admired in her from the first time they met, but which she also thought often got Delia in trouble.

"Why don't you write your nightmares down?" Mattie sug-gested and Delia agreed that would be a good idea. She had been thinking already about doing something like that. Maybe that way she could get to the cause of them.

Hoping to provide an opportunity for Delia to get some relaxation, Mattie told her about her idea to have a costume party on the second of November, to celebrate the Day of the Dead. Delia was enthusiastic about it, and they set out to make arrangements, send invitations after they agreed that the theme of the party would be, of course, anything to do with death.

Delia looked forward to the party and spent a great deal of time in stores looking for materials, and at the public library searching through books for illustrations of the costume worn by various divas who had played the role of Camille in *La traviatta.*

Living dead   Loving dead   Walking this earth With the last look   The last breath

She finally settled on a simple, long, black tafeta dress, with puffy short sleeves, and low-cut back.

Perfect   Just don't ask me to sing

Mattie was delighted to see Delia take interest in something other than books and school work, and watched her dance and talk all night with Fernando Diéguez, a young lecturer in Latin American Studies who was obviously fascinated by her.

As the evening progressed, Mattie looked for an opportunity to talk to him without Delia being present, but that did not happen.

Mattie's intuition told her that Fernando was totally wrong for Delia, but she could not put those feelings into words when she finally tried to warn Delia about him. It was perhaps his arrogance or the way he manipulated Delia so that in a short time he was dictating what she should or should not do.

Then, one day Delia confided in her that he did not approve of her hair, her makeup, or her trips to Los Angeles to see her parents, which he believed were only an excuse to carry on with some secret lover she had there. He was definitely a very disturbed man whose idea of solving the problems between him and Delia was to hurl insults at her.

The good feelings and the attraction Delia had for him wore off during the first few weeks of their relationship and left in their place only anger and frustration, but Delia was not able to stop seeing him even then. Perhaps it was because of pity or fear, but she was quite sure it was not love. *Such stupidity Once I was so angry at Jeff   So little compared with what Fernando does I let him do it to me   Why   Why*

More than his, her own behavior worried her. It was like watching herself from a distance walk of her own accord into a stormy sea, and once in it not know how to begin to save herself or even whether she wanted to survive. Her nightmares, which had become worse and constant, impaired her capacity to deal with the situation in an objective way. There was something in her, however, which had not allowed her to carry out her deathwish; perhaps it was that Fernando's abuse had finally become physical and he had hit her, making her nose bleed.

For a moment, when that happened, she felt as if all the sadness and pain she had suffered through the years had turned into an uncontrollable rage. Delia picked up the first heavy object she could lay hands on, which happened to be the unabridged dictionary of the Spanish language. Before she knew it, she had swung it, striking him on the left temple. Stunned, Fernando staggered and she got ready to strike him once more. "Hit me again, son of a bitch, and I'll kill you," she heard herself saying. And she would have hit him a second time had he not turned around, much to her surprise, and left, never to bother her again.

"And the *word* shall make you free," Mattie said, laughing, when Delia recounted the event. "Poetic justice. Don't you agree?"

Delia laughed nervously, but for many days she alternated between fear and guilt, because she knew she would have hit him again and again had he attempted any retaliation. Yet, she also felt a kind of satisfaction at striking back that made her lightheaded, as if she had gulped down a powerful drink.

Shortly after, Delia woke up one night, aware that the nightmares had stopped. *A sucker for punishment   I should be happy they stopped   Sad   Really* Instead of feeling happy and relieved, she found herself almost sad at their passing; it was the kind of sadness she had experienced when her brothers died, and again when Jeff, Samuel and Sara had left.

Hoping to find something again that would make that feeling go away, she renewed her interest in her studies, and within the next year she had passed her exams and begun her dissertation. Pushing herself to the limit, sleeping and eating little, reading and writing month after month, she followed every rule and regulation until the task was completed.

Mattie wanted to throw a big party for her, but Delia refused.

"We'll celebrate at the Day of the Dead party," Mattie said. Delia was quiet. Much too quiet, Mattie thought, and could not help worrying. During the many years of their friendship, she had seen Delia go through many painful experiences and disappointments and Delia had always managed to survive them. Delia would survive this one, too, Mattie was sure. She promised herself, nevertheless, to keep a close watch on Delia.

For days after she found out her dissertation had been approved, Delia wandered through the campus and the stores on The Avenue, drove up to Tilden Park and sat on a fallen tree at Lake de Anza where the MASC students had held a picnic shortly after she had joined the organization.

She walked to the edge of the lake, caught a glimpse of her face reflected on the water. Not wanting to believe it was her own, she looked over her shoulder expecting someone else to be standing beside her. There was no one else there. She was alone.

Chapter 5

Mother   Father   Sebastián   Ricardo
Samuel   Damn   you   all   No   God   forgive   me
No   Look   at   me   Look   at   my   hands   Shaking
Dark   circles   under   my   eyes   What   did   I   prove   What hap-
pened   to   my   dreams   Where   have   they   gone   Where   do   I   put
this   anger   that   consumes   me   Who's   to   blame   Who

Delia hushed the voice inside her telling her she had been wrong, that all her efforts in the last nine years had been in vain, for she had only pain and a sheepskin to show for her success. She began to feel an emptiness spreading inside her at the realization that nothing had changed in those years. It seemed to her that she was no more able to control her life now than when she had arrived in Berkeley. "But something has changed," she heard a voice say behind her. "You have died." She turned around suddenly and automatically slammed on the brakes, stalling the engine. *Die Die   Die*

She was not traveling at a high speed, but the car skidded a little, stopping a few inches from another car parked at the curb. Almost instinctively, she turned the ignition key and started the car again, backed up and hurried to the first parking space she could find. She opened the door quickly, slammed it shut and began to run in the direction of Mattie's house, two blocks away, turning around every so often to make sure no one was following her, as if there had indeed been someone else with her in the car.

Panting and exhausted, she reached Mattie's front lawn and stopped. Music and laughter trickled out through the half-opened windows. Fog was already rolling in, wrapping itself like cotton candy around the tall pine in the middle of the lawn. A beam from the opalescent porchlight shone through the mist, coloring the dewdrops on leaves and grass.

At any other time, she would have delighted in the scene and would have enjoyed the feeling of peace emanating from it, but all she wanted now was to be surrounded by people, to elude the shadow lurking behind her. She made her way quickly up the driveway toward the back of the house.

There is no one there   If no one is there What's happening to me   Madness   Uncle Simón's legacy   Maybe it's already in my genes   Did he have nightmares at the onset too When did he begin to live his nightmares   When did he begin to believe in them   My God   God   If there's a God there's a devil Shame on you Teresa the devil said Look at you What are you doing Ah praying shitting and smoking   The prayers are for Him the cigarette for me and what's in the bowl is for you I like you Teresa You're my kind of people   You're wasting your time Maybe   Why do you keep coming back Why don't you go and scare some poor soul on a deserted road That's what you're supposed to do   That's boring Child's play No I like talking to you   Why am I thinking about this Stories   Talking to myself She was talking to herself again Marta I don't know what to do   Don't worry   Children do that   You don't think it has anything to do with Simón You know what people say Madness runs in the family That's nonsense   Nonsense I've always talked to myself I'll begin to worry when you start answering yourself Oh Mattie I did Today   But it was the voice of a man James Joyce   Did I create him too No He was real   Was the other one real too then   My God   I don't know what's real any more What's happening to me

The back door was closed, but she could hear people talking inside. Delia was about to open it but changed her mind, stepping aside instead to avoid being seen. She leaned on the wall; the wood felt rough against her cheek, but it was warm. *Come on* She breathed deeply a few times, holding the air inside her and exhaling it slowly. *Get a hold of yourself* She tried to concentrate on her breathing to empty her mind of the voice in the car and her near-accident. When she felt calmer, she sat on the patio chair Mattie kept on the back porch and stared at the misty yard for a while. *I can't go on like this   I have to do something* Her thoughts were clearer. *The first step toward recovery Mattie would say* She smiled at the thought. Somehow she would get through the night and wait until she could talk to Mattie. Delia got up, hung her literary scapulary from her neck, opened the door and went in.

Mattie was nowhere to be seen. A frowning Virginia Woolf and a dandy Baudelaire greeted Delia, looked at her literary scapulary and she at theirs. Following the rules of the game, they folded their hands together and bowed their heads. In unison they exclaimed, "Benediction, dear Saint Theresa." Delia wanted to lose herself in the game, forget everything that had happened that evening. She reached for a plastic tumbler, poured herself some wine from a half-empty bottle, drank it in one gulp, then raised her right hand and made the sign of the cross in the air. Baudelaire and Woolf laughed and applauded.

Delia elbowed her way through the dining room where Emily Dickinson was dancing cheek-to-cheek with Edgar Allan Poe. Ezra Pound lectured T.S. Eliot on the evils of anti-semitic attitudes, while Hemingway eyed Delmira Agustini, Fitzgerald admired Sor Juana from afar, and José Montoya, Luis Valdez and Pancho Villa applauded Alurista's ritual sundance.

Mephistopheles and Faust approached her, extending their hands to her as an invitation to dance with them. She joined them, but after a few steps she felt dizzy. She had not eaten anything since lunchtime and the wine was making her feel sick. She reached the hall and went up the short flight of stairs to Mattie's bedroom, hoping to find it empty so she could lie down for a while. Instead, she found Mattie pouring warm water into a footbath for George Sand. Mattie was happy to see Delia and signaled her to come in. George was obviously in pain.

"Joyce bumped the table and that heavy bust of Beethoven fell on her foot." Mattie winked at Delia.

"Is there anything I can do?" Delia asked solicitously. She welcomed the idea of nursing George's foot and not going out of the bedroom for a while. She moved toward the bed but stopped suddenly. "Who did you say knocked over the bust?"

"James Joyce—what's the matter?" Mattie put down the pan of water she was carrying. *For tonight I am James Joyce* Delia began to laugh nervously. Joyce was there, where she least expected to find him. It had to be the same man. *At last something is beginning to make sense* She shivered at the prospect of seeing him again. What would she say to him? Perhaps more important, what

would he say to her? *I can't face him   He probably thinks
I'm crazy   I could tell him I was rehearsing for the party
That's ridiculous   What do I care what he thinks of me
He's a perfect stranger* There was nothing keeping her there; she
could escape unnoticed through the back door. *I can't go
I'm trapped here   He's out there waiting crouching in the
dark   No he's not   There's no one there Better stay
here just in case   I have to talk to Mattie* She shivered again.

"You look awful," Mattie told her.

"Awful," echoed George between groans.

Mattie hauled Delia toward her dresser. "Come here, look in
the mirror. You look more like a worn-out courtesan than Santa
Teresa. Fix yourself up a little."

Delia looked at herself and saw that her eye make-up had run,
leaving dark, uneven patches around her eyes, and there was no
rouge left on her cheeks.

More like Dracula the undead Delia reached for a tissue to
clean her face and remembered she had kept Joyce's handkerchief.
He was real She found it neatly folded in her skirt pocket, still
moist. *A flapping of wings in the mist   Farewell* Delia
looked at it for a while, then put it back into her pocket. Mattie was
watching her out of the corner of her eye as she applied ointment to
George's foot.

"The crazed and hooded creatures of the heart?" she asked
without turning.

"Yes, crazed and hooded." Delia smiled.

"We'll have to put those creatures in their proper place after
the party, won't we?" Mattie signaled for Delia to help her lay
George on the bed. "Would you mind finding Roger for me? Tell
him Carina—George—is ready to go home." Delia looked confused. "Oops! James Joyce," Mattie explained. "He said he would
take her home. Go ahead."

Followed by a spirited Romeo, a disheveled Juliet sprinted
past Delia and locked herself in the bathroom. Further on, The
Bard explained that Juliet had been flirting with Iago, and that had
unleashed all the furies in young Romeo's heart. Valdez wanted to
know where there was a phone. Murieta and Zapata were late.
Much too late   The revolution was stillborn   Don't

*they know   It died in the hearts of people like Samuel and
me Don't they know*

She felt a lump in her throat, but fought back the tears. If she
started to cry, she would be crying a long time; for her two lost
brothers, her parents whose three children had fallen victims of one
kind of war or another, for all the people like her who believed they
would make a difference and had gotten lost in some obscure corridor of academia. She would be crying for herself.

The knot was loosened, the stream running down her cheeks.
Delia felt the touch of fingers wiping her tears. She recognized the
touch. James Joyce was standing in front of her again. He put his
arms around her. She welcomed his presence.

"George Sand is . . ." She couldn't finish the sentence.

"George can wait. Let's go outside." He was leading her
gently and she offered no resistance.

They went out to the patio. The fog was denser but not very
cold. Delia took off her headdress. They walked to the table and
bench at the far end of the back yard and sat down. She sensed he
was looking at her, but couldn't meet his gaze. His arm pressed
lightly against her. She felt his warmth and had a sudden desire to
put her arms around him, but instead of following her impulse, she
got up and leaned on the table facing him. She observed him. He
had taken his hat and glasses off. She could see that his hairline
was beginning to recede and his eyes were bigger than she had
thought. He smiled. Delia liked his smile. His whole demeanor
invited trust and friendship.

"If you had just been given a potent dose of truth serum, what
would you be telling me?" He lowered his eyes and Delia smiled at
his adolescent gesture. She avoided any thought that would make
her answer with a witticism. Joyce had dared to ask the question
and she would not hide from it.

"That I like you . . . " It was more difficult than she had
realized, but she forced herself to continue. "And I want very
much to have you hold me . . . kiss you . . . It's crazy."

"Is it?" He did not attempt to move toward her.

Delia felt uneasy. She had never said things like those to a
man before. She was walking on uncharted terrain. *Not now Not
again   What's the matter with me* She experienced the same

tingling sensation she had had earlier when she felt herself falling. It ran down her legs and up again to settle just below her navel. It was an aching pleasure and she did not want it to go away. From its center, it spread the whole length of her torso to her arms. She felt her mouth drying up, her heart racing, her hands shaking. She abandoned herself to the feeling and closed her eyes.

A moment later, his arms were around her, his mouth on hers, then on her cheeks, her neck. She pressed closer to him, felt his hardness against her body. Their hands reached up eagerly searching for openings through intricate layers of cloth, finally encountering warm, moist skin. She buried her face in his neck and drew him to her, down to a bed of dewy grass in the mist. In his arms, Delia felt peaceful and secure. Joyce reached for coat and habit and covered her and himself. He did not say anything and she was grateful, preferring to lie there in his warmth, without having to grade his or her performance, as had been the case when she and Fernando made love.

He let his mind wander back to that first moment when he had seen Delia kneeling in front of the rosebush. At first he had been intrigued by the scene he was witnessing, then embarrassed, like a spy in the kingdom of prayer, but he had stayed there, unable to take his eyes off that nun in close communion with God. An old pain came alive somehwere in him. It had been a long time since he had prayed, since that early morning when he saw his wife, half-paralyzed, a drooping eye trying to focus on him. Her hand begged for reassurance, but her mouth could not begin to obey a blood-filled mind which finally lapsed into oblivion, then death. And he had stood there before her, unable to do anything for her except pray to a greater power to spare her and himself.

When it was over, anger replaced faith. The man he had once been was left to roam aimlessly, a shadow in a spiritual wasteland.

James Joyce looked at Delia cuddled next to him. He breathed in the smell of their pleasure, the smell of the ocean. There was no more loneliness, no fear, only the imprint of the precise moment when pleasure and pain joined.

Delia stirred next to him and he tightened his embrace around her. She looked at him, raised her hand and put it on his mouth. He kissed her moist, open palm, leaned forward and playfully pinched one of her nipples with his lips, then the other. She moaned, pressed her body closer to him, and moved her hand slowly down his chest through fields of hair that rose at the touch of her fingers. She cupped her hand over his penis, felt it stirring, growing instantly to fullness. He drew her to him.

For a few seconds she felt as if her soul had escaped from her body through her gasping mouth, and she was dead. She felt his fingers wiping her face, his lips caressing hers. She opened her eyes and looked at him through the curtain of her tears.

"Saint Theresa and James Joyce. Quite a pair we are." He laughed happily.

Delia raised her head to look at him. He pushed her head gently down to his chest again. "I've been thinking about you ever since I saw you kneeling in front of that rosebush. And I felt guilty for wanting a nun. Joyce kept telling me it was all right to want you, but I didn't think I would ever see you again."

The way he had pronounced their assumed names made Delia shiver. *No No   Just another lie   Why must I always impersonate someone   This is wrong   It isn't Yes it is A cheap farce   No   It can't be* She sat up and covered herself with his coat.

James Joyce sensed her tension, but chose to ignore it. He looked at her profile in the dim light—her forehead curving softly at the top of her nose, her lips tightening. What was she trying to hold prisoner? Why was she so afraid? It seemed to him she was someone who had lost a great deal, had perhaps mourned her losses too long. She prompted in him a feeling of tenderness he had not felt in a long time. Would he see her again after that night? Would she let go of her fear of losing one more time? He tried to dismiss those questions as fast as they came to mind.

"Were you surprised to see me here?" he asked in as normal a tone as he could manage.

"Not really." *George   Mattie   Damned* "I was looking for you." Delia looked toward the house and began to gather her clothes. The music was barely audible, and the laughter and chatter had died down.

"Must we?" he heard himself asking and regretted saying it almost at once. He did not want to press her for an answer, but he wanted to see her again. "How about tomorrow? I want to see you again, tomorrow."

"It's already tomorrow." She finished dressing. *There is no tomorrow*

Again, he ignored her brusque remark and helped her button her habit, then kissed her. She felt his warmth again and pulled away.

"I know," he said attempting a smile, "too many complications in your life. Why add one more?"

Delia wanted to answer him, explain her reasons for not seeing him again, but decided to remain silent. *Don't be stupid Tell Who has made you feel that way before   You want him No no   I can't   I don't even know who he is James Joyce   That's who   He's not James Joyce Oh yes he is   Look   He's James Joyce again and he's everything you want   No   No*

James Joyce looked at her and smiled. He reached into his pocket for his wallet, pulled a card out of it and handed it to her. "If you ever want to see me again."

Delia took the card and turned around without saying anything, put it in her pocket next to his handkerchief and began to walk away. A few steps ahead she changed her mind and walked back to him. "Yes, I will call you . . . soon." She held her hand out and motioned for him to walk to the house with her. They said goodbye at the door. She opened it and went in without looking back.

Mattie was in the kitchen readying an icepack. "Gene here—Caesar—got fresh with Virginia Woolf and she smacked him," Mattie said, winking at Delia. "And he fell down and bumped his head on the corner of the coffee table." Mattie put the pack on Caesar's head.

Delia smiled. She felt sorry for Gene; he was a good poet and an easy-going man, but so insecure around women that he always managed to get himself in trouble with them.

Gene wanted to talk and Mattie took him to the living room.

Delia looked at the kitchen clock and was amazed to see it was four-thirty. She began to stack up plates and put glasses in the sink. Then she made coffee.

Mattie came back into the kitchen. "Poor Gene. He has a few drinks and gets so horny . . ."

Delia smiled. *What's my excuse   I wasn't even drunk Mad yes but drunk no   How can I be making jokes at a time like this*

Mattie pulled a frying pan from the cabinet, eggs and bacon from the refrigerator. "I'm starved. I haven't had anything to eat since this morning. Scrambled eggs and bacon okay with you?"

"Uhuh," Delia said absent-mindedly. She arranged plates and cups on two trays.

When the food was ready, they took the trays into the living room, where a fire was already burning. Mattie pushed two arm-chairs close to the fireplace.

"All the props are in place . . ." Mattie looked around. "Ah, the music is missing." She switched the turntable on and the first languid chords of the Albinoni Adagio filled the room. They ate in silence, enjoying the music. It was their private ritual after Mattie's parties, something both of them looked forward to. After finishing their meal, they stretched out on the floor.

"This is my last party, I swear. I spent the whole evening nursing injured bodies and bruised egos. I should have dressed as Florence Nightingale instead of Auntie Mame." Mattie looked at her gown and tried to brush something green and caked from it. "Avocado Dip." She rolled over laughing. "Romeo threw it in Iago's face. You should have seen Iago." She laughed louder. "Thank heaven Moriarty and Holmes stopped them or they would have strangled each other." She coughed a couple of times and rolled back to face Delia, who was hardly listening to her.

"Say, you've got a bad case of the blues." Mattie sat up. "What's the matter? You've been acting very strangely tonight." But it wasn't only that night, she thought. The crisis she had fore-seen some months ago had finally arrived. There was little she could do for her, except be there when Delia needed her.

"Mattie, I just—I made love to a man I don't even know; by the barbecue in your backyard." Delia got up and paced the floor nervously, then sat in one of the armchairs.

"James Joyce, right?" Mattie smiled. She had thought of in-troducing them some time ago, but Delia was having a hard time with her dissertation and her violent affair with Fernando Diéguez still weighed heavily in Delia's mind. "No one better to have an affair with behind the bushes." Mattie couldn't help laughing.

"It isn't an affair," Delia protested. "I didn't meet him until today. I don't even know his real name." She remembered his card and looked in her pocket.

Mattie was already reciting his credentials as if she knew them by heart: "Roger M. Hart, born in Los Angeles, lived there until last year when he moved to San Francisco, works for Marine Resources Ltd., age 46, was a medical doctor and gave it up for a Ph.D. in marine biology."

Delia was surprised. Mattie had never mentioned him before. "How do you know so much about him?"

"He's a distant relative. I don't see him very often. I was really surprised he came tonight." Mattie got up and poked the fire. "He keeps pretty much to himself, ever since his wife died of a . . ."

"His wife died?" Delia interrupted and added, "When?"

"Seven years ago, of a stroke. He took it very hard. For some reason he blamed himself. I guess he thought he hadn't done enough for her, his being a doctor and all that. He abandoned medicine, sold everything and ran away. I didn't hear from him again until late last year." Mattie placed another log in the fireplace.

Delia, aghast, could only listen to Mattie. James Joyce's face flashed in her memory and her hands began to shake violently.

Mattie came closer. "You're not doing well at all." She reached for the afghan on the back of her chair and drew it around Delia's shoulders. "Tell me, what's worrying you? Why are you shaking?"

Delia wrapped herself in the afghan and closed her eyes until her hands steadied. Then she related all the events of that evening, leaving out only the details of their love-making.

"Oh, my poor Delia. How horrible!" Mattie embraced her. "Did you tell Roger about it?"

"How could I?" Delia whispered.

"I guess not. What am I saying?" Mattie rubbed Delia's hands. "You're so cold." She got up and adjusted the thermostat.

"What's happening to me, Mattie? Am I going mad?" Delia shivered again and wrapped the afghan more tightly around her.

"If you can still ask that question, I'd say no, you're not going mad." Mattie smiled and sat on her armchair, looking directly at Delia. "It's called 'battle fatigue,' sheer exhaustion. You've had a pretty rough year—damned dissertation, and that awful relationship with Fernando. Anybody could have told you that relationship was going to bring you nothing but trouble."

"Maybe that's the problem. Everyone else seems to know what's good for me, but I don't. I still don't know how I could take so much abuse from Fernando. I didn't even enjoy making love to him. It was all a mess. But, you know? I kept going back to him and I didn't know why. The proverbial moth playing with the flame." Delia got up, walked to the fireplace, then sat in the other armchair. "I don't recognize myself anymore. I don't know what to do."

"I think it's time you stop punishing yourself for other people's sins and failures." Mattie looked sternly at Delia. "You've been carrying a heavy load." She stretched over and placed her hand on Delia's shoulder. "You're not responsible for your father's weakness or for your brothers' deaths or for anyone else's failures." She turned Delia around to face her. "There's only so much you can do for other people. You can't let their ghosts rule you. You have a lot of living to do yet."

Delia bowed her head and looked at her trembling hands. She took a deep breath. "I have this sense of loss deep inside me, Mattie. I've lost something essential. Maybe some innocence, faith. All these years and I haven't accomplished much. It isn't anyone else's failures I carry with me. It's my own failure, don't you see?" Delia got up and walked to the window. "There were so many things I set out to do and haven't done. I belong to a privileged class now. I have a doctorate—whatever that means. Chicanos can't afford not to be ruled by their ghosts. We're like ants who carry their dead on their shoulders . . ." She turned around to face Mattie.

"Is there any reason why you can't do something for yourself too?" Mattie joined Delia at the window. "After all, it isn't like you haven't done anything for Chicanos. I still remember that year you were carrying eighteen units and volunteering at the clinic in Oakland three nights a week. You're too hard on yourself. You're exhausted. You don't eat properly and you don't get enough rest."

Delia sighed. "I guess you're right, but that still doesn't explain what happened to me early this evening."

"No, I guess it doesn't." Mattie looked down at the floor. "The writer and her ghosts."

Delia was confused. "What did you say?"

"I've always thought you had the imagination and the sensitivity of a writer." Mattie smiled at Delia's loud gasp of incredulity. *This time she's outdone herself* "You've got to be kidding. A writer? I couldn't begin to . . ." Delia stopped in mid-sentence and looked at Mattie. *Why not   You know she's right What did you do when lectures were boring   The journal of nightmares   And the stories you're always telling yourself*

"Why not? I tell you, you'd surely be a better writer than many people who are writing now." Mattie smiled. "Julio Singer, for example. Remember?"

"Will we ever forget him?" Delia laughed. "The bim-bombom poet with that heavy conga he carried everywhere. Samuel used to tease him and tell him that the chancellor granted our demands during the strike just so he wouldn't have to listen to Julio's conga and awful poetry." Delia paused. "It's funny, for the past week I've been thinking a lot about that time. What made you remember him?"

"I saw him the other day," Mattie said. "He was still playing his conga and reciting that poetry of his. He's now a *published poet*. I took him to lunch, for old times' sake. We spent a good afternoon on 'memory lane.' He's kept in touch with a lot of people from that time. You should talk to him."

"With Samuel too?"

"No, not Samuel or Jeff. Jeff Morones. Now, there was a good poet; handsome too."

Delia turned her head slightly as if someone had tapped on her shoulder, then looked at Mattie. "Jeff wrote poetry?"

No matter what I do just go along with me   Ok Jeff what are you doing   Hmmmm   Jeff wrote poetry He never said anything   How could he   I never gave him a chance We think we know someone   Then

Mattie got up and poked the fire. "He was in love with someone. For a while, Sara and I thought it was you, but then he left. I never found out who she was. Did you know about her?"

"No." Delia stared at the fire. "I thought it was me too. I guess I wanted to believe that." She looked at Mattie. "I guess we'll never know who she was."

"Le temps perdu . . . Ahhh!" Mattie sighed. "They were exhilarating times, weren't they? All of you were amazing. Just think. You were only a rag-tag bunch, yet you were able to shake down one of the most powerful educational institutions in the country. That's a story yet to be told." Mattie paused. "The story you must write."

Delia threw off the afghan and got up. She was surprised to find herself so at ease with the idea of writing. Maybe she was grasping at straws, hoping to find a way to get herself out of spiritual deprivation, but a voice inside kept assuring her that writing would help her restore proper order to a world that had collapsed around her. It had before, long ago, when she sat down every day to write in her journal.

Mattie observed her attentively, a grin of satisfaction on her face. After a while, she went into the kitchen and came back with two glasses of brandy. She handed one to Delia.

"I suppose I could try." Delia sipped her brandy. "But it'll have to wait for a while. I have to find a job, some way to support myself, my parents. I've decided to go to Monterey for a while, maybe home after that." She walked back to her chair and covered herself with the afghan.

"You could come with me." Mattie sipped her brandy and put the glass down on the tray.

"Where are you going?" *She's full of surprises tonight*

"I'm not teaching next quarter and I have a sabbatical coming. I've decided to go to Central America."

"Central America? Why? Guatemala, Honduras, El Salvador, Nicaragua. Mattie, there's a revolution going on."

"That's why. There's a group of journalists and historians going." Mattie looked very serious and Delia knew there was no point in trying to persuade her otherwise. "Read the newspapers.

You hardly see any news about it in the papers. We're going to try to change that. The American people must know what the government is doing there."

As always, Mattie was right. Delia nodded.

"You should go with me," Mattie said. "It's important that Chicanos get involved. Who do you think is going to fight that war if we get into it?"

Delia didn't answer. *There won't be a war hermanita* "I agree with you, but I'm not the person to go with you. If Samuel were here . . . Maybe I can join you later, when I have some money." *I could sell my car   That's not enough   I have nothing of value   No I can't go   Not now* "Things never work out the way we want them. The timing is all screwed up."

"It's never the right time for anything. We grab the moment, that's all we can do. And now is always the moment. Write the story—yours, theirs. Plunge in and swim with all your might." Mattie gestured forcefully. "But you're right, you have to stay and begin your book. That's important too. Maybe later you and Roger can join me. He would do a lot of good there. He's a damned good doctor. It's time he forgave himself for not being God."

Mattie walked to the bookcase and pulled out a book. She leafed through it and pulled out a pink paper from it. She began to read aloud.

"You descend, slowly at first, cautiously. You move unrestrained through the water, free. Your heart responds to the tempo of the current. It pulls you in, sucks you into a liquid abyss. Thoughts lie incomplete somewhere in your mind. Fear rushes out of your body with every breath. And all your pores open to the inebriating essence of the depths. You feel the hand pulling you toward the surface and you fight it. You've become one with the sea. Nothing else matters."

"Who wrote that?" Delia asked intrigued.

"I wrote it down, but it's not mine. I extracted it from something a deepsea diver told me." Mattie winked at Delia.

"Joyce? I mean—Roger?"

"Yes, good old James Joyce." Mattie laughed. "A bit romantic, I must say, but useful. You see, he's describing what artists must go through, writers too; actually, anyone who passionately gives himself or herself to something." Mattie's eyes lit up. "Aha! Passion, that's the key word."

Delia felt blood rushing to her face. Mattie was looking amusedly at her but refrained from making a comment. She left the room and went into her bedroom. Delia took the trays to the kitchen.

Mattie came out a moment later with two nightgowns. "We'll have to crowd in the guest room. Roger didn't take Carina home; she's sleeping in my bed." Mattie was speaking in a low voice.

"Why are you whispering?" Delia asked her.

"Let's go into the guest room and I'll tell you." Mattie chuckled, obviously amused at something Delia could not begin to imagine.

"I forgot about Carina," she added once inside. "I don't think she heard us. Just the same we'd better whisper."

"What's so important about her hearing us?" Delia was confused.

"I think she has a crush on James Joyce—Roger, I mean." Mattie shook her head.

"What?" Delia stopped undressing.

"This has been quite a night! Intrigue, passion, jealousy and comedy. Quite a night!" Mattie chuckled softly. "Don't let that upset you. He doesn't care for her the way she cares for him. I'm very sure of that." She felt embarrassed at her indiscretion, but there was no taking back what she had said. "I'm sorry. I didn't mean to tell you this way. It isn't important anyway," she added reassuringly.

"How can it not be important?" Delia said in a whisper.

"Listen. She's a grown woman and she has to face reality. He doesn't care for her, I'm sure." She sat on the bed next to Delia. "Now, don't start feeling responsible for her, too."

"I don't feel responsible for her . . . but . . ." Delia continued taking off her hose, but her hands were shaking again and she stopped.

"Roger needs someone like you and you need him too." Mattie held Delia's hands. "Romanticism and all, he's too good to pass up for anything or anyone."

"I'm not too sure about that, Mattie. Maybe before, but now . . . No, it wouldn't work." Delia straightened herself up and finished undressing.

"Why not?"

Delia didn't answer. She put on the nightgown, got up and walked to the bathroom.

"Is it because he's Anglo? Sourdough balls, as Sara used to say. That Sara. Where did she get all that?" Mattie followed Delia.

"Maybe," Delia answered from the bathroom. She opened the faucet and began to splash cold water on her face. Mattie walked back to the bedroom and looked out the window.

Delia thought of taking a shower before going to bed, but decided against it. James Joyce's odor still lingered on her skin. "Joyce," she said under her breath. "I can't even call you by your real name. You weren't real." But she knew he had been real and, though she chose to think otherwise, he had already become part of her life. She decided not to shower. If only for that night, she wanted to keep his memory close.

Delia walked back into the guest room and joined Mattie at the window. Light was already breaking through the fog. With every thrust of sunlight, another part of the city below them became visible. It was like watching a photograph develop—first the campus, then the marinas, an instant later parts of the Bay Bridge, but the city across the Bay, where James Joyce slept, was still enveloped in fog. Mattie brushed Delia's face with her hand. "We've made it through another Day of the Dead," she whispered.

They smiled at each other, then drew the curtains.

II

I've known loveless nights
  when only music fills the empty space
  amidst black fires,
  eyes of the tigers
  waiting for my soul
  to leave its boundaries,
  and then I've written verses
  prayers
  incantations
  to exorcise their dark power.

I've known passion and pain and joy,
  I've been hurt and
  I've brandished silence
  This double sharp-edged blade
  that wounds two hearts at once.

Chapter 6

"Asunción Aguirre Cadena, your great grandmother, was a skilled silversmith. Her smiles were as bright as the silver chains on her table at the end of the day. I can close my eyes and still remember the rhythmic murmur of her voice at night telling us stories and legends of long ago—the color and texture of the landscape, the sorrowful song of La llorona, the hoofbeats of the horse the devil rode and the prayer that sent him away the night your great grandfather died.

"Other nights I would sit next to her listening to the song of the crickets and cicadas, watching hundreds of fireflies circle the night. I knew she was thinking of Simón, her brother, who had gone mad, people said, because of his libertine ways. After supper, she would take him out to the lot next to their house to watch the fireflies. One night she forgot to bolt the door of his bedroom from the outside and he escaped. She found him sprawled face up on the ground, his hands and mouth full of fireflies. He was dead. Everyone in the town suspected Asunción of poisoning him, because fireflies don't kill, but if she did, she took the secret to her grave.

"Vicenta, your grandmother, was a curandera and every morning I would help her water the herbs she grew in pots, in the back corridor of her house. She prepared oils and powders, and people would come from far away to be treated by her. A man was saved from snakebite; a woman finally conceived after years of waiting.

"Diego, your grandfather, was a grain broker and would go to the *sierra* to trade with the mountain villagers for textiles. He was one of the few travelers the villagers would trust and they would let him spend the night in their homes. One night, darkness fell before he could reach Zamora. He came to a hut on the skirt of the volcano and decided to try his luck. The people at the hut were very friendly. They offered him a place to sleep and soup with lots of fat, tender meat that smelled like chicken. He asked for their permission to wash his hands before sitting down to eat. They pointed the way to the rain tank at the other end of the corridor. As he walked through a semidark room, the pungent smell of fresh blood struck his nostrils and he stopped to see where it was coming from. He was dismayed to see half a man hanging from a meat hook. He remembered the white meat he had thought was chicken and his stomach turned. He knew he could not leave because that would mean sure death. He ate the soup and complimented the woman serving him. The next morning his skin had turned pale yellow and no matter how many remedies Vicenta tried, her curative powers were useless against it. He stayed that way until he died, a week before the world, our world, came to an end.

"It was a beautiful morning, and your father and I had gotten up early to go with Uncle Chinto to the marketplace. It was *tianguis* day, and all the Indians were coming down from the mountains to sell their crafts. José Guadalupe and I played hide-and-seek under the tapestries and ponchos, and spent a long time just looking and smelling the wooden boxes whenever a customer let us do it. Uncle Chinto bought us two small boxes from which snakes with sharp metal fangs sprang when you opened them.

"Uncle Chinto had finished his business at the marketplace and we were walking slowly back to the house when we felt a trembling under our feet. In the next few seconds the earth shook for what seemed an eternity, giving no one the opportunity to run or even scream. When it was over, nothing remained standing except the main building of the town church. Of our family, only Uncle Chinto and your father and I survived. After we buried our dead, Uncle Chinto decided to try his luck across the border and he brought us with him.

"Imperial Valley, San Fernando, San Joaquin, Salinas. My first menstrual flow fertilized the soil where onions grew. I was becoming a woman, only I didn't know I was barren. My blood would never nourish another being; my arms would never hold my own child.

"I was sixteen when I met your uncle Jack, and seventeen when we were married. Since he was a U.S. citizen, we applied for my residence and I got it. Jack was a foreman at the lumberyard and was able to get your father a job there; we helped him get his residence, too. He enrolled both of us in night school to learn English. José Guadalupe and I had gone to grammar school in

Mexico. Although we hadn't finished it, at least we knew how to read and write. I liked going to school, except when we had to study English prepositions. The Devil's language! Since I couldn't get pregnant, I continued my education until I got my high school diploma. Imagine! I was already twenty-four years old by then.

"Your father was laid off and decided to move to Los Angeles where he met your mother. Rosa Elena had moved to Los Angeles, after her mother, Eva Gallardo, died. They had been living in Stockton. Eva was thirty-seven and pregnant with your mother when she left her husband, Laz Cardona, because she found out that he was in love with Silvia, Eva's cousin.

"Eva found work at a sewing factory, but she already had poor eyesight, and doing that kind of work made it worse. She went blind. Your mother was sixteen—your age—when she went to work to support her mother and herself.

"For two years, your grandmother refused to leave the house. Then one day, for no apparent reason, Eva walked into the street when Rosa Elena was at work. She didn't hear the car coming and it hit her. She died instantly.

"Your mother tried to find her father, but she knew very little about him. As far as she could tell, Eva and Silvia had been raised by their grandmother, who had died before Eva married Laz, and your mother didn't know of any other relatives.

"Living in Stockton was becoming very sad for Rosa Elena. A friend of hers at the sewing factory told her that she could get a better job in Los Angeles and start a new life. Rosa Elena gathered her few belongings and left for Los Angeles, where she met your father. A few months later, they were married.

"Sad and happy memories, but I wanted never to forget any of them. And here they all are: our family, always with me, and now with you, Delia. As I have told you their story, so must you tell it to your children and their children."

Delia had spent every summer since she was eight years old with her aunt Marta. Delia and her mother would take the late night bus and would arrive in Monterey early in the morning. She loved those night rides and almost never slept. Through the window she would see the downtown buildings, then other cities she had never visited, and finally the open road flanked by walls of darkness blending at the horizon into a starry sky. Closer to Monterey, she would strain her eyes to catch a glimpse of the great ocean and the boats, imagine the cypress towering in the distance, half hidden in the early morning mist.

There was something special, almost magical, about the peninsula. Perhaps it had to do with her aunt Marta's love for it and for her, Delia thought as she pulled into the driveway that early December morning, happy at having left Berkeley behind, ready to start anew.

Her life in Monterey had been different, fuller, she wanted to think, perhaps freer. It always amazed her how limiting life in a large city could be. People didn't know how to cope with the vastness and set up invisible borders beyond which they would hardly step, so that in fact, it seemed, as though they lived in small towns. They would warn one another about the dangers and horrors the rest of the city had in store for those who ventured off the tribal grounds.

"Funny, isn't it?" Mattie had said when Delia tried to explain her preference for Monterey over Los Angeles. "We crowd into huge hives, thinking all the time the city will protect us from danger. And now the city, with all its light and power, has become our worst enemy. And yet, look at all that beauty."

They were standing at the water's edge in Sausalito, looking at the city of San Francisco across the bay, guarded on the east and north by two concrete and steel giants rocking in the December wind. It was the evening before Mattie's departure for Mexico City, where she was to board the plane that would take her and her colleagues to Honduras and then to Panama. Delia had left for Monterey a week later.

Ever since their encounter in early November, Roger had been constantly on her mind, but knowing that she would be gone soon, Delia had not called him. She gave herself all kinds of excuses, but secretly she hoped that somehow he would try to get in touch with her. When he didn't, she tried to put him out of her mind and busied herself with packing her own things, running errands and helping Mattie clean her house.

"One day, all of this will be only a memory," she told herself many times, but every night before falling asleep she would conjure the memory of their night together and make up accidental encounters at the airport or the wharf, at a restaurant overlooking the Monterey Bay, in the spring, in the rain, near the produce at a supermarket, in a small shop on Paseo de la Reforma. They would always end their journey in a bedroom she had designed piece by piece, with tall windows opening onto the San Francisco Marina and the Golden Gate Bridge. In the mornings, all the fantasies would evaporate like night fog at Delia's first awareness of light streaming through her bedroom windows, leaving a dull ache just below her navel and lines of poems she would write in her journal while having toast and coffee.

They were harmless fantasies, she thought, and she even laughed at the prospect of meeting Roger, still dressed as James Joyce, while fondling cantaloupes and smelling strawberries. She wanted to tell Mattie but had changed her mind, for she was adhering to her decision not ever to see him again, and she did not want to reopen the subject for discussion.

Delia was happy to be back in Monterey, in her room where she had spent many happy summers, talking with her friends, listening to her aunt's stories, or reading undisturbed. She would never tell anyone, but ever since her first visit, she had thought of that room as her true home.

In Los Angeles she had lived a more restricted life, under the ever vigilant eyes of her mother. She liked school but was almost never allowed to venture out on her own, except to the neighborhood grocery store to buy something her mother needed for dinner. That almost always meant two trips because, no matter how well they calculated the exact amount for her purchases, she was always short. Prices seemed to jump from day to day, and Mr. Hassan would not give credit to anyone, despite having known all his neighbors for years.

On spring Sundays her father would take them for a ride in the old Chevy, or they would pack the Coleman coolers and thermos for a day at the beach where they would meet the Martínez and the

Saldaña families who lived in Ventura. Mr. Saldaña would play the guitar and they would all sing. Sometimes they would just listen to his tenor voice that made even people who didn't understand Spanish look for the owner of such an instrument.

Sebastián was the only one who would not take part in the singing. As soon as the guitar was out of its case, he would leave for a stroll down the beach. He lived in a world all his own.

"Funny," she had told Samuel when she first spoke to him about her family. "Brother and sister, living in the same house and I can't say I knew him."

"You hardly got a chance," he commented. "How old were you when he died?"

"Fourteen. Ricardo was sixteen. He was the only one who knew anything about Sebastián's life away from home." Delia paused then continued. "One day Ricardo told me that Sebastián was in love with a married woman, a gringa by the name of Laura. Sebastián hung around her husband and other men who were into drugs. I don't know when he started shooting up. I guess it just happened, or maybe he wanted to get her to notice him."

"Did your *jefito* know about it?"

"Not until he went to claim Sebastián's body." *He probably wouldn't have done anything anyway* Delia swallowed hard, then coughed a few times as if something had gotten stuck in her throat. "Ricardo and I tried to tell my mother about it, without giving away the whole story, but she didn't listen to us." *No sabe lo que quiere todavía Ya encontrará el camino   He's a man He'll find it   The needle   Es hombre   Es hombre* "If maybe my father had forced him to go to Monterey."

"I don't think that was the answer," Samuel replied.

"What then?" Delia pressed him for an answer. "What?"

"It's the system." Samuel put his elbow on the table and rested his face on the back of his hand. "White supremacy. Colonialism. Whatever we want to call it. It spells racism, oppression. No choices." He looked at Delia hanging onto every word. "Your brothers were both victims of it."

"You mean . . . But parents should do something about it, too." She lowered her eyes. "My mother could have done something. At least tell Ricardo not to enlist. He wasn't drafted. He enlisted. But she wouldn't do it." She bit her lower lip. "And she said she loved him." *I loved him too   She let them kill him She did   She's to blame   She doesn't love me I love you m'ijo   She thinks I don't know   I don't hear She never said that to me   Buenos grades m'ijita Papá Te traigo ice cream   Inteligente m'ijita   Mira mamá Saqué muchas A's   Pon la mesa   Do the dishes That's all I'm good for   M'ijo So handsome in his uniform*

"Yes, I suppose they could. We all could." Samuel stopped to think. "This may sound like I'm pro-establishment." Delia raised her eyebrows and Samuel smiled. "I really think that until our people exercise the power of the vote, there's little hope that things will change in the community." Delia nodded.

"How do we do that?"

"Have voter registration campaigns in all the barrios. Infiltrate both the Democratic and Republican parties." Samuel rubbed his chin. "That's where it's at."

"The Republicans, too? Reagan is a Republican." *Join the enemy   Really*

"Yes, the Republicans, too. Especially the Republicans." Samuel laughed when he saw Delia frowning. "I told you it would sound pro-establishment." He was pensive for an instant, then asked, "Do your parents vote?"

Delia thought about his question for a moment. "My father. Once. For Kennedy." She pinched her nose. "We had an old Motorola. The picture was so bad. Anyway, I remember we watched Kennedy's funeral. My father had tears in his eyes. He made Ricardo and me stand up during the procession. He put his hand on his chest." Delia paused. "Then . . . That sound of the bugle. Long. Sad."

Three years later Ricardo was dead   The bugle played My last summer in Monterey   It would never again be the same Samuel was right   It wouldn't have made a difference Aunt Marta   I sent her their pictures   I wanted them to be there   Next to Diego   Asunción   Vicenta Simón

Ricardo and Sebastián had spent only one summer in Monterey, despite their father's wishes. Ricardo would probably have gone a few more times, but Sebastián easily convinced him not to go.

Ricardo was very enterprising and talked Mr. Hassan into giving him a job in his store every summer. Mr. Hassan paid him very little, but he didn't mind and used the money to buy meat, rice, *frijoles* and *tortillas*, and convinced his mother to make *tacos* and *burritos* for him to sell in the street.

Every time Delia came back from Monterey, he would lay his profits on her bed for her to see. The next day they would walk to the bank where he would deposit his money. *If more Mexicans were like you young man your people would not be in such a precarious situation We'll take good care of your money What does he mean Don't pay attention These gabachos are all the same   But he thinks we are lazy and look at Daddy He works very hard And Mr Saldaña and Mr. Martínez too   We'll show them hermanita We'll show them*

Everyone praised Ricardo's enterprising spirit, especially his mother, who would take out his savings passbook and show it to anyone willing to listen. Ricardo was saving his money to go to college, because he knew his parents would not be able to afford it. He didn't know then that his savings would one day pay for Sebastián's funeral.

Delia saw her father, dressed in the only suit he had ever had, stand before Sebastián's grave, distant and serious. For an instant she felt angry at him. For days afterwards, she could not stand being in the same room with him, and would not respond to the inquiring look in his eyes every time she moved away from him. Every night she would hear him walk down the hall to the living room when he thought everyone was asleep and she would wait until his footsteps returned and the door to his room closed. This was something unusual because it was his daily routine to go to bed early.

One night, she decided to find out what he was doing up until so late and she followed him. She saw his silhouette against the window and heard the muffled sounds of his sobbing. Her first impulse was to go to him and comfort him, but she found herself fixed in her place, unable to move toward him or leave, until he turned around and saw her. He walked slowly to her and opened his arms and she held him. She wanted to say something to him, confess her anger, ask him why he hadn't done something to prevent Sebastián's death, but every question and every recrimination made the lump in her throat grow larger until she could hardly breathe and her body went limp. She woke up a few minutes later in her room. Her father was kneeling beside her bed, rubbing her arms. He didn't say anything to her but he smiled, tucked her in and left the door open behind him.

The next evening, her father came home with a box of bitter chocolate truffles and handed it to her. She was surprised because it was only on Sundays, from time to time, that her father would buy truffles and they would eat them after supper. She opened the box and they sat in the living room, smelling each one before biting into it, savoring each tiny piece until they were all gone.

That night, Delia's father went to bed at the usual time and she fell asleep still waiting to hear the sound of his footsteps. It was the first time since her brother had died that she did not cry herself to sleep.

As time went by, Delia was able to understand her father better. His was the story of a man who was sensitive, perhaps too sensitive, uprooted and left at the mercy of circumstances not of his own choosing. He had been a migrant worker, uneducated, and perhaps because of that his greatest ambition was for his children to have a good education; yet he believed that not everything was learned in school. He couldn't afford for them to travel, so he welcomed his sister's offer to have them spend summers with her in Monterey.

Delia learned later, secretly, because they had never spoken about it, that her father was very happy she was at Berkeley, although Sister Marguerite and Aunt Marta had had to talk him and her mother into letting her go. His dream of seeing her graduate from one of the most prestigious universities in the country was the only thing that made her absence from home bearable for him, especially after the death of his sons. Neither Delia nor her father realized then that his dream would be her prison for a long time.

Although they were brother and sister, Marta was very different from José Guadalupe Treviño, but they were very close. Delia would know when her aunt was on the phone because her father, holding back his laughter, would say, "Yes, this is José Guadalupe Treviño, son of Vicenta Jiménez de Treviño and Diego Treviño Aguirre, who was the son of Alberto Treviño Zamora and Asunción Aguirre Cadena, the same one who had an uncle Simón who went mad, at your service. Is this Marta Treviño de Ciotti, the keeper of all the souls in the family?"

Halfway through his recitation he would start chuckling and his eyes would light up. He treasured his sister's letters and kept them in old cigar boxes on his dresser. He would read each letter to his children after dinner, then fold it exactly as it had come and place it in the top box with the others.

Sometimes Delia wouldn't understand some of the words in her aunt's letters, because she wrote them in Spanish; she'd copy those words to ask her aunt about them on her next visit, and her patience had always been well rewarded. Marta would not only explain their meaning, but would also add plenty of examples. Sometimes, she would make up chants or rhymes using them; at other times, she would tell her stories about their family.

Listening to her was a pleasure for Delia, a treat topped only by the tasty hot chocolate and *pan dulce* Marta made for both to have during their linguistic expeditions.

For seven summers Delia had lived in a bountiful place where music, legend and family history were consumed every day like food to keep alive and healthy. It was there she began to understand what people meant later by the "living language" and "the dynamics of culture."

Through the years, her aunt had kept Delia's room intact. There were the dolls her uncle Jack had given her, the stack of Mexican records next to the phonograph, the gallery of family photos—the last few frames empty, awaiting memories, as her aunt would say.

Eva   Was she beautiful   Do you look like her mother Talk to me about Eva mother   Did she hear the car coming Did she want to die so you could go on with your life Talk to me about Eva mother   About Sebastián   Ricardo I would understand   I would

There was also the altar of the dead they had made during Delia's third summer in Monterey. Marta's *comadre* Cloti had asked for her help in designing an altar for the church for the *Día de los Muertos* in November. Delia wanted to know all about it, so, although it was only August, they busied themselves making an altar. They made the traditional candy skulls and the bread for the dead while Jack made the shelves.

One for Asunción One for Vicenta Another for Diego One more for Matilde my sister a little rose on the forehead Just one rose Let's make it blue One for my brother Manuel a marigold for him bright yellow One for Simón fireflies in his mouth

They made the *papel-picado* cutouts and Delia glued them on long, thin sticks to be installed at the ends of each shelf. There were also tiny pictures of Kennedy and Pope John next to a medal of the Sacred Heart; two embroideries Marta had made years ago showing the heads of Tiburcio Vásquez and Joaquín Murrieta hung on each side of the picture of the Virgen de Guadalupe. Marta was a great admirer of both folk heroes, and their feats and exploits were part of her storytelling repertoire. *Quite a group I'll have to change some things before I show it to Cloti Pagan she'll say sacrilegious*

Delia lay on her bed, pulled the pillows and propped them under her neck to have a better view of the photographs on the wall opposite her bed. They stared at her in silence, but their stories were engraved in every gesture, in the eyes at rest, in the smiles and the inaudible words.

Being in that room always gave Delia a feeling of well being. She was someone special there, but was also a part of a larger family and of a community whose history in California was forever present. Like the cypresses with their twisted roots searching for nourishment, she and her family stood on the rocky shore. One day, she hoped, they would not have to trade beauty for survival any more.

Chapter 7

The icy lyrics of the moon shine on the tiny pools in the yard
Beat egg whites until stiff and set aside   October will be
here   Blend masa and cream thoroughly   Add butter
or margarine and beat well   Summer will be over
Mattie Gone ten months   Her last letter   Postmark
Miami Add salt and egg yolks one at a time   I wish she was
back   Symmetry of petals   It'll give me time to finish
the novel Takes so long Add baking powder   Add add add
Sit there until my back aches   My eyes are red
Petals caressed by the swollen tongue of the sun   The words
don't come Hmmm Fold in the egg whites   Without warning
They're there on the page She'll have a lot of stories to tell It'll be
good to see her again   For the filling wilt onion in hot oil
Add tomatoes Tomato lies cheerfully with onion or something like
that Add chiles   Tomato loves   Onion wants and here
comes chile to upset it all   Picardía chicana   I'll ask
her to spend a few days here I don't want to go to Berkeley
No she'll probably be tired   Olives   Raisins
A dash of salt   I'll have to go   Where fog ends sadness begins   Place half of the masa mixture at the bottom of
a casserole   This is all so stupid What are you afraid of
Top with filling   He won't be there and even if he is
Hmmm   This is going to be some dinner Hunger There's a
kind of hunger only a greasy tamal can satisfy A hunger
The solitary rose in November   Pre- heat oven to 350 The
collective memory of spring on a bare limb No   On a naked
branch   That's it Bake for 30 minutes The soul is bared The
body naked   Everything I write is so personal And now to
wait My life is one big waiting room Corny corny No one has to
read it   The light of the decaying sun   The branches
of the sequoia   Say the things I can't tell anyone Pain Passion Loveless nights Weakness   Despair   Does he
ever think of me   There won't be fog tonight   His
name is Roger   An absurd name James Joyce   That's

95

better   The light etches long and slim blades of shadow on the wall   I still think of him When the wind becomes a whisper and fog rolls in from the ocean It's getting dark   I was once afraid of night Now I like darkness The tiger's dominion It's mine "Tyger Tyger Burning bright In the forests of the night" Burning bright Does he remember me   What's the use Why can't things be simple   Nothing ever is Pick up the phone Call him No I kissed you once under a bloodstained flag Oh Jeff I do love you I couldn't sleep that night I was thinking of you It seems so long ago   A lifetime How old were you Jeff Twenty one going on ninety You never did again   What   You never kissed me again We were never alone No one was alone then I thought you didn't want to be alone with me Maybe I didn't Why I'm not sure Angry Afraid I suppose Everything was happening so fast   I should have sent my sidekick   Your what   You know In western movies there's always the cowboy hero A loner Rage pouring from every pore but shy and sensitive deep inside and in love with the girl but can't let her know 'cause she fights him and he's not sure and besides it would destroy his macho image and the sidekick knows all this so he tries to explain to the girl Where do you get all this   From the movies I told you Well who was your sidekick   My Harley Davidson but it didn't speak caló Seriously   There was Samuel but he wouldn't have done it Why not   Big brother No one dared get close to you while he was around and then I left Berkeley Why did you   There was nothing for me there Well there was you but you were only a dream like everything else then A wet dream Thanks a lot   You know what I mean I know   I have no regrets   I do I stayed Why didn't you leave then I tried many times and I couldn't It sounds like a Buñuel movie It was a Buñuel movie

The sun was rising east of the mountains and a few tufts of fog still hung between them covering the pines, but the ocean was at rest, a blue rippling canvas where April's first light etched the silhouettes of sailboats. All winter long the storms had come and the waters had surged, mimicking the thundering liquid symphony of the sky.

Everyone had complained about the harshness of that particular winter, but not Delia or her aunt Marta, who went for a walk to Cannery Row every Saturday morning in boots, raincoats, wool hats, scarves and gloves.

Delia had welcomed the storms that gave her time for herself. She had intended to stay only a few weeks in Monterey, enough to catch her breath before the journey to Los Angeles, but as time went by, she found herself more and more reluctant to pack her suitcases and head south.

Her aunt was delighted at the prospect of having Delia close, so she could nurse her back to health; it was obvious to her that her niece was not well. At first Marta thought Delia had lived a busy life in Berkeley and had simply not been taking care of herself; she made a point of preparing all of Delia's favorite dishes, but nothing seemed to whet her appetite. She knew there had to be another reason, but she couldn't begin to guess the cause of the malady that made her niece toss and turn at night and talk in her sleep. Marta became so concerned that she would get up in the middle of the night and check on Delia. One night, on her way to her bedroom, she heard Delia sobbing. At first, she stood by the door wondering whether she should go in and find out once and for all about the problem. When she finally decided to go in, Delia seemed to be asleep.

Marta was puzzled. She touched Delia's forehead lightly to check her temperature and found it normal, but noticed that her cheeks were moist. Delia stirred but did not wake up. Marta stayed in the room for a while, as she had done so many times through the years, watching Delia sleep, thanking God for the pleasure the young girl had brought her. She was grateful to Rosa Elena and José Guadalupe for letting Delia spend the summers there, for writing her with news about their daughter to compensate for the times when Delia was not in Monterey.

They had all spent Christmas together in Monterey and Marta expected them to inquire about Delia's health, but they didn't seem to be concerned. Perhaps it was needless worry, she thought, as she walked to the door. It was then that Delia murmured, "Joyce. The rose is dead. Dead." Marta repeated the words to herself as if to learn them by heart.

Walking by her side, the next day, Marta tried to think of ways to ask Delia about her dream, but she could not find an appropriate opportunity to approach the subject. It was when they reached the front garden of her house that she noticed that the rosebush had one bud, a yellow one.

"Look, Delia, the first rose. Isn't it beautiful?" Marta said joyfully, ready to use that as an excuse to guide the conversation to the subject of Delia's dreams and problems.

Delia looked at the rosebud with no apparent discomfort or apprehension and Marta was again confused. Delia was ready to go into the house when she heard her aunt ask behind her, "Why is the rose dead, darling?"

Delia turned around to look at her aunt and Marta saw the puzzled look in her eyes, something that confused her even more. "What did you say, Auntie?" Delia moved back to where Marta was. "The rose isn't dead, Auntie. Is there something wrong?"

Marta smiled. "No, darling, not this rose. The rose in your dream."

Delia looked at her aunt and leaned against the wall. *The rose in my dreams* She remembered her dream from the night before. If her aunt had simply asked what she had dreamt about (a question she had interpreted as a morning greeting on previous occasions), Delia would have said as always that she had not dreamt at all. Indeed, she could not remember dreaming about anything in particular, until her aunt inquired about it.

"I talked in my sleep?" Delia did not wait for her aunt to answer. "What else did I say?"

"You talked about a woman, Joyce, I believe. Who is she?" Marta took Delia by the arm and they walked toward the door. "Let's go in. It's cold out here."

Delia went to the kitchen, served two cups of coffee, and sat down at the table in front of her aunt. "It's a long story, Auntie, one only Mattie knows about."

"We have all day, darling. Your uncle won't be back until nightfall. When he and Cerdeño go fishing . . . Anyway, tell me."

Marta poured more coffee into Delia's cup and her own.

"It's not a woman. It's a man. I call him James Joyce." Delia spoke slowly at first, trying to choose the right beginning for the story her imagination had broken into disjointed episodes, so that at times she could not remember the chronological sequence of events. She was giving herself time to figure out how to tell about making love with James Joyce without actually saying it. *Writing by implication   The poet's task*

She began telling it in Spanish, which she always spoke with her aunt, but as she related the episode about her near-accident and her fear of being mad, she switched to English, something that Marta found very amusing and interesting but not strange, as she herself would on occasions do the same thing. "There are things," she had told Cloti many times, "that one can only express in mother's language."

"And you still think of him? It's been three months." She held Delia's trembling hand in hers as Delia finished her story. "You must love him very much. Why didn't you call him?"

"I don't know, Auntie. Sometimes I think I did the right thing. There are times I'm sure it wouldn't work." Delia was relieved to be able to talk about it at last. "Why wouldn't it work?" Marta was intrigued. She had always been glad Delia was a cautious person, but believed that the mere fact of being in love threw fear out the window.

"He's Anglo, Auntie. I've seen too many conflicts in mixed couples who don't know how to make two cultures work together. I've seen Chicanos grow to hate their Anglo wives they once loved above all. And then, the children get torn apart. Some of them have actually been abducted by their fathers because their mothers were Anglo." Delia was angry. *Is that really why you won't see him Who cares   But it's true   Roberto Cadena Sal Casas Why did you marry her then Why didn't you think about it   I was in love man I was in love   "The greatest crimes have been committed in the name of love"   And love ends and she becomes a bitch   And a bitch must lose her children because now he wants to be a two-hundred percent Chicano*

Marta was baffled and was trying very hard to figure out what Delia's real reasons were for not seeing Roger again, yet Delia thought about him so much that he was even in her dreams. "I've never thought much about those things. I suppose if I had, I wouldn't have married your uncle."

"It's not the same case. Uncle Jack is Italian and his heart is all Latin. No, I am talking about real WASPs, Auntie." Delia paused.

"Is he . . . a WASP?" Marta asked.

"Joyce? I don't know." Delia looked directly at her aunt.
She's right   I know so little about him   Is he a run of the mill WASP   Is he Catholic   Did he vote for Nixon Does he like what he does   What does he do when he's not working What does he do at work   I know nothing about him What's the use of knowing anyway   I'm not going to see him again The chances of our meeting again are so slim   Then why do I think about him all the time   One time only One night That's all we had together   One night This is crazy Why has he become so important   Is he really that important   Am I just fooling myself again   Again I'm always waiting for something to happen   Call him If you really want him call him No   I don't want to call him He's not that important   How can he be One night That's all   Then why do you keep him alive He's only alive when I want him to be   When I want him to be

"You've told me before about what it is to be a Chicano, but I never considered it as great a conflict as you seem to think it is." Marta said bemusedly. "Something interesting in that conflict. I saw it happening while you were telling me the story of James Joyce. You know? You can only express fear and anger in English."

"I know." Delia said with a smile. Her aunt's keen intuition had detected her ambivalence. "And I'm letting my fear and anger get in the way of my heart, as you would put it."

"Exactly as I would put it. Don't you know, darling, that there are no rules in matters of the heart? We love another human being; that's all that matters."

"I'm not sure I love him." Delia touched her forehead. "It's more like an obsession, a delusion."

The oil was sizzling and Marta removed the pan and put it aside. She turned and looked at Delia. "There's only one way to find out what it is."

"See him again?" Delia shook her head. *No   I can't I
won't   Pursue   another   dream   Another   dream
I   can't   I   won't   Why   do   it   Why   not*
She wasn't sure she could pinpoint her reasons for not seeing Roger
again. Something in her adamantly forbade it. All she could do was
to wait it out until the time when she would no longer remember
what he looked like, when he would be only a name and a face
packed away in her memory. She was certain that day would come
in time. There was sadness in that certainty, just the same.

*We know the story well   The tearful gaze   The
trembling hand but let's read on my love   Let's read on
So romantic Such a romantic   In love   with   an   ideal
Is that why I fight so hard not to love a man   Fiction is
always more interesting than real life   "Not Ideas About the
Thing but the Thing Itself"   Who's to say   A barrio
street   A scrawny girl tossing a dirty blue ball into the air
From where I stand on the roof the ball looks like an earth globe
Dark continents Ocean blue   A toy for her   Perhaps
the only one   For me the world   Who's to say we're
not both right   Still Have I ever loved a man   True
love   Love   Bare   Without   qualification
Who's to say   Do I love Joyce   If I do why do I
hesitate   Who or what stops me   I don't have to do
anything I don't want to do   But you're not even doing the
things you want to do   Always hoping   Always waiting Never making a decision   What are you waiting for*

Lunch was ready and they sat down to eat. As usual, Delia
had a frugal meal. Marta wished there were something she could
do. She prayed for something to happen, to make Delia snap out of
her depression.

"I've decided to stay on, Auntie, if it's all right with you and
Uncle Jack. I don't know exactly for how long," Delia said after a
while.

Marta was pleased to hear Delia say that. She had already
been asking her friends to tell her about job openings in the area
that could interest Delia. "I'm so glad, darling. You know? Cloti
has been telling me this young man who's working at the

library . . ." Marta caught Delia's amused look. "It's not that." She laughed.

"You and Mattie! No wonder you two get along so well." Delia began to wash the dishes. "Matchmakers."

"No. It isn't that! I was thinking that he'll be leaving his position at the library soon. He wants to become a cowboy or rancher, something like that. Anyway, you could apply for that position," Marta said enthusiastically.

"I suppose I could," Delia agreed. "What would I do? Do you know?"

"I don't know exactly, but he can tell you."

"Who?"

"The young man." Marta paused trying to recall his name. "John? Jack? I think that's his name." Delia smiled. "Anyway," Marta continued, "the library has been having an auction. Cloti found a few wonderful books on the history of this region and bought them for me. This Jack is bringing them to me. Maybe he'll be able to tell you more about it."

"Let's hope it works out. I'm down to my last few pennies, and I need something to do. I have to start a new life, make my dreams happen."

Make my dreams happen   Wash the dishes   If only it was as easy as washing dishes   Why haven't I made my dreams happen   I'm almost twenty-nine   When am I going to do it Maybe Professor Ruvalcaba was right Am I afraid of success Taking the bull by the horns   The way he said that   The famous line   You Chicanos You people   The man is from Texas   Doesn't the mirror tell him   Brown like me   I should have said that to him   Kidding myself   I never say what I think Never do what I want   Why is it so hard I didn't want to stay in Berkeley and I did   Afraid of hurting them   Following their dreams   I wanted to go to jail with Samuel and the others and I didn't   Samuel insisted I didn't I had to be protected   Spared   Why   Because I was weak A woman   Was it that   But the other women went to jail And I went home   I couldn't sleep that night   I cried You're special Delia he said the day he left Berkeley What's so special about someone who never has the guts to do what she wants   Life goes by   We watch the dreams go under So many regrets   Daggers shining in the night   It's so much easier to bear the pain than inflict it   To do what others tell me   Why

Delia finished washing the dishes. She looked out the window. "I'm going to call home tonight. They're expecting me to go back and settle there." She was speaking in a low voice, almost to herself. "I hate to disappoint them."

"They'll understand, darling. They do," Marta said in a comforting tone. She knew how important it was for Delia to take care of her parents. Ever since Sebastián and Ricardo had died, her niece had felt she was responsible for their happiness and well-being. "But you must start taking care of yourself, too."

"I have to get my act together first. That's what I have to do. Forget all this nonsense about Joyce," Delia said emphatically. "Forget all those years in Berkeley."

The doorbell rang and Delia went to answer it. A man was standing with his back to her and turned slowly as he heard her. He was holding a box, so she immediately knew he was the man from the library. He looked at her and began to laugh, startling Delia.

"I once kissed you under a bloodstained flag," he said in a sonorous voice, and laughed again as he went past Delia and deposited the box on the floor.

"My God! Jeff Morones. What are you—How? I can't believe it!" Delia was aghast. A thick Zapata moustache tickled her nose as he kissed her on the cheek.

He doesn't even have a moustache and he's friends with that campus policeman I'm telling you Samuel Jeff's a cabrón That vato's not one of us   I don't think so Julio Jeff's OK Lover boy is a vendido eh Delia   Shut up Julio   Vendido Vendido

"You haven't grown an inch," he whispered in her ear.

Delia took a step back from him and smiled at seeing him blush. "But you've changed." She placed her index fingers above her upper lip sliding them toward each corner of her mouth. "You finally grew one."

"Yes. Julio would be happy now." He laughed. "I'm finally a

bonafide Chicano."

"That you always were." Delia looked at him again. He was no longer the young man Julio mistrusted. *Cowboy boots and hat No Boycott Grapes button   It was such a silly quarrel* He had gained some weight, which she thought made him look better, and he was darker than she remembered. *We'll go riding* He still seemed to be a happy man, someone who genuinely delighted in human nature, someone who had kept his sense of humor, even during the most bitter moments of their student life. *Only once That look   Hurt   Anger   What was he trying to say I wouldn't listen   It doesn't matter   Gone from his eyes*

Delia searched in herself for the anger she believed would be there if she ever saw Jeff again, for the pain when confronted with a reminder of the most turbulent time in her life, but that wasn't the case. Jeff's mere presence made her feel better. More than happy, she felt grateful he was there.

Marta, who had been standing at a safe distance watching the exchange between them, made the sign of the cross to thank God for what she believed was a miracle. Delia's face was illumined by a contentment she had not shown in a long time. Not wanting to intrude, Marta waited for a short while, then introduced herself to Jeff and without hesitation invited him to join them for dinner and meet her husband. He accepted.

It was a lively dinner, a joyful occasion Marta and Jack would talk about for days. Jeff was very entertaining, recounting humorous moments during the strike, overshadowed by the tragic events around them.

No wit no wisdom   Mattie's right   So involved in the pain   Laughter gets lost   Pain   Hurt Anger He can still laugh   I wish I could

At eleven, Marta signaled Jack that it was time to leave Delia and Jeff alone and they went to bed. Delia and Jeff moved to the living room. He looked at a silkscreen huelga poster Samuel had given Delia in 1968, that now hung above the fireplace. He studied the raised fists of the farmworkers, the Virgin of Guadalupe, the red flag with the black eagle in the center.

We were happy then "It was a good year. 1968." Delia said, standing at a distance, then sitting on the sofa across from the fireplace. "Probably the only good one."

"I can't believe that." Jeff turned around and sat in the arm-chair next to the sofa. "There must have been others. After I left." Jeff wanted Delia to tell him about her life, her feelings when he left, but Delia was not about to discuss that, he thought. After all, she was not interested in him then, so why would she talk about that. Even now, he could not find words to tell her how he had felt about her.

"We never got our college." Delia sighed.

"No. But if it hadn't been for the strikes at San Francisco State and Berkeley, many Chicanos would still be dreaming about going to college," Jeff said with assurance.

"That's true, yet . . . Well, it wasn't enough. We could have done so much more." Delia was quiet for a while.

"You're right. It wasn't enough, but it was a start." Jeff looked at her and smiled. "Still an idealist, eh?"

"A romantic, you mean. I've been told that before." Delia looked down. "Maybe." *You can't fix it Nothing you can do about it It hurts but it's the truth   Maybe but I have to try We've become so easy to please Stay Samuel Stay   You're a dreamer Don't you see A romantic There's nothing more to be done here Finish school and get out Delia Get out   The day after the revolution   What happens the day after   People expect everything to work perfectly   Impatience sets in Despair by any other name   A few stones   A sack of cement   So little gained   Why not take what you can while you can Plunder   Destroy   Human nature We are no different from any other people in this world   Fear the day after the revolution   That's when the real struggle begins*

"I should be the one to talk." Delia sighed. "I haven't had anything to do with Chicanos in a long time."

"On sabbatical, eh?" Jeff tilted his head and looked at her for a brief moment, then down at his open palms. "Neither have I." He rested his elbows on his knees and looked at Delia, expecting her to ask him why.

Delia observed him without saying a word. There was very

little she could say when his unspoken question echoed her own.

Jeff got up and leaned on the chair he had been sitting on and laughed softly, then looked at Delia. "You're not going to help me, are you?"

Delia tapped on her lips with her fingers. "How about this? Deadly. Bombom. The fucking knowledge. Bombom. La cucaracha Bombom. Sucks. Bombom. From the poisoned honey. Bombom. Bombom. Bombom."

Jeff laughed. "One of his better 'Conga Songs.' That Julio, he was good sometimes."

"Mattie saw him recently. Julio is now a *published poet*." Delia nodded. "He's actually not a bad poet now. Not as good as you, Mattie said. I didn't know you wrote poetry." *So many things we didn't know about each other   Never any time* She watched for his reaction, but Jeff did not bat an eye or make a comment. "Did you ever hear from Samuel?"

Jeff was not surprised at her question. He had been waiting for her to talk about him. "No. I've thought of him often," he said in a quiet voice. "He was so angry at me. He was right, too. But . . ."

"Would you do it again . . . I mean, if you could live that part of your life all over again?"

"Yes, I would . . . and so would you." He smiled at her. "I know," he said. "We didn't get our college, but we put up a good fight." Jeff rubbed the end of his moustache. "We did what could be done. Isn't that enough? There are a lot more Chicano professors and students in colleges and universities now than there were then. They have to carry the ball now."

"But so many more in prison, dying of drug overdoses in the barrio, or in the fields breathing in death." Delia sighed. "It wasn't nearly enough."

"I did write poems. Then," Jeff said without warning. "I still do." He laughed. "It's funny. The only time Julio and I talked without daggers was about writing poetry. Mostly, he talked and I listened."

Jeff stretched back in the armchair and began to recount his conversation with Julio, his long talks with Mattie and Samuel about politics, their plans, their dreams. Delia listened with attention, interjecting a question from time to time when she needed to clarify a detail. *Why couldn't we do this then Talk   Like friends talk   We couldn't   There was never any time We were never alone   So much happening   Now we could I need his friendship   He needs mine   I'm glad we found each other again*

The clock in the living room struck two and they heard it, but made no effort to move. A few minutes later Jeff got up, put his jacket on and began to move toward the door without saying a word. Delia went with him.

"I'm so glad you're back," he said and put his arms around her. Delia rested her head on his chest and sighed. She breathed in the scent emanating from him, familiar yet new. She stood at the door until the noise of the engine became a humming in the distance.

The next morning, she realized she had gone to bed thinking about all that Jeff had said and not of Roger. *Maybe now the nightmare will end   Lay the past to rest* She woke up early and after having coffee and toast, she went back to her room and looked for the folder where she had put the two chapters of her novel, written since her arrival in Monterey.

At first she had had a hard time getting started, and nights would go by when the only semblance of writing were the smudges left on the white paper by a green eraser. But an urgency she could not explain made her sit at her desk every day. Slowly, almost painfully, the words began to form one night.

"On the day I left Berkeley, almost ten years after my arrival on campus, I remembered the evening my father brought me a box of dark, bitter chocolate truffles and we sat beside the coffee table in the living room, looking at them at first, then snipping off their little crowns, biting into them and letting the sweet nectar of rum and cherries flow down our throats. It was a happy day, one of so few I had at home."

She had written and rewritten the paragraph many times that night, only to throw it into the wastebasket the next morning, and frantically look for it in the garbage can in the evening. She copied it onto clean paper and put it away in a drawer of her desk. She had no desire to write about herself, to put her most intimate thoughts on paper for anyone to see, but everything she wrote then and afterwards was of an intimate nature. She promised herself that no one would ever see what she wrote, and discovered that the idea did not bother her. It was the writing that had become important. She alone lived in that world, had control over it, created chaos or order as she pleased, at times. At other times, it controlled her, demanding every inch of space in her mind. She would curse it then, busy herself with other things, uselessly, because she knew that eventually she would get back to it.

The past   I wish I could write about something else I can't   No one is ever rid of the past   It hurts like a piece of loose skin at the edge of the wound   Cut off the skin Relief   Words   Tiny blades   Trimming the loose skin around old wounds   Silence   Double sharp edged blade   I've brandished silence   Silence

For the past two weeks she had fought the desire to write, giving herself all kinds of excuses not to do it. Talking with Jeff the night before had brought back that urgency to make sense of things, to find answers to the questions that had plagued vigil and sleep during all those years. *Why do I fight it It's the only thing in my life that makes sense   Passion Pain Hunger   Toil Everything is resolved   Here nothing can hurt me*

Delia had been writing for quite a while when her aunt, smiling, came into her room announcing that Jeff was in the kitchen having coffee and waiting for her.

"I'll be there in a while, Auntie. I'm about to finish this, but I still have to take a shower and get dressed."

"I don't think he's going anywhere," Marta said. "He's going to have breakfast here."

She should have been surprised, Delia thought as she applied mascara and checked herself in the mirror, but there was no need, because she had in a way been expecting him.

They spent the rest of the morning looking over a ranch on the outskirts of Salinas. His father, a retired car dealer in Phoenix, had died the year before, Jeff told Delia later, and had left him a sizable amount of money. He was planning to invest it in a ranch, a dream he had held dear ever since he had ridden his first horse at the age of eight.

Delia watched him ride a bronco that had arrived a week before, a beautiful but dangerous palomino that had already been responsible for a few broken bones.

"That man musta' been born on a horse," Delia heard the owner of the ranch say behind her. "He's good! Damn good!"

Delia felt a sudden wave of heat move upward from her legs to her face, and back down her shoulders and spine to settle in her lower back. She shuddered and tried to close her eyes that had been fixed on Jeff's steady moving in counterpoint to the bucking of the horse. She blinked rapidly a few times and moisture came to soothe the burning feeling; perspiration trickled down the nape of her neck, racing to that spot on her lower back where Jeff had rested his hand the night before. It was then that the palomino surrendered its will to the rider's and began to race around the corral stopping suddenly and rearing onto its hind legs. Someone opened the gate and Jeff and the palomino darted out at full gallop toward the open fields.

"Why don't you sit over there, Seño,? It'll be a while before they come back. *Los dos tienen que sacarse el coraje*," Delia heard someone say behind her. "It's cooler there." An old Mexican ranch hand was pointing at a bench under the poplars a short distance away. She nodded and touched the man's arm in a gesture of gratitude; she felt that words could not even begin to form in her parched throat. The man came back a while later and handed her a glass filled with water and ice. She cleared her throat and thanked him.

Sitting under the poplars, watching the leaves dance in frenzy at the slightest touch of the eastern wind, Delia let her mind wander through the fields, uphill to the forests of pine and madrone, old cathedrals where the scent of earth still wet from night rain mixed with the smell of madrone berries.

Home   To the precincts of this day   I've come
To these forests   Circling the night   Firefly in search
of light   I've come

Half an hour later, Jeff walked slowly toward her and paused at seeing her so still, bathed in the frantic symphony of light and shadow under the poplars. He immediately turned around to look for the owner of the ranch and make him an offer.

Delia saw him approach a moment later waving a paper. "You bought it?" she asked, with great enthusiasm.

"Not quite. My lawyer has to look at the papers first, but I want to buy it." He put his hands on her shoulders.

He began to stroke Delia's hair and pushed it behind her left ear, uncovering the skin between her neck and her shoulder. He bent forward and kissed the spot, not giving Delia a chance to withdraw and was surprised when, instead, he felt her lips press against his cheek. He raised his head slowly, careful not to make a sudden movement that might frighten her away.

Delia enjoyed the caress without hesitation. It seemed natural to be there with him, as it had been during that winter in 1968, before anger and silence had come between them. Somehow, thinking about the future didn't produce in her the usual feeling of despair.

Jeff held her tightly, almost as if he were afraid that if he loosened his embrace she would go away, and relaxed only when she made no move to withdraw from him. He kissed her with his lips only, sacrificing the urge of his tongue to taste hers. She had always been friendly toward everyone, even Julio, Jeff thought, but, with the exception of Samuel and Mattie who had gotten to know her well, no one else had been able to get close to her. Ironically, everyone would have done anything for her had she only asked, but Delia never asked. Even now, as he held her in his arms, she seemed unreachable and Jeff wondered if he was again pursuing a dream.

He had left Berkeley because it had finally become unbearable for him to suffer the humiliation he was subjected to by the other students during the strike. In retrospect, he had made peace with that situation and was glad he had participated in it, so that when Delia asked him whether he would live that part of his life again, he had said yes without hesitation. He also believed he had made the right decision in transferring to Riverside. It had, however, taken him years to reach the point where he could look back and find humor rather than bitterness in his memories of that time.

The only hard part in leaving Berkeley had been the thought that he would never see Delia again, but he had been certain that she felt no more than a passing attraction for him. Through the years, he had thought he was in love many times. He became infatuated with the idea that he could make sense of everything around him only through his relationships with women. He threw himself into innumerable affairs, but not one of them seemed to provide the meaning he searched for, except for Rita. Quite accidentally, she had given him a clue to what was happening to him.

She was an intelligent, independent woman, ten years older than he. She had been married to a former rodeo champion whom she had divorced after catching him in bed with the wife of one of their best friends. Instead of accepting half of their savings and alimony, she had taken equal partnership in the ranch they had bought just before their divorce.

"Why be stupid?" she told Jeff when they met. "The Champ and I were good business partners before. A pair of hustlers. That's what kept us together. Y'see? I own half the ranch, signed and sealed, and it's doing real well."

"He didn't object?"

"Are you kidding? He was the one who suggested it." Rita laughed. "He knows a good thing . . . I work as hard as he does and he can trust me. He even built me the house next to his."

Jeff had been looking for a place to keep a horse his father had offered to buy for him. Rita and her ex-husband agreed to lease him a stall if he bought one of their horses. Jeff went there to ride as often as he could get away.

The Champ, as everyone called Rita's husband, had seen him ride and been very impressed. He immediately offered to teach him all the skills and tricks a good rodeo rider needed. It was something new and exciting and Jeff devoted himself to it with the same ardor he had used before in pursuing women.

One Sunday, The Champ had to be out of town, but Rita insisted that she could give Jeff as many pointers as her former husband. And Jeff, much to his surprise, found that she did know as much as The Champ. Later that afternoon, she prepared lunch for them both and after eating she took her clothes off and invited Jeff to follow her to her room.

Jeff liked Rita's sparkling eyes and her entertaining manner, and though their sexual relationship was not particularly exciting to him, he enjoyed spending time with her. He found himself confiding in her about his previous involvements with women. Once, he even took photographs to show her. Rita straightened the bed cover and laid them all in a row, and studied each of the women in them.

"You look like a fortune teller." Jeff laughed.

"There's no fortune here, but there's telling," Rita said smartly. "You know? You're looking for one woman. If you put them all together you have only one woman."

He went home that day and laid all the pictures on the table and looked carefully at each one as Rita had done that afternoon. Suddenly, it came to him that Rita was right: they all had something in common. He got up and searched frantically through the boxes of papers, leaflets and posters he had from Berkeley and found the photos he had taken of Samuel and Delia on the day they had gone swimming in Lake De Anza.

Rita was right. He had been looking for one woman all along. Later, he showed her Delia's photo and she laughed wholeheartedly.

"Any chance of you two meeting again?" she asked him.

"Nope. I don't think she was interested in me," Jeff said, trying to sound casual.

"Then find another like her, but you have to give the second one a chance or it won't work."

There had been very little time for looking. What time he had between working and riding he devoted to his schoolwork. He wanted to get his degree, but he already knew he would work toward getting a ranch of his own one day.

The day after graduation Jeff decided to go on the road with The Champ and the other men he was training, to try his luck on the rodeo circuit. It was a demanding life—long journeys where even the breakdown of a car was a welcomed change, dingy motel rooms or the haystacks for those without campers, the nauseous ache at the pit of the stomach that went on for hours before the competition began, the cramps in hands and legs, the sharp pain of twisted muscles after falling, and the sour taste of defeat.

By the second time they made the Salinas rodeo, Jeff realized he did not enjoy competing as much as riding, and he made up his mind to quit and establish himself in the area, buy a ranch and, in time, look for that other woman and marry her.

And now he was holding Delia in his arms again. If she would only show him she wanted him too, he thought, but although Delia did not shun him, she was keeping her feelings to herself. Perhaps he was expecting too much, too soon, he told himself. No matter how long it took to win her over, he would not give up so easily this time, he promised himself.

I've tried before   I can't love anyone   Daniel Mario Fernando   Cruel words   Anger   I won't do that to him Not to Jeff   I want to be around him always   I don't want him to go away   If we tried What if it didn't work He would go away   Hurt each other Silence between us I couldn't take that   No

During the weeks after their first encounter, he tried to guess her feelings for him, but doubt still made him hesitate about showing his own to her. Delia was always happy to see him and went gladly with him everywhere he suggested, but did not seek to touch him or have any other physical contact except for an occasional kiss on the cheek. A few times, he thought about not going to see her, but his fear of losing her was much greater than his desire to know the truth about her feelings for him. The moment he caught sight of her and they began to talk, all his doubts and fears would disappear.

He felt exhilarated when talking with her and many times went home to search for the poems he had left unfinished in a drawer and ended up writing new ones. He had always written humorous poems and stories which he considered trivial and insubstantial, though Camille and the tenants at the old Victorian house where he had been living in Salinas found them amusing and clever. They lacked something, pathos, he told Delia one day, when he finally mustered up enough courage to show them to her.

"That's what poetry is supposed to be all about, isn't it? Feelings."

"Joy and pain. They flow from the same source, like ice and heat. Humor is one way to express them." Delia stopped. "I sound like a lecturer." She laughed. "What I've never wanted to be."

"Sound like a lecturer; it's okay. Just tell me what I want to hear." Jeff brushed her cheek with the back of his fingers.

"I can't do that, because I like your poems." She looked at

him. "You seem to think that sadness is a better emotion than humor. Who said such nonsense?" Her face was flushed.

Jeff smiled. "I did. You just told me that." He thought about the futility of trying to stay away from her. Even if she did not say another word at that moment, her silence would be as intense as her arguments; he would be caught in her intensity. If only she could talk to him about her own life, her own personal feelings, like she expressed her ideas about literature, human emotions, art. But she never gave him a chance to look into her inner world, never let down her defenses, and he felt at a loss.

"Anyway," Delia continued, "as Mattie says, where there's wit there's wisdom."

"Or cynicism or the same bull . . ." He laughed. "Cheap philosophy."

"Are you going to send them out? You probably have enough for a book," Delia said, leafing through the manuscript one more time.

"No way. I don't mind being trampled by a horse, but critics, no," he said emphatically.

"People would read your work, other poets." Delia was trying to persuade him without exerting too much pressure.

"No, thanks. I don't want to be a published poet, underline published."

"My, my, my, Mr. Dickinson." She teased him, but she understood his hesitation. She herself had not had the courage to show him or even her aunt what she labored to write late at night, like a fugitive with darkness as her only accomplice.

It was like having two love affairs, being two different people at once, but she felt no remorse for her illicit activities. Sometimes Delia would get up in the middle of the night to write, especially at those times when she would remember Roger. Nothing seemed to have any effect on her memory of that night in early November. Most of her waking hours she was able to relegate it and its host of fantasies to a dark corner in the back of her mind, but she was always aware that it only waited in ambush. And on any night, when she was unable to sleep or was troubled by something, it would come back.

Her fantasies had changed in nature, it seemed to her. There were no streets and no markets, no journey to a room overlooking the marina, no bridge spanning the waters, only the two of them making love in a dark space, then the echo of her voice calling him as she fell asleep.

Why are you still here   *Why* "Why? Why?"

During the following days, she would avoid seeing Jeff, or talking to anyone, and rush home to write frantically about anything at all, everything that came into her mind. In a ritualistic manner, she would read the words aloud as if, in doing so, she could exorcise the power that held her prisoner and could liberate herself by restoring the order she had upset.

Chapter 8

"I'm twelve, perhaps thirteen, sitting on a tall stool like the ones in bars. I'm wearing the light blue dress my mother made for me when I was ten. I'm writing something because I can see paper and pencil at my feet, but I can't make anything out clearly. I feel tired and begin to walk through a long corridor. I know my room is at the end of it. I open the door. The bright sunlight blinds me. I'm not afraid even though I sense he's there behind me. I turn to face him. I can't explain it, but I know who he is and why he's there. He looks at me. His eyes are bloodshot. He must have been crying because his nose is red. I think he suffers, too. His right hand hangs hidden, but for an instant I see what looks like the blade of a knife, a clean shiny blade like new. We don't speak. He raises his left hand to keep me at a distance when I try to move closer to him. I open my mouth wide and stick my tongue out as far as it'll go. He holds it tightly by the tip, raises the blade, and swiftly slices my tongue. I don't remember screaming or feeling pain in my dream. I drop my head. I watch my blood pouring out black as ink. It turns red when it hits the floor."

The old Victorian mansion where Jeff lived in Salinas housed an assortment of odd people, who seemed to fit there but nowhere else. It was like a purgatory of sorts, filled with transient souls, waiting. For what? Delia didn't know. No one in that house seemed to know either, although when asked they all seemed to have definite plans.

Casto, the Chilean exile, would go back to his country when the Pinochet regime crumbled. In the meantime, he worked as a janitor in a local school. Lizabeta, a young Russian, waited for her stranded husband to arrive from Italy. She had already been waiting a year without a word from him and had begun to work as a nurse's aide in a convalescent home. Carla, who had been named after the

116

tango singer Carlos Gardel, believed fate had decreed that she be a singer and dancer. She had gotten a job as an aerobics instructor and was saving money for a ticket to Paris, where a childhood friend had opened a cabaret. El Andaluz, who could have been a model for the portrait of the bullfighter Manolete that Delia had seen at a small Mexican restaurant in San Jose, said nothing about his plans except that he loved horses and enjoyed tending the stable at a ranch nearby. Jeff had already hired him. Camille, the owner of the house, had come into a fortune when her grandfather, a well-known criminal lawyer in Boston, had died. She read everything she could get her hands on.

"I joined a commune but I could never be a good hippie. Contemplation was never my forte and the land could wait, as far as I was concerned, until I finished whatever I was reading. Trash novels," Camille explained to Delia while giving her a tour of the premises on her first visit to the house. "Reading was my only redeeming grace, my grandfather used to say. I guess that's why he left me all that money."

Camille ran the cleanest house in Salinas, Jeff had told Delia earlier, and after seeing it, she agreed with him. The stairs, the garden, the bookcases in the basement, the halls and the landlady's own rooms were immaculate. Camille charged her tenants very modest rents on the condition that they each contribute to pay a cleaning lady, which they did not mind after the housekeeper's first visit to their rooms.

Once a month, on the second Sunday, they and their friends and other guests would get together at the house. These "Anything Goes Soirees," as Camille called them, were attended by artists and musicians who would travel from Monterey and Carmel to Salinas for that express purpose. Camille provided plenty of food and wine and the guests took care of the entertainment.

Even Lizabeta and El Andaluz, who kept to themselves most of the time, would join in. Camille was happy to see them laugh and, at least for a day, forget the cause of their sadness.

"His real name is José Juan Hernández Montero," she had explained to Delia and Marta the first time they joined the group. "I know only bits and pieces about him, but I think he was in prison and escaped. It was during the Civil War in Spain. How he ended up here, I don't know."

Camille seemed genuinely interested in the well-being of her tenants and took their problems to heart. She had become as indispensable to them as they were dear to her, but she particularly liked Jeff and was extremely happy to see him keeping company with Delia. She made her approval immediately obvious to Jeff.

Camille and Marta quickly struck up a friendship, and sat in the love seat for quite a while exchanging confidences about "the kids," mapping out the relationship which naturally would lead to the altar, and enjoying the idea of having several beautiful "grandchildren" to spoil to their hearts' content.

"Delia looks radiant," Marta commented, "and so does Jeff."

"Yes, I haven't seen him this happy since before his father died," Camille said in a low voice. "He was literally sick for weeks. They were not very close, you know? Jeff's mother died when he was very young and Señor Morones remarried."

"Did the stepmother mistreat him?" Marta asked, also trying to keep her voice low.

"No, but she was always very cold. She never made any effort to be close to him. I met her when I went to Phoenix with him for the funeral. She was very upset that Señor Morones had left half of his money to Jeff. But, tell me, what injustice is there in that? After all, he was the only son."

"Of course. Did they have any other children?"

"From what Jeff told me, she miscarried a couple of times and after that, I guess, they just never tried again." Camille sighed loudly.

Marta sighed, too. In a way she felt sorry for Jeff's stepmother, because she knew quite well how embittering it could be to want children and not be able to have them, to live the pleasure of being a mother only vicariously. "I can sympathize with her, not having children of my own."

"I can, too, except I chose it that way. But here he is, Jeff. He has been my consolation, ever since he walked into this house looking for an apartment," Camille said and waved at Delia and Jeff, who had been looking in their direction for some time.

Jeff seemed to fit well into that group, Delia thought, though he was probably the only one whose dream was becoming a reality.

Much to her surprise, Delia felt comfortable among them, perhaps because she felt she was also a misfit, a transient soul waiting to find the place where she belonged.

"Odd people. All of us, there." Delia commented to Jeff on their way back to her house from Camille's soiree, five weeks after their first encounter. Delia's car was at the repair shop and she asked Jeff to pick her up, since he had to meet with someone in Monterey that morning. "From so many different backgrounds, yet they get along well. I like them, odd and all."

"Oddballs? Yes, we are all oddballs. This whole country is one big box of oddballs," Jeff said. "And German balls, and cueballs," he continued, "and bullballs, Irish balls." He paused and Delia waited, for she knew the litany hadn't ended. "Chicano balls? Ah, and baseballs, *bolillo* balls, French balls and last but not least, my *compadre* Samuel's balls."

"Did you forget anyone? We don't want to be guilty of omission," Delia chuckled. "I know. You forgot Carter."

"Carter's balls? Naaah! Cotton balls go a longer way."

"How about yours?" Delia asked, placing her hand on his leg. *What are you doing   God   How could you say that   Why not   What's he going to think   Shit   Why did I do that*

"Very well, thank you," he answered and was quiet for a while. Suddenly, he pulled off on a dirt road and turned off the motor, leaving the lights on. "Don't tease me, Delia. I couldn't take that from you." He looked seriously at her, then turned away and slammed the light button with his fist.

Delia had seen that look in his eyes, hurt and angry, only once before, on the day of the strike victory dance, the day before he left Berkeley. It confused her now as much as it had then. She realized she had been the cause of his hurt and anger that other time, but still could not figure out what she had done wrong now or then. *The last thing in the world I wanted to do I never learned to flirt He talked to her all night Sonia didn't have any trouble making her intentions known He's probably still thinking about Sonia She's so beautiful A good dancer Bet she'd be a good rider too He wasn't just dancing with her   He was dancing for her I thought we could still be friends   I tried to show him that*

Why is he behaving this way   Shit   It's all a mess now   I can understand Emma's or Anna's passion Paper people   Another human being That's different Maybe I don't want to know anyone Really Maybe I want people to be like I want them to be I'm not making sense   It's been so long since anything made sense   This is hopeless Hopeless

During the weeks that followed their first encounter, Jeff had been tender and affectionate with her, but he had not shown any obvious signs of wanting her. Unaware that Jeff had decided to wait patiently until she showed her feelings to him, Delia came to think that she had misread his attitude, or that he had changed his mind. But the last two times they had been together she had felt him shudder whenever she would touch him or kiss him on the cheek, and he would withdraw from her.

That whole afternoon and evening he had seemed so distant, spending most of his time talking to Sonia, a dancer friend of Carla's and a newcomer to the "Anything Goes Soirees."

Delia had ventured looks in their direction whenever he was not looking. Once, she had walked over to them, but Jeff had not introduced them. She placed her hand around his waist and felt his muscles tense, but did not move her hand away during the time she was there. She wanted to reassure him that everything was all right, that she understood he wanted to be with someone else. *Only friends   That's what we've been anyway   Why not Only friends   That other girl   She was beautiful too Nine years ago   Go on   Cut in   I'm glad I didn't*

Jeff was surprised and confused. For a moment, when he saw Delia at his side, he wanted to believe she had joined them because she was jealous, but he changed his mind when she started talking to Sonia about him—what a good rider he was and a good poet, and he was buying a ranch! It sounded to him as if she was trying to convince Sonia that he was worth having, a good catch. Why was she doing that? How simple it was to give him over to another woman. How could he go on loving and wanting a woman who did not want him? He felt angry and moved away from her.

Delia thought she was doing the right thing, but could not

understand her sudden desire to cry when he withdrew from her. She tried to ignore his indifference, but it became increasingly difficult as the evening progressed, and she began to imagine all sorts of encounters between Jeff and Sonia, watched them laugh and later move to the dining room where Casto the Chilean had begun to play the guitar. "Why should I care?" she whispered to herself, but moved closer to the fireplace so she could continue her surveillance without being noticed. If anyone had asked her at that moment whether she was jealous, she would have denied it emphatically.

Jeff, Sonia and Carla began to dance. This in itself was not unusual. He had danced from time to time with Carla, who had taught him the tango and several other Latino ballroom dances, in exchange for lessons on *salsa* and *norteña* dancing. Jeff had agreed at first to join the dancing lessons because they needed a second male partner, but he had soon begun to enjoy himself. Sometimes, Delia had joined them, but more than dancing with him, she enjoyed watching him. His movements were precise, and he instinctively exerted only the exact amount of energy on every step, creating the illusion of effortless motion.

El Andaluz had taught Jeff and Carla the basic steps of what he called "tablao achulao," a mixture of flamenco and Spanish folk dance steps, that was further modified by adding a Latin rhythm to it.

Casto had begun to play de Falla's "Canción del fuego fatuo." El Andaluz grinned and got his guitar to accompany Casto, something he would rarely do in public. Carla left the group, but Jeff and Sonia continued dancing. Everyone gathered around them.

This time, Delia sensed there was something new in the way Jeff danced. He was totally absorbed in it, dancing for himself and for his partner only, it seemed to her. The thought sent a chill down her spine, but soon she was transfixed. She followed each one of his movements, intensifying it in her mind until she was there, inside him, moving with him as one. She felt the same wave of warmth she had experienced at watching him ride the palomino. It rose from her feet to her neck, nestling there at the moment the music stopped and people applauded and cheered.

She saw Jeff standing in the middle of the room looking intently at her for an instant. He turned around then and left the room. The thought crossed her mind that he had been dancing for her and not for the other woman, but she dismissed it, and spent the next hour making small talk with some of the other guests but thinking about Jeff, wondering whether she should look for him. He came back bathed and changed, ready to take her back to Monterey.

Jeff was exhausted, Delia was certain, because every time he got tired he would start one of those litanies, almost as if he needed a word game to recover his sense of humor or work out the intensity of an emotion that left him spent and bedraggled. Afterwards, he would become very quiet.

Delia did not mind his silences. She actually welcomed those moments with him. There was no pressure to make small talk or analyze something, and she never felt left out or uncomfortable. But this time it was different. Silence stood between them, darker and denser than the darkness around them on that dirt road between Salinas and Monterey, where they were now parked.

Delia looked at the window, then at Jeff. Seeing him still so intensely caught up in whatever was causing him pain, she realized the dancing had only exacerbated his unhappiness.

"I am not teasing you." She looked for his eyes and put her arms around him. "What's happening to us?"

"I think you know the answer to that." He pulled her to him and kissed her. "I want you. I can't stand being near you and not making love to you."

Delia did not answer. She unbuttoned his shirt and took it off. She closed her eyes and her fingers traced the outlines of his muscles, while her mouth and tongue looked for the hollow of his mouth, guided by the warmth of his breath. She pulled her skirt off and he helped her to slide off her panties and hose, while she snapped open his belt buckle and unzipped his pants pulling both sides apart at once. She felt his fingers moving softly down her clitoris on their way to the moist opening between her thighs. She trembled and moaned.

Without letting go of her, Jeff pulled on the lever to make her seat recline to a more comfortable position, but in his eagerness he pushed too hard making it go all the way back. In her effort to

122

fasten on to something, she grabbed Jeff's head pulling him with her while he struggled, trying to find support for his feet which were caught in the legs of his pants.

"Oh, shit! *Qué cabrones* . . . ," Delia heard him say and she began to laugh. He laughed, too. "I feel like I'm in a Peter Sellers movie."

He pulled the seat forward slightly. "Did it hurt you?" He asked apologetically when their laughter finally subsided.

"No. I'm not hurt, just hungry," she said with a sigh.

"Hungry?!" Jeff exclaimed, disappointed more than annoyed. He rested his head on her stomach. "I suppose . . . I don't know what's open now."

"Not that kind of hunger, *tonto*." She ruffled his hair. "Let's start again. The bed is unmade already."

" 'Tis, isn't it?" He laughed, then held her up to recline the seat completely.

They finished undressing each other slowly, stopping on every newly discovered rising or hollow, letting their tongues speak in their own language until the new territory of their bodies had been negotiated.

He entered her, thrusting and pulling away slowly, then more rapidly responding to the pressure of her hands on his buttocks, resisting the urge to surrender to the squeezing of her warm and moist vagina as the rhythm of her pleasure quickened. They were caught in the power that impelled them, until there was nothing left but a point of light that grew larger and scattered in all directions, obliterating everything but their pleasure. Then warm, humid, peaceful darkness.

"I love you. I always have," Jeff whispered and pushed gently into her. She heard him from that distant place where her soul had gone and was soaring, a place where her nightmares could not follow. She held him tightly, feeling the throbbing of his penis still inside her, then relaxed her embrace and gasped softly as he pulled out of her.

He moved to the side and turned her around until she was resting on him. "I don't want you only for one night. You must know that," he added, thinking that her silence meant regret.

"I know that," she answered after a while. "I can promise

you forever if there are no nightmares there."

"What? You're delirious." He raised his head to look at her and wiped the sweat from her forehead, then stroked her buttocks. She shivered.

"Is that passion or cold?" He laughed softly and rubbed her leg.

"Cold, I'm afraid." She pressed lightly against him. "I'll tell you on the way home." She sat up, reached down for the lever to bring the seat to an upright position, and rested her head on his shoulder.

Jeff pushed her hair away from her face. "Tell me what?" He licked her neck with upward strokes.

"Hmmm. About my nightmares." She pressed her lips against his shoulder, then bit it playfully. "How come you never kissed me again?"

"When?"

"After that night. The spray-paint raid. Remember?"

"We were never alone again." Jeff began to talk about western movies, cowboys and the girls they were in love with, and the know-it-all sidekicks, and Delia listened to him thinking that he did not want to talk about the past. Jeff was quiet for a while, then said, "I left Berkeley."

"Why did you?" Delia pushed slightly away from him to see him better.

"There was nothing there for me." He caught her look of disappointment at not hearing she was the cause of it. *Thanks, a lot* "Well, there was you, but you were only a dream, a wet dream." Delia giggled and lay her head on his shoulder again. "I wanted you so much, I couldn't sleep that night," he added.

"So much happening." Delia sighed. "So many dreams that didn't come true—wet and dry." She chuckled. "I wanted to leave Berkeley, too."

"Why didn't you?"

"I tried many times, but every time something happened and I didn't. Hoping that things would change, not wanting to disappoint my father, thinking that perhaps my mother would love me when I finally got my degree. I was trapped in that academic Hades."

Delia shivered and Jeff cupped his hands on her buttocks and held her tightly. "It sounds like a Buñuel movie."

"It was a Buñuel movie." Delia laughed softly. "Only a movie." They fell silent.

After a while, thinking that he had fallen asleep, she began to look around for her clothes. He stirred next to her and she reached down for his pants, and put his feet in them, then helped him pulled them up. "We better get home. Aunt Marta must be getting worried." She began to get dressed.

"I think your aunt will figure out what's happened. She's one smart lady." Jeff held up his shorts for her to see. "What do I do with these?"

Delia laughed and snapped them away from him. "I'll keep them as fetish." She folded them and put them inside her blouse. "We better get home. I start work tomorrow, at the library."

"Why didn't you tell me?" He was surprised. "They took their sweet time in hiring you."

"Well, I was going to tell you today, but . . . Anyway, I start tomorrow."

"Hmmm. I wonder what it would be like to make love to you among the stacks. Good fucking in the middle of all that knowledge, with the ghosts of the Californios bearing witness." Jeff was amused at the idea and began a name litany. "Vallejo, Moraga, Martínez, Cabrillo . . ."

Delia grinned and shook her head. She decided he was really at the point of total exhaustion, and without asking him, got in the driver's seat and started the car.

When he finished his catalogue of names, she began telling him about her journal and its narrative of nightmares. She had forgotten about it until the day before, when she found it in a box of things she had left unpacked. Writing longhand was becoming a burdensome task, now that it was clear to her she was on her way to writing her novel. She had been looking for an old manual typewriter her uncle kept in the basement and the typing paper she had brought with her from Berkeley.

Jeff buttoned his shirt and leaned back on the seat with his eyes closed, turned his head toward her and began to listen attentively. Delia's voice had dropped almost to a whisper over the sound of the engine.

125

"For a long time—almost two years—I had the worst of nightmares. I don't know why. I think it was all the pressure I was under. The dissertation and my . . . *relationship with Fernando* things happening . . . Anyway, sometimes I feared going to sleep. I drank cup after cup of coffee to stay awake, cleaned the house at odd hours. Two o'clock in the morning and I was mopping the floor like a madwoman. I even joined an exercise class at the Y to exhaust myself and sleep soundly. Nothing seemed to work and I was making myself literally sick, so I tried self-hypnosis, sitting every evening in front of a mirror repeating, 'When the dream begins, you'll wake up'; or I would lie down in bed and visualize my toes falling asleep, then my feet, my legs up to my shoulders, then I would fall asleep. But all that was useless; every night, like clockwork, another nightmare began. Sleepless nights. But days seemed to go by fast. Reading and writing chapter after chapter of my dissertation. I was working at the Admissions Office. You know that office. Never a quiet moment, phones ringing off the hook, papers lost, students found.

"Anyway, Mattie suggested that I start a journal where I'd record my nightmares to get at whatever the problem was. I had tried everything else. So I thought, why not? Every time I woke up after a bad dream, I would turn on the light and write it down, and add whatever comments came to my head at that point. That helped some; at least I was able to sleep better afterwards.

"I began to study them and after a while I could see a pattern; so I began a catalogue of nightmares. Useless, because they all seemed to be somewhat similar to one another. Someone pursued me, but I'd wake up in time not to be overtaken; or someone pursued me and I'd try to fly away, but would fall downward, unable to make my arms flap long enough to keep me airborne. I never knew who was after me; I didn't even know if it was a man or a woman."

Jeff was very quiet. Thinking that he had fallen asleep, Delia turned around to look at him. He reached up and brushed her hair with his fingers to let her know he was still listening.

"Yesterday," Delia continued, "I read the catalogue and journal through in one sitting, and, you know, I didn't feel afraid any more, except for the last one. Very different from the rest. It puzzled me."

To her best recollection, Delia recounted the details of the nightmare about the man who had cut her tongue. She felt Jeff's hand squeeze her knee.

"Weird. It was the most terrifying—its blinding light and sacrificial ritual. I wrote in a simple, almost elementary English. I couldn't begin to describe the horror of it all. This time it was clearly a man, and he sliced my tongue. Who is he? Why did I have to be punished? What frightens me most is that I didn't fight him. I let him maim me. He took away my tongue. My tongue! The very instrument of voice."

She saw the exit to Highway 1 coming up and she stopped talking until they entered it. Jeff sat up, but did not say anything. It was the first time Delia had opened up to him and he did not want to do anything that would make her withdraw from him again.

"I don't know what it means. All I know is that whoever pursued me had finally caught up with me and made me pay with my tongue whatever it was I owed, but I can't, for the life of me, figure out what that is. Funny, I didn't write anything after that dream, and then the nightmares stopped. That was the last one for a long time until one night in November last year. I was going to a costume party at Mattie's . . . *Watch it   Watch it What if I told him about it   No   Don't be stupid Joyce Never tell him   No* Anyway, there was only that one and it was the same as the others. Then I left Berkeley. I dream sometimes—silly things—but I don't remember much except bits and pieces. I guess it's better that way."

They reached her house and Delia turned off the engine and the lights. She fell silent; Jeff was quiet, too. He searched in his mind for something to say to her, but could not think of anything that would comfort her. He knew enough about her life to realize it had been full of sacrifices and disappointments. There was also Delia's conflict with her mother that Sara had mentioned many years ago. Delia had referred to it in passing when she talked about her reasons for not leaving Berkeley.

He did not know much about her life in Berkeley after he left, except for her unhappy experiences on campus and her struggle to finish her degree and leave. What else was there hidden from him? The question hit an emotional nerve somewhere that made him hold his breath and tighten his fists, and that set his heart racing for a short while. He let the air out slowly and relaxed his hands.

He looked at Delia, her hands still on the steering wheel, gazing into the semi-dark street. Under the poised and demure face and manner lived a woman haunted by fury and sorrow, a woman he loved and yet did not know well.

The memory of so many lonely nights, and of his anger at his father, that even after his death left a bitter taste in Jeff's mouth; all this rode across his mind in quick succession. He put his arms around her, not to comfort her, but to share her pain and her victory as well, to be stronger in her.

Delia felt lightheaded, rested her head on Jeff's chest, and listened to the steady beating of his heart. *Where darkness travels at the same speed of light   I've looked for you For your body Your soul   Brown like mine   Love If only it could be like this always   Always is such a long time So absolute No   It is now   Now is the only absolute we can hope for   Ever ever ever ever ever ever* "Ever, ever, ever, ever, ever . . ."

The sound of her own voice woke Delia up and she opened her eyes slowly, expecting to see sunlight streaming into her bedroom, seeing instead the clarity of early dawn through the windshield. She raised her head and looked at Jeff's smiling face. "I fell asleep?"

"Uhuh. Were you having another dream?"

"I don't think so. Why?" She straightened up and yawned. "Oh, yeah, I was saying 'ever' or something like that. I don't know. I don't remember. What time is it?"

"About 5." He combed her hair with his fingers.

"Hmmm. Did you get any sleep?" She rested her head back on his chest. "A little." Jeff looked for Delia's handbag and handed it to her. "Let's go in. I'll make breakfast while you shower and then I'll take you to the library."

"If Aunt Marta lets you fuss around her kitchen." She got out of the car and waited for him.

"She will. I'm a whiz with the cheese," Jeff said and shook his head.

"Corny, Mr. Dick, that ain't going to get you the Pulitzer,"

Delia teased.

He took Delia's keys from her hand and opened the door. "I'd rather have *you* for breakfast." He bit her earlobe while trying to push the door shut with his foot, almost making them lose their balance.

"Is it going to be like this every time we make love? You're dangerous!" She looked at Jeff who had thrown his head back as if hit by a flying object.

She tried to hold back her laughter for fear of waking up her aunt and uncle, but finally had to let it out. It gushed out of her, echoing his trailing behind her down the hall, into the bathroom, joining the chorus of running water under the shower. Delia felt alive and content.

This is what love does to people   It makes us children again   Silly children   Love   I'm in love   I am finally in love   The many nights counting and recounting the cracks in the ceiling   Wondering why I couldn't love anyone Fearing it and wanting it   Living it only in novels   In the midst of paper walls where nothing can harm us   The inorganic matrix of organic desires   Passion and love   I wish there were some good Chicano love stories   Love poems No We are still afraid of writing about love   I wonder why All that love stuff is corny   Carnalismo   La raza La causa   But not love   Or eroticism for that matter We live in fear of being found out   Passion and love Passion   I once had a dream of passion Joyce Why are you still there   Go away   Why won't you go away

Marta and Camille were very pleased that Jeff and Delia had found each other again, and showed their approval at every opportunity, commenting on their being a perfect match or hinting at the need for a steady feminine hand at the ranch.

Jeff would wink and smile at Delia. She did not know if he simply assumed that one day they would get married or live together, or whether he preferred things as they were. She would only think about it when the two matchmakers were at work, but never seriously. Perhaps it was selfishness on her part not to want things to change, but, for the first time, she was able to laugh and enjoy life without worrying about the future or her obligations to anyone.

She and Jeff spent weekends together; once a week they went to the movies or attended a cultural event, and often they would meet for lunch or speak on the phone. She was glad he did not insist on seeing her every day, because she wanted time for herself as well as for writing, something that became more important as time went by. Now, there was nothing therapeutic in it, as when she had written in her journal during her years at the university. Writing seemed as natural a need as eating or breathing and Delia could no longer envision her life without it. Sometimes, she sat down at nine in the evening and when she looked up at the clock again four hours had gone by as in a whisper, and she had to force herself to go to bed, to be able to work the next day.

Marta, who had been intrigued by the sound of Delia's typing every night, finally asked her about it.

"I'm writing a series of articles on the Third World Strike at Berkeley," Delia said, resisting the temptation to tell her aunt the truth. *I'm a writer   Self-conceited   I'm not a writer An apprentice   Laborer   A writer   I don't even know if it's good   It doesn't matter   It makes me feel good   Maybe I'll show it to her   One day To Mattie   Maybe*

Marta was satisfied with the answer and didn't inquire further since it was obvious Delia was happy. Every so often, the typing would stop for days and Delia would seem moody, but that would quickly pass as soon as Marta heard the clicking of the typewriter again.

Delia did not mind the sleepless nights or the backaches, but the silences that would come every so often without warning, just when she thought she was making progress, drove her into quiet despair. Unable to understand why they happened, she would stubbornly sit in front of the typewriter, but the words she searched for eluded her.

Silence   Always   silence   I   hate   you You've always been my enemy   My enemy   If Mattie were only here   October   Almost a year   November   There won't be a Day of the Dead party this year The solitary rose in November   Joyce   Why do I still

think of you Why do I sometimes wake up in the middle of the night
You're there wiping my tears   I want to touch you
Lose myself in you   Forget everything   Like that
night   Afraid and lonely   He came upon me on the
Day of the Dead   His mouth on my breasts   All my
lips   Burning bitterness of his   Why am I thinking
this way   It turns around and around in my head   A
mystery   The loose ends I can't find Jeff   Jeff
This has nothing to do with him   How can it not   Oh
God Please   Maybe it's this need to confess   I should
tell Jeff about it   Maybe it's just my guilt   No Lose
my tongue first   Lose my tongue   What am I saying
Code of silence   Endless sand   Endless sand
This has to end   I have to make it end   How I can't
even write about it

Then, one day, without warning, the silence was broken. She rushed home from work, anxiously sat at the typewriter and felt relieved when, past her initial hesitation, she resumed her writing.

During those periods of silence in her writing, the image of Roger dressed as James Joyce loomed persistently. The memory of their only night together recurred as perniciously as the memory of her sacrificial nightmare. Afterwards, the tailend of a thought, a fractured image that wouldn't come together in her head would surface for an instant and go out of sight again. *Code of silence* *Code of silence   No flowers   No trees   End-less sand   First time   First time What does it mean*

At times, the need to tell Jeff about Roger and face the consequences was almost irresistible but she fought it. *I've been lying for so long   No   Not lying   What good would it do   I would hurt him   I've hurt him enough I'm moody   Despondent   He's there for me always No Telling him would help me not him*

She would have to find the answers on her own; then, there would be no need for confessions, because there would be no guilt. Still, she feared the moment she would see clearly the path to be followed and the possibility that such road would lead away from Jeff. The thought of losing him made her postpone the decision of seeking a second meeting with Roger, though she knew that one day she would no longer be able to keep herself from it. Silence for now, she told herself, was best.

Silence A blade of light crossed her mind, leaving behind a feeling of emptiness in her stomach.

Chapter 9

From solstice to equinox   No   Summer is a solstice Autumn an equinox   Or is it the other way around
Who cares That's it   Who gives a damn   Summer
comes followed by autumn   One season on another
Yellow to ochre to brown to gray   Soup today   Tama-
les tomorrow   Work day in and day out   Sisyphus
rolls the rock up the mountain   The rock rolls down the
mountain   Sisyphus runs down after the rock Day after day
One day he gets tired   Not of rolling the rock up the mountain   There's nothing he can do about that He gets tired of
doing it exactly the same way every time   He designs a hoist
He likes making it   It's finally ready And the rock is suspended at the top of the mountain   He climbs up He sees
tiny wild flowers growing all around   It's the first time he's
seen them   A miracle   He swears they hadn't been
there before   They were there all along but he hadn't seen
them   This is a silly story   I'm bored Jeff   I
wonder what he's doing   Probably putting up a fence
Fixing the house   What for   I don't see him anymore
So busy all the time Perhaps it will be good to go to Berkeley to see
Mattie One thing about my life in Berkeley it was painful but never
boring   Maybe Mattie was right   I should have gone
with her to Central America   No   The could-have-
beens of my life I wanted a stable life   No I was told that's
what I wanted Maybe I'm more Anglo than I care to admit
Mobility   The Lawrence of Arabia complex Jeff says
Camille agrees   Go to a distant place   Find yourself
The formula   Eliot Pound   Hemingway Stein
But not Williams   I wonder Given the same choices would
Montoya leave   Alurista Anaya Valdez Méndez So very few
Chicanas   Portillo Zamora Corpi Poems in kitchen drawers
In hope chests   Mostly men Hinojosa Arias   Herrera
deep in the snows of Kilimanjaro   He was not made for
snow   He loses his uptown step Salsa caliente no longer his

style His poems flatland racers lie frozen at the bottom of a
gorge No he was not made for snow He was made for noon
and ocean as yellow and blue as his brown eyes may take
Cute Cute Mattie would say Soon She'll be back soon
It'll be good to see Mattie Will he be there Why
would he Why not You have an excuse Call him No
It's easy Pick up the phone It's been so long He
won't remember Oh yes he will What do I say
This is Delia We met at Mattie's Day of the Dead party and we
made love by the barbeque in the backyard Remember This
is absurd He could have called He didn't Why
didn't he You could have called him Liberated eh
Still waiting by the phone The clock of my destiny is off It
always is So you think he's your destiny You see It's
not over It won't be over until you see him again There's
too much at risk Jeff Do you really think you can be happy with him
You bite your lips not to say his name Joyce He's a fantasy
Jeff is real Only because you won't see him again
What if it's not over then What if it works out
Would I marry Joyce How could I I can't even call him by his real
name I don't want to marry period That's what you tell yourself I'm
never going to get married Why do you say that Delia
See if I get married I'll have children God granting yes And
I'll suffer Who says you will Mamá says that Do you suffer
Auntie No I don't I'm very happy especially now that I have you
Why does Mamá suffer Maybe it is that she and your father
want the best for you and they feel sad they can't give you everything But Mamá says that all women suffer It is hard to be a woman
But Papá loves her I know he loves me too Well sometimes
women want other things besides love What does Mamá
want Why don't you ask her She won't tell me She
says I ask too many questions Is that bad No darling it's
not bad She probably feels it's too late for her Too late
Why We all have dreams that sometimes never come true
Dreams The lethal dose swallowed What did she
dream of doing She lies in the cradle of unfulfilled dreams
She lulls herself to sleep And I thought all her dreams had to do
with us Ricardo Where does the dream end and the nightmare begin

She once had two sons The man came and took one away
Sister listen to my story Sister holding back my tears I demand from
him   Go on Lay your platitudes on my table   And she
gave him   Tell me that to die for God and country is right
She could have said no but she didn't Tell me that the killing must
go on to ensure the welfare of the world   There won't be a
war hermanita and I might just come back with a career
Tell me that I was wrong to bring up men of peace   Why do
mothers allow their sons to go to war   But before you come
for my sons man Build a concrete wall around you For my heart
knows inch by word your dark designs And you You're in danger
Beg   Fight   Go to jail Organize   Mattie is
right   Brown brother against brown brother   Young
Chicanos will buy again the politics of self-destruction
Central America   If we could organize Chicano mothers
How   Aunt Marta   Camille They don't have children
My mother   Maybe she could do it   No she probably
wouldn't   Just another dream   Another dream
Or another nightmare nightmare   Why not   Even if it
is What if it doesn't do any good   It didn't do any good ten
years ago   It seemed all so useless No   Jeff is right
It's useless not to try to do something   It wasn't fair But
then life has nothing to do with fairness   No He hasn't done
anything for Chicanos   I haven't either Okay We got beaten
over the head I will get beaten and I'll get up again and again and
again   I'm here to stay   Do you hear me Stubborn
Relentless   That Delia is dead   Something has
changed   You're dead   I don't fight for anything anymore Maybe my staying in Berkeley had to do with that Delia
I've been fooling myself Blaming everyone Even Jeff   He's
happy I must do something   What   How
When   Go to the canneries   To the fields   Talk
to the mothers who have sons No To the mothers of daughters too
because one day they may also have sons I will one day have a son
A son   And he won't go to war I won't let them take him I
won't   Listen to me I don't even want to get married
I could have a son anyway Chicano Mothers for Peace   My
father would probably have a heart attack   Maybe not

*My mother   Probably wouldn't talk to me again   We
hardly talk anyway Silence between us   So much silence in
me Around me So much silence Silence*

Delia's parents had traveled to Monterey for the holidays and
the whole family had joined the group at Camille's house for
Christmas. She introduced Jeff to her parents and judging by their
smiles, she knew they approved of him, something her aunt Marta
confirmed.

Delia's salary at the library was not very much, but she insisted on giving her aunt some money for her room and board.
Marta accepted it because she knew it was very important for Delia
to feel she could take care of herself. Delia was sending money
home, as well, and had been to visit her parents as often as she
could. On one of her visits she went to the cemetery with them and
much to her surprise she did not cry or feel anxious at the sight of
Sebastián's grave or at the memory of Ricardo as she had seen him
before he left for Viet Nam.

*M'ijo looked so handsome in his uniform   Why didn't
she ask him not to enlist   He would have done it for her
He adored her   But she didn't   Why*

Delia looked at her mother, who had tears running down her
cheeks. It was still very painful for her mother to go to the cemetery, but she went faithfully every last Sunday of the month, her
hands full of seasonal flowers.

Over the years, Delia had learned to live with the idea that no
matter how much she tried to earn her mother's approval, she
would never gain it. Delia's presence and her accomplishments had
not been enough to fill the emptiness in her mother's heart at the
loss of her two sons. *Lose a son and the world comes to an end
Lose a daughter and nothing is lost   Would she cry for me
like this   Would she bring marigolds and lilies to my grave
Would you Mother   Would you   Guess I would have
to die to find out   Then it wouldn't matter anymore
It doesn't matter   Time heals all wounds Cliches*

True though   Why does she still cry   Guilt Maybe
Time doesn't heal that   I never asked her   I had my
own pain   Her mother dead   Never knew her father
So much sadness in her   Talk to me mother Why won't you
talk to me

Delia had been so engrossed in her own feelings that she had
not considered her mother's pain. Did she blame herself for her
sons' deaths? Had she sought comfort in Delia and had Delia un-
wittingly ignored her plea?

All those years, Delia had blamed her mother for Ricardo's
death. Pain and guilt had bound them together, yet set them apart
from each other. She had never stopped to think about her mother's
reasons, about her frustrations or her own dreams, besides those
she shared with her husband for their children. Whether she was to
blame or not seemed unimportant at that point.

Later that afternoon, Delia watched her mother sitting at her
usual place by the window, crocheting, her hands skillfully moving,
looking out on the street every so often, her head tilted slightly to
the left.

Delia's mother turned around, looked at her daughter and
smiled. "*Mi* pacifier." She raised her crocheting. Delia sat on the
floor next to her and rested her head on her mother's knee as she
used to do when she was little and they would both wait for her
father to come home. It was nice to sit there beside her mother, to
recall their life together and for once think of the good times they
had had. Their dreams had been different, Delia thought, but she
hoped one day they would both be able to talk about them, and
perhaps about their nightmares as well.

Maybe she would accept   It would have to do with her
sons   Talk to other mothers   It would help her too
How do I ask her   My father would object   Maybe
not He came over and hugged me   Waits patiently for her to
stop crying He knows why

"I felt so close to her," Delia told her aunt, after her return
from Los Angeles. "But I still can't talk to her."

"It'll come, darling," Marta said reassuringly. "You'll find
the way."

"Maybe it's time for me to go home," Delia said.

"What about Jeff?" Marta asked. "You know what people say: Amor de lejos . . . Love at a distance . . ."

"Los Angeles is not so far away."

"What if he asked you to marry him? Would you?" Marta asked with hesitation.

Delia smiled at her aunt, kissed her on the cheek and did not answer. She took her suitcase to her room and began to unpack. *What if he asked me to marry him   I don't know   I'm too tired to think   Silly question anyway   He won't ask He's not the marrying type either*

On her way back from Los Angeles, she had thought about her reluctance to consider marriage as a possibility in her life. Through the years she had come to believe that she was one of those women who was not meant to be a wife, and that her consideration of the subject had more to do with her family's and her friends' expectations.

It was true that until the day she and Jeff had made love for the first time, she had believed that she had not met a man with whom she was willing to share more than bed and breakfast. Perhaps that was the reason for her choosing relationships that she well knew would not require a permanent commitment from her. *I love you   I never said that to anyone   Jeff   He knows I love him   I don't have to pretend with him Words are not important   There's no need for them We know where it's at for us*

During their year-long relationship, Jeff had made plans for them to spend occasional weekends away from home. Delia had accepted without saying anything, despite it bothering her that he would not consult with her first.

A few days before Delia's return from Los Angeles, Jeff made arrangements for them to travel to Oregon to attend a horse auction. He wanted her to choose a horse he intended to give her as a birthday present. Delia had been riding Paloma Negra, a peaceful black mare Jeff had chosen for her to learn to ride, but the mare was getting old and Delia was ready for a younger horse.

After getting the tickets at the travel agency, he went straight to the library to give Delia the good news.

"Why didn't you ask me?" was Delia's abrupt response. Jeff,

taken by surprise, was speechless, then hurt. He turned around and left without saying a word, slapping his leg with the tickets on his way out.

Oh God   There I go again   What's the matter with me Why do I do this to him   I love him   I do I always manage to hurt him   I'll go see him after work Shit I'm a cabrona   No   I'm not   He has to learn to ask me what I want   I've always been told what to do

Jeff got to the ranch and went directly to the stable. El Andaluz was waiting to tell him that he had a crew of five men to repair the fences around the corrals and they had been waiting for him to start work.

"Take care of it then," Jeff said in an irritated tone. "You know what to do." He saddled Pal, the palomino he had broken when he and Delia had first visited the ranch, and rode out at full gallop.

El Andaluz watched him go. "*Problema de faldas*," he muttered to another ranch hand. "I know the look." He shook his head.

Two hours later, Delia drove into the ranch and asked for Jeff. El Andaluz shook his head, then nodded as if confirming to himself his suspicions.

" 'E's angry," he told Delia. " 'E's been riding for a long time. *Le vo'a ensilla' al Turco. Mejor caballo.* La Paloma is slow."

"*Por favor*," Delia said, oblivious to the fact she had never ridden Turco, an impetuous brown horse that Jeff had recently bought. When he returned with the horse, she asked him which way Jeff had gone; El Andaluz pointed west.

The horse was restless and Delia patted its head, rubbed its mane gently, then mounted and rode off toward an oakgrove on the west side of the ranch, one of Jeff's favorite spots, but he was not there. Delia looked in all directions, taking off again when she spotted his horse grazing on another slope, a short distance from her.

Turco began to race and Delia pulled on the reins and squeezed its ear, and was delighted when the horse slowed down. She then prompted the horse with her legs and rode on at a steady stride.

Jeff was lying, as in a hammock, on the branches of an oak,

and looking at Pal grazing nearby. He had ridden his horse and himself to exhaustion, but was still upset at Delia. "I'm mad at her and I still wish she was here with me," he told Pal. "Moaning and fiery and quiet. I've never known any woman like her. A wise old woman one day; a playful, passionate girl the next." He pulled up his leg and hit the branch with his boot, and the horse neighed. "I know there have been other men in her life. That doesn't bother me now." Pal came closer and Jeff rubbed the side of his head. "Almost a year. Once, just once, I want to hear her say she loves me."

He sat up when he heard the sound of hoofs in the distance. He looked in that direction expecting to see El Andaluz.

"What the hell," he exclaimed and stood up and caught sight of Turco and Delia's smiling face and waving hand. "Hang on," he shouted. "Don't let go of the reins!" He watched her prompt the horse with her legs, so sure of herself. "This woman is going to drive me crazy." He smiled. "Has a mind of her own, for sure. For sure."

Delia was giggling like a girl with a new toy as she dismounted. She threw her arms around Jeff's neck. "This is the horse I want to ride from now on. No other." She was panting.

"Yes, ma'am." Jeff buried his face in her neck. "I'm so stupid. Forgive me."

"I'm sorry, too," she whispered in his ear. "I don't know what comes over me sometimes."

"Sssh. We'll talk about it later." Jeff was unbuttoning her shirt, stroking her nipples with his tongue, smiling when she began to moan.

"Let's go home." Delia pushed him gently, but saw that Jeff had no intention of moving. "Right here?"

Jeff took off his boots and the rest of his clothes, and made her lean on his jacket and pants, against the trunk of the tree, then pulled her boots, pants and panties off. "Uhuh. You're always telling me you get bored doing things in the same way."

Delia wrapped her arms and legs around him. She closed her eyes in anticipation and opened them again when Jeff made no move to enter her and she heard Turco's neighing. The horse was rising onto its hind legs, then striking with force at the ground.

"A snake." Delia heard Jeff saying. He put her down, and ran toward the horse, checking the ground for the snake. He got hold of the reins and pulled Turco away, followed by Pal.

Delia put on her boots, buttoned her shirt and ran toward them, laughing. She stopped laughing when she looked at the dying rattler, still twisting; she ran back to the grove to find something to strike the snake with and kill it. She found a piece of wood heavy enough to do the job and went back, but the snake was dead. She stared at it, lifeless, yet beautiful, its long dark body stretched over the May grass that was beginning to turn pale yellow. *"Life contracts and death is expected"* *Quickly it comes* *Short the instant to love before its call*

She dropped the log and walked slowly back to the grove where Jeff had the horses already tied to a tree. She threw her arms around Jeff's neck and rested her face on his chest. "I love you," she said in a mournful kind of way.

Jeff smiled, wrapped her in his arms and kissed her head. "Let's go home."

Even if she never said it again, Jeff thought, even if she had said it sadly, almost as if resigning herself to something she could not fight anymore, Delia had said the words and he felt happy.

"I've been told all my life what to do," Delia said without warning when they sat down to supper. Jeff put down his fork and looked at her. "Only once, I did what *I* wanted to do." *Only once* *What I wanted to do* *One night in November* *It seems so long ago* *So long ago* *For the first time I did what I wanted to do* *First time* *First time*

"I'm sorry I didn't ask you if you wanted to go with me," Jeff said after a while. "I wanted you to choose a horse . . . *I* wanted. I see what you mean." Jeff shook his head and smiled. "What do you want?"

Delia passed her fingers through her hair. "I want time."

Jeff pushed his plate away and bit his lower lip until it began to hurt. "You want to stop seeing me?" He was breathing hard and his hands were shaking. "That could be arranged . . ."

Delia sat up in her chair as if pinched by something. It was the second time in one day that they had quarreled. Delia chuckled.

"What's so funny?" Jeff's voice was growing tenser.

"We are," Delia answered. "Do you realize, this is our first fight? One year and we never once argued."

"Not because I didn't feel like it," Jeff replied. "Damn! You make me so mad sometimes." He laughed. "And then . . . Pass the tequila, please."

"Then what?"

"I'm about to make a fool of myself. I need a glass of tequila in front of me. No self-respecting *vaquero* is going to cry for his girl over a plate of *enchiladas con frijoles*." Jeff got up, walked to the kitchen and brought back two glasses and a bottle of tequila. He opened it and poured some into each glass, then placed one in front of Delia who, up to then, had been laughing.

"You're serious," she said, no longer laughing when Jeff gulped down his drink. She grabbed the bottle and held it against her chest.

Jeff laughed and walked around to where she was, took the bottle away from her and put it back on the table. Delia rose to her feet. *He's in a strange mood tonight   I've never seen him like this   Joking but almost at the point of tears*

Jeff bent down and kissed her. "I don't understand you, but I love you." He looked at her. "Whatever it is, you can tell me when you're ready," he said crypticly. "Com'on, I'll walk you to the car."

Dumbfounded, Delia searched in the pocket of her jacket for her keys and walked outside in front of him. She started the car and drove off. All sorts of things zigzagged through her mind, none clear enough to explain what had just happened.

That night Delia was awakened by a noise like that of glass when it shatters. She threw the covers off and cautiously went to check the windows in the house, but they were all intact. *I must have been dreaming*

She was shivering and went back to bed, drawing the covers up to her shoulders. She closed her eyes. *Where are you going Delia   Joyce Where are you   I'm here   Where No trees No flowers   Only sand   A hat lying on the sand There it is   Glasses   I'm afraid They're waiting for me Crouching   There's no one here We're alone You and I alone   They're coming Can't you see them   There's no one here I'm afraid They're there   No one can hurt you I*

*won't let them   Where are you No I don't Don't touch me
No please   I don't want you   Jeff JEEEEEFFF I am
Jeff No you're not He doesn't wear glasses   I'm Jeff Don't
come any closer I'll kill you I'll kill you I will I will   Delia
wake up   Wake up   Wake up*

"Delia. Wake up, darling. Wake up." Marta was standing at Delia's bedside, shaking her lightly. "Mattie is on the phone. She's back. Wake up."

Jeff doesn't wear glasses "You're not Jeff. You're not Jeff."
You're Joyce   Joyce

"Of course I'm not Jeff, darling. Wake up." Marta pulled open one of Delia's eyelids.

"What? Auntie, what's the matter?"   Delia opened her eyes and, seeing Marta sitting on her bed, sat up. She rubbed her eyes with the tip of her fingers. *Weird dream   My neck hurts My throat too   Nightmares   Again   My throat really hurts   I was shouting   Calling Jeff Or was it Joyce It's all so confusing   Auntie   I must have awakened her with my shouting   Poor Auntie She doesn't understand what's happening   I don't understand it myself*

"I was dreaming," Delia said, opening her eyes wide.

"I can see that." Marta wiped the sweat from Delia's forehead. "It must have been quite a passionate dream." Marta pulled the covers off Delia. "Mattie is on the phone, darling."

"Why didn't you tell me?" Delia got up, put her robe on and walked out. "What time is it?"

Marta shook her head and chuckled. "It's 6:30 in the morning, and it's the third Wednesday of May, 1979, *para ser más precisa.*" Delia laughed as she picked up the receiver. "I'm so glad you're back."

"So am I. Sorry about calling you this early, but I'm still on Panama time. Anyway, I want to see you. Either I'll go there or you come here." Mattie paused. "No. Would you mind coming to Berkeley? I have to see about . . . Never mind. I'll tell you when I see you. Is there a chance?"

"Well. Memorial Day is coming up. How about then? I'm taking a two-week vacation after that. Believe it or not, I've been working at the library eleven months already." Delia laughed. "Oh,

Mattie, it's so good to hear your voice."

"Gosh! Has it been that long? Did you get all my letters?"

"Yep! So many things to talk about. I can drive up Saturday morning. How about that?"

"Sounds good. I'll have all the props ready. See you then."

Delia closed her eyes and sighed as she put the receiver down. She went into the kitchen and began to prepare breakfast. Marta watched Delia go about sipping her coffee, running to the stove to stir the beans, cracking eggs, humming a tune, then sitting down to have her breakfast, talking about Mattie and the things they were going to do when she got to Berkeley.

"I have to see Joyce. Find the pieces for this puzzle," Delia said, as she ran to shower and get dressed, then out the door to work.

Marta wanted to say something when she heard Delia speak about Roger, but Delia had not given her a chance. She had not thought about him since Delia and Jeff had started seeing each other. It was needless concern on her part, she thought, since she was sure Delia loved Jeff.

It was during her morning break that Delia thought about the incident of the rattlesnake, Jeff's perplexing behavior and her nightmare.

I don't understand you but I love you   Tell me when you're ready   When am I going to be ready   When Tell him about Joyce   Tell him what   That I love another man Do I love Joyce   Do I love Jeff   They were one and the same   No trees   Passion   Jeff doesn't wear glasses Passion No flowers   Endless sand Passion and love That's what I feel for Jeff   Then what Why Joyce He has become my obssession   Maybe it's just me   The way I am Lack of commitment Run away I've been running for so long So long   Blades shining in the night   Maybe that's what my nightmares are all about A shining blade like new   He sliced my tongue Somehow I knew who he was   I knew who he was   10 o'clock   Have to go back   Black as ink Turned red when it hit the floor   Hit me again son of a bitch I'll kill you   I'll kill you

Delia gasped, making people around her turn to see her. She smiled to reassure everyone she was all right. She had not thought about that unfortunate episode when she had threatened Fernando with the Spanish dictionary until that day, and she was surprised to recall it immediately after the nightmare about losing her tongue.

"I'll be damned," she said under her breath. "I was making myself pay. *Code of silence* Victim and victimizer." *The code of silence   Silence   Silence   I sliced my own tongue   Dios   What have I done to myself* "Do I hate myself so much that . . .? Joyce and Jeff. It's all so confusing." *I have to find out   Once and for all   Once and for all I can't go on like this*

Instead of going directly home after work, she went to the ranch, but El Andaluz told her that Jeff had gone to Camille's house where he was going to have dinner. Delia knew that once she got to Camille's house, she would end up staying for hours, so she called her aunt and told her not to expect her for dinner.

"*Y esto, qué es?*" Delia asked when she saw a pile of rubble and wood next to the wall of the house. "It wasn't here yesterday."

"*No lo vio, ayer,*" El Andaluz told her and smiled. "Now, 'e wants to make a room. There, next to 'is room." He pointed to the side of the house. "*Los carpinteros empezaron ya.*" He arched his left brow. "*No anda bien.* 'e's riding a lot."

"Maybe he's getting in over his head with all this," Delia offered, trying to sound casual, but worried about Jeff, too.

"Maybe." He stared at her and Delia lowered her eyes. *He blames me   Maybe he's right   I'm to blame*

She drove to Camille's house, but Jeff wasn't there either.

"He was here, but he went to Monterey." Camille opened a window. "It's so warm today. So unlike May." She sat on the sill. "He'll be back for dinner. Why don't you stay? It's only the three of us. Everyone is off somewhere."

Delia agreed on the condition that she help prepare dinner and Camille welcomed her offer, since she did not look forward to cooking in such warm weather. She served Delia a glass of wine and poured another for herself and began to chat about astrology, birth planets, progressions, tarot readings and other things that Delia did not have the vaguest notion about. Camille was a great

145

conversationalist, witty and lively, and Delia did not mind.

"Now, you must be a Gemini," Camille said, sipping her wine.

"I don't know," Delia replied.

"When's your birthday?"

"June 12." Delia sat in front of Camille after covering the pot where the rice simmered. "What sign is that?"

Camille pounded on the table. "I knew it! Oh yes, a Gemini."

"Is that good or bad?" Delia raised her eyebrows.

"There is no good or bad in astrology. Only in-ter-est-ing." She looked at Delia bemusedly. "You must have Saturn in one of your Houses; Mars too, I bet. You're an interesting Gemini. A bit melancholic, but restless; you have a strong intellect and an equally strong libido."

"Would that be a reason for having nightmares, awful ones?"

"Definitely. Two people, equally strong, live in you. Always fighting each other, keeping each other in check." Camille looked up. "I think the rice is ready, don't you?"

Delia looked into the pot and turned off the heat. *Wouldn't it be funny   All in the stars   Maybe there's something to it   A Gemini   Two people   Equally strong Loving two men   It's ridiculous   Maybe not*

"It's all ready. I'll broil the steaks when Jeff gets here." Delia poured some more wine into Camille's glass and her own. "What's Jeff's sign?"

"He's a Saggitarius, with the sun in his First House and Venus in his Third." As if reading Delia's mind, Camille proceeded to explain the meaning of it all. "He's generous, but make no mistake, he's proud. Independent. Amiable disposition and very fruitful intellect. Love of music, the arts, poetry."

Delia stared at Camille and smiled. "That's him! Can you really tell all that from planets and signs?" Her curiosity was piqued.

"Oh, yes. And much more." She sipped her wine. "The only part I can't figure out is his love for horses. It must have been some astral disturbance when he was born." Camille laughed. "You must think I'm crazy."

"No. This is fascinating," Delia said in all sincerity, and Camille smiled.

"Tell you what. Give me your exact birthdate, time and place, and I'll have a chart done for you." She raised her index finger. "As a birthday present on June l2. Matter of fact, we should have a party, music, dancing, mirth." She paused and looked straight at Delia. "You and Jeff can announce your engagement then." She nodded once.

"Camille. Really." Delia felt blood rushing to her face.

"Why not? You two are made for each other." She looked inquisitively at Delia. "Is there someone else?" Camille shrugged. "I'm sorry for asking, but these days . . . relationships are very complicated."

Is there someone else   My God Delia sighed. "It's not that." She played with the wine glass. "How do you know he wants to get married? Has he told you that?" *Let the answer be no Please   Please   I need time   Time*

"Not in so many words, but I know him." Camille paused. "You have to remember, he has the sun in his First House. He's proud. He won't ask you until he's sure you'll say yes. Will you?"

"I don't know." Delia breathed a sigh of relief. *Not now Please   Not now   I'm so close to the answers I can taste them   All the pieces are there   I know it I need time   Piece them together   Now is the moment The only absolute   Please God Just a little while longer I sound like a pleading child* "I haven't thought about it."

"Will you?" Camille smiled when she heard the front door. "Let's eat. I'm starved and half-drunk already." She went to set the table.

Delia turned on the broiler, then adjusted the thermostat. Jeff came into the kitchen wearing an old flannel shirt and the stubble of two days. He looked tired. Delia began to breathe hard and had a sudden desire to cry. She walked to him and held him in her arms and felt better when he returned her embrace. *Make no mistake He's proud*

"Let's eat fast and get out of here," he whispered in her ear. "We can drive up to our very own, private dirt road and I'll read you some romantic poems." He brushed her lips with his tongue and laughed when Delia, pushing away from him, looked at him and crossed her eyes.

Delia turned around inside Jeff's arms and dragged both of them to the broiler to check on the steaks. "Are you still mad at me?" he asked.

"I never was. Is that what you thought?" She looked over her shoulder at him. Not waiting for an answer, she said, "Mattie's back. She called me this morning."

"Is she?" Jeff let go of her, opened the refrigerator and pulled out a bottle of beer.

"A hair of the dog that bit you, eh?" Delia put the steaks on a platter. "That's why you wanted me out of there last night. Party pooper."

Jeff smiled and took a long draught of beer, then pounded his chest and brushed the foam from his moustache.

"Why do men always do that?" She carried the tray to the dining table. "Why?" she asked again when she walked back into the kitchen.

"Get drunk or party-poop?" He took another draught and pounded his chest again.

"That. What you just did. Like a gorilla." She imitated Jeff.

"Ah, that! Part of the ritual, like eating popcorn at the movies." He smiled and offered Delia a sip of his beer.

"That's one taste I haven't developed. Now, brandy . . . That, I like." She tugged at him, then pushed him to the table.

"I didn't know you liked brandy," he said amusedly. "Brandy. What do you know!" He looked at Delia then at Camille.

"A good, hearty spirit." Camille nodded. "Perfect for a Gemini." She winked at Delia.

"You two have been talking about astrology and all that jazz?"

"And all that jazz!" Camille waved her finger at him. "Don't knock it."

"I don't. I think it's interesting, but a bit inaccurate." He served himself some rice and salad and reached out his hand, asking Delia to pass the steak platter. "So what's new with the stars?"

"Camille was telling me something about me—Gemini, I mean." Delia handed him the platter. "It's fascinating."

Camille related her and Delia's previous conversation, but made no mention of a party for Delia's birthday nor of her engagement to Jeff. Delia was grateful and smiled at Camille, who winked at her.

"Yeah. She's all that, this woman. And stubborn, mischievous and sexy." Jeff smiled at her, then laughed when Delia blushed.

Camille was delighted and went on with the subject until they had finished eating. She brought a bottle of brandy and served glasses for all of them. Delia closed her eyes and sniffed her glass. Jeff and Camille smiled at each other. Camille got up when Delia finished her brandy and started on another. "I better make coffee."

Delia's face was glowing. Jeff stopped drinking and sat back in his chair, watching and listening to her tell him about her plans to drive up to Berkeley to see Mattie. The whole idea made him feel uneasy. Dangerous ground, he thought, but he interpreted his reluctance to see her go to Berkeley as protectiveness on his part. Everything else was only the garbled sound of a voice inside him, warning about some incomprehensible danger.

"What would you like me to bring you from Berkeley?" Delia came closer and knelt in front of him. *This brandy is making me horny   No   I'm always horny when I'm with him What if I took off his clothes and mine   I better stop drinking I'm already wet and he hasn't done anything yet*

"Bott's ice cream, strawberry, a loaf of sour dough." He caressed her cheeks. "And thou. And thou."

Camille came back with the coffee. "Why don't you go with her?" Delia froze, but the liquor had taken effect and she could not quite figure out why. Just a moment ago, she had been counting the minutes to get out of there and make love to Jeff.

"I wish I could, but the carpenters . . ." Jeff looked at Delia who had gone back to her seat and was helping Camille pour coffee into the cups. "You and Mattie will have a lot to talk about."

His instinct told him it was better that Delia went alone, though he could not pinpoint why. It was a nagging feeling, the same one he had had the night before when Delia had begun to talk about a day in November, the only time she had done what she wanted. The idea that Delia might not come back made him cringe, but he would just have to wait it out, he told himself.

149

Delia was breathing in the aroma of the coffee, then sipping it slowly. Camille decided she did not want any coffee and said goodnight, after clearing the table and taking everything to the kitchen. Jeff helped her. "I think you two better stay here tonight. In your room," she told Jeff.

He kissed her on the cheek. "What would I do without you?"

Jeff looked for Delia and found her staring out the open window in the dark living room. She turned around when she heard him enter. "There are so many things I haven't told you."

"You'll tell me when you're ready," Jeff said, walking to her and putting his arms around her.

"I've been such a spoiled brat." She sighed. "A child."

"You've been through a lot and it still hurts." He kissed her forehead. "You'll live through this one, too. No matter what." He swallowed hard at the thought of her not coming back.

"Yes, I'll tell you when I come back." Delia began to kiss him. Jeff lifted her and carried her upstairs to his room, careful not to miss a step.

They got in bed but did not make love until just before dawn. Jeff talked to Delia about his relationship with his father, and she listened quietly. *So many things we never told each other Silence So much silence*

They drove to the ranch and watched the sunrise from the grove where two days before Turco had killed the snake. Then she drove back to Monterey and sat down to write, hoping to finish the chapter she had been working on, but what she wrote was of a different nature.

"I learned silence, painfully, slowly, as one learns to write, stroke by stroke until the letters form and sound is etched on the whiteness of the paper, and voice uncovers its reason for being.

"Silence then is simply the pause between words, the breath that keeps them alive, the secret element that spans the territory between them.

"I have feared you so, Silence, my oldest enemy, my dearest friend. I surrendered my tongue to you once, freely, and I learned your secret. I learned to write."

Delia put down the pen. In a few days, she would drive to Berkeley, walk the streets alone and stare at the empty buildings, looking for the lifeblood and the heart she had left there.

III

Can't you see the liquid footprints,
the scars still crimson at the edges
on the thin and purple fabric
that has become the lining of my heart?

Chapter 10

The open road   The tearful gaze   May
No more rain   We know the story well   Open the
window   A little   We know the story well but let's
read on   I once had a dream of passion   Damn
I missed the turn I've been on this road so many times   Left
Overpass San Mateo Bridge   Now   I guess it's not
good to know it so well Easier to miss the turn   Miss the
beauty too Overconfidence I guess   Take a wrong turn and
keep on going It's warm Steady   Hold the wheel
Pull the left sleeve   There Now the other   Oops
I'm good at that   Stubborn I hate change   But I get
bored with routine after a while Are you bored now   With
you you mean   Yeah   No I don't get tired of things I
just want to do them different   Good Let's explore the possi-
bilities   Stop kidding Let's go home Right here You're always saying you want to do things different Jeff   Junction 17
2 miles   I like May   It's warm Flowers every where
Children in the park   People smiling I'll be thirty in two
weeks   A Gemini   I don't want to celebrate it
Birthdays are important   All the good things to come
Music dancing mirth You and Jeff can announce your engagement
too   Camille Really   You two are made for each
other   How do you know   The sun in his First House
Proud Won't ask till he's sure you'll say yes Will you   I
don't know   Is there someone else   No Lie
Lie Will you   How can you marry him   You would
destroy everything Why not   There's something between us
No I don't know Something Eliminate   I can't go at it as if it
were a research problem   Probe and poke and bite a work of
art until it lies bleeding in my mouth   It's sad There's pity in
sadness Sadness in loneliness   No Passion in loneliness A
need to have what we don't have to want what we can't have I once
had a dream of passion   That line keeps coming back Over
and over   I can't find where it belongs   I once had a

dream of passion On an early November night In a place called
Berkeley   It ain't working   Maybe it's the ending and
not the beginning   I should work up to it Slowly   It's
not a bang bang job   Drop your panties and   open
your legs and that's that   Why not   That's what it
was Don't be gross 580 Coming up   1 1/2 miles
Work it slowly easy   It all begins with a look   The
way he sits on his horse   The way he moves when he dances
His eyes halfclosed   Away from me Walking slowly toward
me   His fingers barely touching my nipples   His
tongue that knows my skin inch by inch I want him to touch me I
want him in me   Until I want no more   I want to
wake up beside him every morning   Hear his laughter in the
morning dispel the darkness   And not have to explain myself   Know that I am Delia even when he is in me That's Jeff
not Joyce   How can I even think of my life without him How
can I think of leaving him   Then why do you still want Joyce
I don't know why Yes you know   Passion Loneliness Fear I
was once afraid and lonely   He came upon me on the Day of
the Dead   He took his hat and glasses off and I unbuttoned
his shirt and trousers and he snapped open my habit and loosened
my hair and we touched and passion stalked across every inch of
skin every neuron every pore and his hands were warm and moist
and salty like his mouth and his tongue on my neck and my breasts
and all my lips and I tasted the burning bitterness of his sex and
drew him into me and his pleasure was mine and we were of one
breath and one body and one mind once and again   I
I   I can't write that   Why not   I would have to
explain Would Jeff understand   He doesn't have to know No
one has to know Mattie knows Joyce knows   I know I know
He'll always be there between us   Why do I keep him alive
He's only alive when I think of him   Why do I Really
24 Berkeley Walnut Creek   No He's alive somewhere in San
Francisco Flesh and blood   Does he think of me
Does he remember   Watch it This is an obsession
Think of something else Jeff   I wish I could go   The
carpenters   What's the rush He's building another room
He's been riding a lot   Don't Don't Don't That's my favor-

ite word Where   When did I learn to tell myself NO It's Okay Jeff No It is Really   Even when I say yes I'm saying no You'll tell me when you're ready Why in hell are you so understanding Jeff   Why don't you say I don't want you to go That's true Liar   Why don't you tell him your other reason for going Berkeley Bring me a loaf of sourdough and Bott's ice cream And thou And thou   The Claremont Hotel The campanile Passion How can you be so stupid   Everything is so green   Obsession I can't make out the time It must be about one Claremont exit to College Avenue Mattie must be worried There it is Derby Street   Everything looks different in the spring   Come on   Keep on going Don't stop   I'm tired of running   Always on the road somewhere Always the road someone else has chosen for me Always wondering what lies at the end of the path not taken This is stupid   I lived 19 years of my life in LA Almost nine in Berkeley   Berkeley does this to me   I don't know who I am here   What I want   A long war A soldier who has forgotten the reason that made him take up the gun Death everywhere   Cadavers eaten by frantic buzzards Trees that may never bear fruit again Towns gone under Empty fields   Ruins   He finds his soul among the ruins Once children roamed the fields They will again he thinks They will again   Soon he tells himself Soon Soon is the sound of a bullet racing through the air Strife has found its target The heart is silenced Ricardo   Ricardo "Death is absolute and without memorial" No   Each new heart is a memorial   A new contract that must be negotiated Open ended   Chance is accepted   But not war Channing Way to Piedmont to Hearst to Euclid to Grizzly Peak My heart knows what I must do If I only listened   If only I had the courage to do what I must Don't look back Forgetting takes so long So long Kill the dream I'll kill you   I will   I will

Mattie opened the door as soon as she saw Delia's car pulling into the driveway and ran toward her with opened arms. Delia laughed and hugged her.

"You look great," Mattie said holding Delia at arm's length. "Monterey has been good to you." She picked up Delia's overnight bag and they began to walk toward the house.

"So do you. I like the silver streak in your hair." Delia pushed away some strands from Mattie's face.

"It's all natural, I'll have you know. I earned each white hair the hard way in Nicaragua." Mattie stopped to pull out a few long blades of grass from the azalea bed. "We'll have lunch in the back yard. I'm barbequing." She turned to look at Delia. "You do remember the backyard, don't you?"

Delia looked at Mattie and smiled, turned around, went up the short flight of stairs to the guest room, and put her bags on the bed. She noticed that the old walnut dresser was gone and so were the desk and bookcases, and she remembered not seeing the rocking chair and Mattie's favorite love seat in the living room. The walls had looked somewhat empty, as well. *What's she up to now*

"What did you do with some of the furniture?" she asked as she went down the steps, stopping to take a second look at the dining room.

"You noticed, eh? I'm closing shop here and going back to Central America, Honduras to be precise."

Delia wasn't surprised. In her last letter, Mattie had hinted at that possibility. "When are you leaving?" She moved toward the kitchen.

"As soon as I can rent or sell the house. I don't know which yet. I want you to have some of these things. You can choose them before you go," Mattie said at the top of her lungs, and laughed when she saw Delia standing at the kitchen door. "Something I picked up in Panama. No one whispers there. I had a sore throat for two weeks."

Delia laughed, too, and picked up the tray with glasses, plates and silverware, while Mattie secured the salad bowl between her arm and waist and flung the screendoor open. Delia moved cautiously down the stairs and smiled when she saw the single rose in the slim crystal vase on the center of the table. *The symmetry of petals caressed by the swollen tongue of the sun Oh Mattie Mattie   So much has changed and yet   Yet*

"Living in Monterey has done wonders for you. You look absolutely gorgeous." Mattie put down the bowl, walked over to the pit and turned the pieces of chicken over. She looked around and walked back to the house. "I forgot the dressing."

Delia sat down and looked at the rose, smelled its fragrance and closed her eyes. *I once had a dream of passion* She opened them quickly, not wanting to think about the past. She got up and began to set the table and was putting a chicken breast on Mattie's plate and another on hers when she heard the screendoor creak.

"Everything is ready. Let's eat." Mattie tossed the salad and passed the bowl to Delia. "Like old times. I'm so glad you came. And now . . . Where were we? Ah yes, Monterey." Mattie nibbled at her salad. "I was so happy when I got your poems, but you sent me only a few. I read them again last night. I love 'Delia's Song' the best. It's a bit shaky at the end. You'll have to rework that. I was right, wasn't I? You are a poet."

"I don't know about that—the poem, I mean." Delia signaled Mattie to wait while she swallowed. "It sounds so self-indulgent." She followed the flight of a blue jay. "There's so much I need to learn."

"It's a good poem. I don't see the problem." Mattie threw a few crumbs for the birds. "Are you going to write the novel?"

"I've been writing it already." Delia got up and poured some water in her glass. "Do you want some water?"

Mattie nodded. "You hadn't told me about it. When am I going to read it?"

"One of these days, when I feel brave enough." Delia placed another piece of chicken in her plate. "This is so good."

"Hmmm. What are you afraid of?"

"Nothing in particular," Delia answered. "It's just that it's all so intimate. Baring the soul."

"That's the best kind of writing." Mattie looked at Delia.

"I have no trouble with the writing. I have trouble with people reading it; even you," Delia explained.

"Many women writers do, but that's no excuse." Mattie shrugged. "So what if some busybodies point the finger at you? They'll point it even if you're not a writer. Please yourself." Mattie pushed aside her plate. "I don't eat very much now," she explained at Delia's puzzled look. "I guess we went too many days with too little to eat. I got used to that."

"Where? I never knew exactly where you were. Everything

was postmarked in Miami."

"Most of the time we were in Honduras, but we crossed over several times and traveled with the guerrillas around Ocotal and once to Esteli. Illegally, of course. After that we went to Panama where we had to wait weeks for our documents to go to Managua as tourists." Mattie spread an old army blanket on the grass and sat down. Delia poured coffee into the mugs and handed one to Mattie. "I'll tell you. War tests your every belief, even when you think you're sure of them." Mattie lay down on her back. "I made copies of my articles. I'd like you to read them."

"Yes, I want to do that." Delia switched positions to see Mattie better. "Are you resigning or taking a leave?"

"I have to teach this term, then we'll see. I'll probably have to resign. They aren't going to make it easy for me to take a leave. It's ironic, isn't it? I fought so hard to get tenure. Oh, well. Life changes and we change with it or perish, one way or the other." She got up and served herself another cup of coffee. "Would you like some more?"

Delia shook her head and looked at Mattie who was walking down to the edge of the yard to inspect the dahlias. Delia joined her. "Why are you going back?"

Mattie sighed but did not turn. "It's difficult to explain. No matter how informed we are here, how many photos or newsreels we look at, we really don't understand what's happening." She spoke slowly, almost as if giving herself an opportunity to choose the right words. "We don't know what it is to have our country torn in two, to lose parents, children, brothers or sisters, our homes. To watch a mother put a rifle into her son's hands and send him to a sure death . . ."

To lose brothers   Lose your children   Have no home A mother puts a rifle into her son's hands and sends him to a sure death   Ricardo   We do know what that is We Chicanos know what that is   Oh Mattie   We don't have to go that far   We've been at war here

Mattie turned around and began to walk back to the table. Delia followed.

"I suppose people during the Civil War knew what that meant," Mattie said. "But we now don't know what war does to

157

people. We even try to ignore what it did to our young men in Viet Nam. We cannot afford to waste another generation so that regimes like Somoza's can stay in power."

"Maybe white people don't know what war is all about, but we Chicanos know all about it." Delia faced Mattie. "For us the Civil War never ended. We're still fighting it," she said, with a sad smile.

Mattie looked at her, amazed at first, then nodded. "You're absolutely right. We white people don't know what that's all about." She laughed. "Touché! The student has become the teacher."

Delia also laughed, then passed her arm around Mattie's shoulders. "But why Honduras now?"

"Saunders, a British journalist I met there, predicts a Sandinista victory in a matter of weeks." Mattie walked to the table, then sat down. "There are plenty of U.S. troops, armament and equipment at the Honduran border; 'though reading the newspapers here you wouldn't know about it. No, it isn't over. I'm afraid it's just beginning," Mattie said sadly. "I have to go back. There's enough of a network now, and perhaps if we start making enough noise, the American people will listen." She fell silent.

Delia sat quietly next to her. So much had happened to them in the last year, things that had changed their lives forever. "It's strange how we go on doing the same things day in and day out, and suddenly it all gets turned around," she said after a while.

Mattie nodded in agreement and patted Delia's hand. "Perhaps you'd like to go in and lie down. I'll clean up," Delia said as she got up and began to put things on the trays.

"No. We'll do it together. I want to spend as much time as possible with you. We'll listen to some music and then I'll make us a light supper." Mattie picked up one of the trays and the salad bowl and walked toward the house. Delia watched her go until she stepped through the door. Delia finished picking up what was left and then sat down on the bench. She looked up at the clear sky and followed the flight of the blue jays. *I have this feeling   She's just going to Honduras   It bothers me   So thin   Drawn   She may resign   No   She feels she has to do this   That's all I left too   And nothing wrong happened   I don't want her to go*

She checked the pit to make sure the fire was out and threw some crumbs on the grass for the birds. She watched them swoop down and pick the pieces up, then she threw some more. *For the little ones in the nests* She picked up the tray and went into the house.

Mattie turned on the stereo and walked back into the kitchen. *The Albinoni Adagio   Of course*

"Do you ever think of him?" Delia was surprised at Mattie's sudden question, but she understood immediately what it was about.

"Yes." She had wanted to ask Mattie about him ever since she had walked into the house, but did not know how to approach the subject. She finished putting the dishes into the dishwasher and turned it on.

"He came to see me in Panamá. He asked about you." Mattie was standing right next to her.

"Really?" Delia tried to speak as normally as possible, but her mouth felt parched and her hands trembled slightly.

"Really. Don't you want to know what he told me?" Mattie held Delia's hands. "Come, let's go to the living room and I'll tell you. You know I'll tell you, anyway."

"I don't think I want to hear. What for?" Delia said, but followed Mattie and walked to the window, then turned around and sat on the floor resting against the wall. "Okay, I'm listening." She laughed.

Mattie's eyes lit up. "Aha, I knew it. If you must know, he asked a lot about you."

"Why didn't he ever call? That's the only thing I want to know," Delia said peevishly.

"Tch. Tch. You were the one who was supposed to call. I want a glass of wine. Do you want one?" Mattie went to the kitchen and brought the bottle and two glasses without waiting for Delia's response. "Do you know that when you didn't call he went looking for you?"

"How did he know where I lived? I didn't tell him. Did you?" Delia took the glass Mattie offered her.

"He went to personnel on campus and gave them some cockamamie story. Oh, he's a charmer when he wants to be." Mattie laughed. "They didn't give it to him, but they sent him to the Registrar's Office and they sent him to Graduate Admissions which sent him to the Alumni Association and he got it. There, in a nut shell." Mattie got up and turned the record over.

"When did this happen? Why didn't he call you?"

"He says he called me but I was never home. It must have been when I was getting ready for the trip. I did get a note from him the day before I left, but how was I to know?" Mattie went to her desk and pulled out a piece of paper and showed it to Delia. "You see? The note just says that Carina had told him I was leaving town and he wanted to say goodbye. He didn't say anything about you. I didn't have time to call him, so I wrote him from the Mexico City airport. Our plane was delayed and I had some time. I told him when and where I would be in Panama and suggested he join me there. And he did."

Delia looked at Mattie and smiled. "You're enjoying this."

"Of course I am. Anyway, he went to your old address and found out you were not living there any more. And your landlady wouldn't give him your address in Monterey." Mattie looked at Delia, who was now pacing up and down.

"Did you tell him where I was?" Delia finished her wine in one gulp.

"Slow down. No, I didn't. I wasn't sure you wanted to see him again." Mattie changed her mind and handed the bottle of wine to Delia after pouring some into her own glass. "We might as well get drunk today."

Delia laughed. "Yeah, might as well." She sat on the arm of the sofa. "There's something you're not telling me. I know you well, Mattie N. Johnson. What is it?"

Mattie sighed. "It's not easy to tell." She paused but decided to continue. "Remember I told you Carina was in love with him?" Delia nodded. "I also told you he didn't love her." Delia slid into the sofa. "You have to understand Roger is a very sensitive and caring man. That's what makes him special."

"And he married her?" Delia sat up. *Strange   Life is We think we have it all figured out   I guess I'll never know now Joyce   How could you*

"Relax. He didn't marry her, but she tried to commit suicide." Mattie went to sit next to Delia. "Apparently she had tried it before. A very sick lady."

"What did he do?" Delia began to play with the glass, then put it on the floor. "Don't tell me. I don't want to know any more." She was going to get up but Mattie held her down.

"He got the best psychiatrist he could afford for her. I talked to her last week and she seems to be getting better. You see now why I wouldn't give him your address?" Mattie smiled at Delia. "None of this means he's not interested in you. Are you still interested in him?"

Delia looked at Mattie out of the corner of her eye, but did not answer right away. *Am I   Am I   What do I want I'm crazy   One minute I want to see him so badly The next minute I   So complicated   Jeff   I don't have to see Joyce I won't see him   It's* "Over. No, I'm not. I think I'm going to marry Jeff." *I think*

"Oh dear, oh dear, oh dear! We're going to need something stronger." Mattie got a bottle of brandy but didn't pour from it. "We've got trouble. Jeff Morones." She poured some into her glass and into Delia's. "I knew you were seeing him, but I didn't think it was that serious. You treated the whole affair so casually in your letters."

Delia smiled sadly. "I guess I don't always say what I think." *Tell the truth   For once in your life tell the truth* "There are so many things I don't understand. Have you ever had the feeling that . . . No, I'll start again. You have a puzzle and you're looking for a piece. Color. Design. Shape. You're almost sure it'll fit. You try. It's almost, but not quite right." She closed her eyes and shook her head. "What I'm trying to say is that I sometimes think that I have the pieces and then, . . . It's useless. I can't explain it."

"Why don't you start at the beginning?" Mattie suggested and Delia nodded, but didn't say anything for a while. She then began to relate events, beginning with her fantasies about Roger, her encounter with Jeff, the things they did together, her writing, her resentment toward her mother, her feelings for Jeff, and ending with her quarrel with Jeff and the nightmare about Jeff and Roger being one and the same.

161

"I have all the answers; I know it. I just can't make the pieces fit." Delia closed her eyes and rubbed the bridge of her nose. "Some do. That whole affair with Fernando and the nightmare. It was the first time I received a blow and I was ready to do . . . I did something about it."

"You certainly did!" Mattie laughed.

"I've been so afraid all my life." She looked down. " I do love Jeff. A part of me wants to spend the rest of my life with him. Is that so wrong?"

"Of course not. Jeff is as good as they come and he's always been in love with you." Mattie moved to the edge of the sofa to look better at Delia, who was playing with her glass.

Delia sighed and looked at Mattie. "But then, why the fantasies? Why J—Roger?"

Mattie raised her eyebrows. "Quite a quandary. Imagine. How many women dream of being in your position? Two good men who love you and want you. Quite an interesting problem."

"One man who loves me. How can J—Roger love me? He hardly knows me." It was the second time Delia had said his real name. For a long time, Roger had been the shadow of James Joyce, the other side of fantasy, but the dream was taking on flesh and blood. "I don't know why I'm afraid of seeing him again, Mattie. I give myself all kinds of reasons why I should and why I shouldn't, but I'm still afraid. I just don't know." *I'm afraid Of what Afraid* Delia got up and began to pace up and down the room again.

"I don't see how you're going to find that out if you don't see him again." Mattie smiled. "Maybe you won't like him anymore. Maybe he'll say the wrong things and you'll hate him. Maybe it isn't as big as you thought it was."

Delia chuckled. "Same old Mattie."

"I'll say one thing for Jeff, he's taught you how to laugh."

"That he has."

Chapter 11

"There are no clouds, only the bright red sky above and endless sand ahead of me. No flowers. No trees. Not a sound. A tower in the distance. I walk to it but it recedes from me at every step. The heat is unbearable even at twilight. I'm drenched and exhausted. I look for a rock, some place to sit down, but there's only sand, hot sand. I don't want to go on but something pushes me toward the unreachable tower. I'm quite sure I'm alone in this desolate place, but someone must be here with me; I feel the cold touch of hands on my hot back. I don't want to go on. It's useless. I know I'm dreaming and all I have to do is to wake up, but I can't open my eyes. In my dream I reach for my eyelids and try to push them open, but in my dream they're open. I am conscious enough to know that I must open them in real life; I try to raise my arms but they do not obey me. I'm paralyzed. I fight the power that pushes me toward the tower. To no avail. I'm now struggling hard to open my eyes. I don't want to sleep, I shout; I want to wake up. I am so afraid I will never be able to wake up. I pray, say the words louder and louder; I'm shouting, I'm sure. I wake up and hear the muffled sound of my own voice saying, 'Forgive me.'"

Why am I always asking for forgiveness   What have I done but be beaten and get up every time   Is that my sin
Is that my sin   No trees   No flowers   Endless sand Being asleep forever   Never waking up   Sleeping Beauty In the flesh   No rescuer   You're on your own girl I'm on my own

Delia finished writing down her dream and looked out the open window. It was only six-thirty, but the breeze blowing in already felt warm. This time, the urgency to make sense of her dream was not there. She closed the small notebook she now carried everywhere to write notes for herself about her novel. She left

163

the pen inside to mark the place where she had stopped. *All the dream analysis in the world couldn't help me now   I'll get back to it later   Tomorrow   Tomorrow   It's already tomorrow Famous last words   Make that call After breakfast   Yes I'll call after breakfast*

She woke Mattie up and busied herself making *huevos rancheros* served on lightly fried tortillas with plenty of *salsa picante* on them. *I need all the furia I can get   Fury No Vehemencia Courage   Hot blood and cold mind Nothing like chile to make your blood run hot*

After breakfast, she helped Mattie get ready for the open house. The realtor was expected at ten and prospective buyers at noon. Mattie disliked the realtor but he had been highly recommended by her friends; nonetheless, she wanted to be around to talk to people herself.

"That's just not done," Delia said. "Besides, why do you want to be around when people come, poking under the sink, looking for *cucarachas*, termites? I wouldn't."

Mattie shrugged and Delia decided to leave the arguments to the realtor. She wasn't looking forward to being there, watching people talk about bugs, foundations, exposed wires and rusty pipes to take a few thousand off the price, with no concern for the feelings of the woman who called that place home.

She decided to spend the day out, walk to campus, browse around at Moe's and Cody's, perhaps have lunch at Larry Blake's and visit the rose garden before returning home in the afternoon. She thought of calling Roger before leaving the house, but decided against it, and started from Mattie's house on her way to campus, thinking that a good walk would help her clear her head. Half way down the hill, her feet ached and her shirt was already soaked, so she sat on the bench at the next bus stop, took her sneakers and socks off, and wiggled her toes.

It was a splendid Sunday morning, clear and warm. The bay shimmered in the distance. Down below, the campus and the downtown area already buzzed with activity. The end of the term was approaching and students hurried unhappily to the libraries when they would have liked to go to the beach or play frisbee in the parks.

She put her socks and shoes on and was ready to resume her walk when she saw the bus approaching. She waved to the busdriver to stop. The ride was relaxing and she was almost sorry it had ended when she got off on Euclid and Hearst, on the north side of the campus. She thought about walking through the campus, but decided instead to go around it and turned right on Piedmont Avenue, on the east side. She passed International House, and a few blocks from it she stopped in front of a student co-op at the sound of *salsa* music blaring out of a stereo somewhere on the second floor.

She crossed the street to get a better look and saw two young Chicanos talking. Freshmen, she thought, and smiled. They were no different than she, Sara, Samuel or Jeff when they had arrived at Berkeley. *Sara   First things first A stereo and a phone Top of the list for any student   January 1969 Viet Nam peace talks resume   LBJ's farewell speech to the Press Club Inauguration of Richard Nixon   Duke Ellington and orchestra play at his inauguration   Antiwar organizers in Washington stage anti-inaugural   Sara's scrapbook   TWLF strike at Berkeley Manuel   Ysidro   Richard   Fernando   Sal   Thelma Guillermo   So many names   I have forgotten so much Samuel was right One day somebody would be looking for us   I'm so glad he went around collecting things and made me do the chronology And my journal   Strange   I've relived the events so many times   Yet Disjointed   Pieces in my head Jeff probably has a lot of things too*

She remembered her conversation with Jeff on the day of their unexpected meeting in Monterey. The two Chicano freshmen were not aware that all of them had fought ten years before to help them realize their dreams now. They would probably never learn the price such an undertaking had exacted from the students who had held the door ajar for their generation. Perhaps some of them now were thinking of majoring in math or literature, without the political burden of "What's a Chicano doing in English when we need lawyers and doctors and social workers?" Hadn't that been what they, ten years before, had chosen to fight for, after all?

Even philosophy   Philosphers   The last ones to

165

come Delia smiled. A month ago, she and Jeff had been walking along the waterfront in Monterey for quite some time. "We need to stay in shape," she'd told him, not wanting to explain about the disquietude a sudden break in her writing produced in her.

"I like your shape. Please, let's stop." He pleaded. "There's The Tinnery." He pointed at a restaurant. "Let's go in and have lunch."

Delia puckered her lips, shook her head and kept on going, but Jeff didn't follow her. Exhausted, he took off his boots and lay on the grass of the small park in front of the restaurant. Delia went a few feet until she noticed he wasn't anywhere around her, headed back to the restaurant and looked in the windows of The Tinnery, expecting to see him waving at her from one of the tables. Jeff was not there, so she went across to the park and looked around until she found him.

"I'm a rider and a dancer, not a walker."

Delia sat next to him. "Lucky for you you didn't get your M.A. in anthropology. Lots of walking and digging."

"Those are archeologists," Jeff said. "They're the ones who do the diggings."

"That was another thing Julio had against you. Your being in anthropology." Delia was restless and got up. "He told me." She found a pebble and threw it in the water. "He was trying to convince me to go into law."

"He had so many things against me." Jeff sat up. "Come and sit down." He stretched his hand to Delia, but she refused. "Are you uptight about something?"

"No, I was just thinking. I want to start a group." She knelt behind him and started massaging his back.

"Feels so good. What kind of group?"

"A group of women to talk to Chicanas about their sons resisting the draft." Delia sat down behind Jeff. "I know. There's no draft now, but there will be if we go into Nicaragua."

"Yep. And Chicanos will be the first to be called." He swung around to face Delia. "It's a good idea. You should talk to Camille about it. She'd be happy to help."

"I already talked to her and Aunt Marta." Delia got up again and jogged in place for a short while, then stretched out her arms, palms down and turned her torso left and right a few times. "I don't know. I just feel I have to do something. Literature won't solve our problems as Chicanos." *Funny thing to say when I just started writing   Phd in literature*

"I'm not too sure about that. The pen is mightier than the sword, or so people say." Jeff smiled and got up. "Okay, you win. Let's walk, but back to the car." He put on his boots. "And slowly." He put his arm around her shoulders. "You *are* tense."

"Do you think we'll ever have philosophers?" Delia ignored Jeff's last remark and he smiled. She would always get tense when she wanted to discuss something, speak as if to herself most of the time and not relax until the subject was exhausted.

Jeff was tired and hungry and didn't feel like discussing anything that sounded in the least serious.

"We already have those. Cheap philosophers, taco philosophers, cafe philosophers, cantina philosophers . . ." Jeff stopped his litany when she poked him in the ribs. "Cow-boy phil-o-so-phers."

"Stop it!" Delia was trying not to laugh. "It isn't funny. You can be such a cynic. Agh!"

"Cynical philosophers." Jeff held Delia at arm's length. "Sexy philosopheuses."

She made a fist and was going to push it against his stomach, but decided to tickle him instead. "You and your . . ."

"Cheap philosophy?" He snorted and held her hands. "Is that what you were going to say?"

Delia burst out laughing. "Yeah."

"You're right. We'll have Chicano philosophers. Maybe by the year 2000, to welcome the new century." He expected Delia to go on with the discussion, but she was quiet.

"I'll be over 50 when 2000 comes around," she said after a while.

"If we don't blow up the world before then." Jeff began to laugh.

"What are you laughing about?" She looked at Jeff who could hardly speak. "Com'on. Stop laughing and tell me." In a short while, without knowing the reason, she was laughing and clutching her stomach.

Jeff sighed a few times. "You know that friend of Carla's, the *argentino*. What's his name?"

"Corelli," Delia said.

"Yeah, that one. I walked into Camille's house and she was running after him with the scissors. Ready to cut his balls off. Poor *vato*." He breathed in deeply. "Apparently, they'd been discussing the dangers of nuclear weapons. Things like that." He wiped the sweat off his forehead with his hand. "*El pendejo* told her it was okay for the gringos and the *rusos* to blow each other out of existence. Then the *argentinos* could have the whole world for themselves."

"He must have been kidding. I can't believe he was serious." Delia cleared her throat and wiped the tears from her eyes. *Laugh when crying   Cry when laughing   Ice cream in winter Hot coffee in summer*

"He wasn't." Jeff rubbed his stomach, but could not contain his laughter. "She was furious, running after him with the scissors, shouting: 'Pray that you get to see that day, you, you.' Corelli got out of there like *alma que lleva el diablo*."

Como alma que lleva el diablo   Oh Jeff   Such a silly story   But we laughed so much   What am I doing here How am I going to tell him   Tell him what   I haven't even seen Joyce   No   Roger   Roger Why can't I call him by his real name

Delia went back to campus and looked into the student union building, then sat on Ludwig's Fountain to watch the passers-by. She did not recognize anyone and no one recognized her. There was something pleasant in her anonymity.

Somewhere in the damp basement of a campus building, in steel boxes—a kind of common grave, she thought—the dossiers F.B.I. agents had compiled on each of the students who had participated in the Third World Strike lay stacked one on the other. *Chicano   Black   Asian   White Native American All equal there   Paper people   No longer dangerous   In black and white   The colors of bureaucracy   I'd love to see those dossiers   I should go to the library and check some things while I'm here Sometimes I forget dates Sequence of events   I need to do*

*that   Check   Now I'm also in this business of
dossiers   Mine tell a different story   All there
In that common grave   It's sad though   To know
we're only as thin as paper   Paper and death   The
great equalizers   Color blind   Only black and white
And finally yellow   Then dust   Dust And not to leave
anything behind to be remembered by   Frightening Asleep
forever   Knowing it   All the things we could have
done and didn't   Could now be doing if we could only wake
up   The tower   Did I really want to reach it Conform
to the rules   Not anymore   Lived with regrets Too
long   Sorrow   Loneliness   Have to call
Don't think about it just do it   Go back to ASUC
Pick up the receiver   Follow the instructions Deposit the
dimes   Wait for the dial tone   Dial the number
Wait   Not hang up   What if Carina answers
What if he answers Identify yourself   Speak clearly   I
always speak clearly When I speak that is   Do it
Easy   Follow instructions   Whose instructions
Your own for once Think of it as a dialogue in a story   Re-
move yourself This is not a story   This is real life*

Delia did not want to give herself time to change her mind
about calling Roger and searched in her coin purse for dimes, but
found only a nickel and a quarter.

*Use the quarter   What's a nickel anyway   Do it
now Go to the phone* Her hand was shaking as she inserted the
quarter and her heart was beginning to race. *Where's the card
I don't need the card   I know the number by heart*
"921-6ll5."

"Deposit 50 additional cents, please."

"Operator, I don't have change. May I charge this call to my
phone number in Berkeley?" *What's the number   Shit
What's Mattie's number   Hang up now   No No
You know the number* "548-3391." *Ringing*

"Hello." *It's him   Answer   Say something*
"Hello. I'd like to talk to J—Roger, please."
"This is Roger."
It's him   Steady   Say something   You're

169

taking a long time   He's going to hang up   I "You might not remember me. My name is Delia. Delia Treviño."

"Ah yes! Mattie's friend."

Mattie's friend   Mattie's friend   A perfect stranger   Why did I call   Mattie's friend "Yes, Mattie's friend."

"Are you in Berkeley?"

I should have said Saint Theresa   He would have remembered her   She wasn't Mattie's friend   She was James Joyce's lover "Yes, I'm in Berkeley."

"I can be there in an hour. Where would I meet you?"

Where   Where   I don't   Think "Do you know the Berkeley Rose Garden?"

"No, but I'll find it. What street is it on?

Damn   This is going too fast   Is it on "Euclid. I think."

"I'll be there in an hour."

Hang up now   Now

"Hello? You won't disappear again, will you, Delia?"

Disappear "I'll be there." *Now it's done   Not shaking anymore   No wondering   No waiting around It's done   The garden*

There were only a few people in the rose garden. They moved slowly and spoke in each other's ears or in whispers, as if they had just entered a sanctuary, pointing discreetly or bending over this or that variety to inhale its fragrance. They all turned around at the tinkling of a poodle's tags and looked admonishingly at the small blonde woman who was getting ready to free her dog, but who soon realized she and her pet were in danger and turned to leave.

A poodle in paradise Delia chuckled.

"Really! It's all organic, anyway," the blonde angrily uttered. "Look at him." She directed her comments to Delia, standing nearby, and pointed at a tall, white-haired man in a gray suit and bow tie. "He does research for the government at the Lawrence Rad Lab." She spat on the ground. "What does he think is going to happen to his precious roses when the damned thing explodes?" She rushed out, dragging the poodle behind her.

We come here to be tested like pieces of metal   To be

*dipped in sulphur infusions   An alchemist's dreampieces
Are we the real stuff   Nuclear winter in May in the middle of
a rose garden   And all because of poodle shit   Jeff
would love this one   Jeff   Jeff   I've done
something terrible   I wish   No   It's done
He'll be here at twelve   Ja   No   Roger
The least you can do is call him by his real name   Will I
recognize him   I could hide   No   I'm always
hiding   The air is so heavy Trapped in this garden
Eve   I need a drink of water*

Delia walked to the water fountain at the west end of the
garden. After a long drink, she sat on the stone guard next to the
fountain. *I'm sweaty   I'm not even wearing make up That's
funny   He's already seen me at my worst*

"Hurry," she heard the alleged professor's wife whisper to
him as they passed in front of her without turning to see her.
"We're going to be late to the service."

"Just in time. Look who's coming," he answered disdainfully.

Delia looked in the direction of the entrance, where a Black
couple with two young children were walking into the garden. *Now
is when I need you Blondie   Tell them off   I wonder if
she would   Dogs are one thing   Blacks and Chicanos
are another The Calibans in a world that is neither brave nor new
Nothing has changed   Everything has changed   Plus
change Enough I'm getting sick of this garden   That's what
Eve must have said   And so she ran across the garden God
and Lucifer and he had built myth by myth stone on stone
She ran barefoot Naked   Eve they called after her
Eve echoed the wind She was gone It was long ago   In the
winter of the gods When evil and good were one*

Delia felt flustered and began to fan herself with her hands.
The campanile clock struck twelve thirty. *He's not coming It's past
the hour   He's probably lost   It's so easy to get lost
in Berkeley   Berkeley   I've tried to run away and
here I am again   In an infamous rose garden   Waiting Eve   You've betrayed yourself*

Delia got up and started to walk slowly toward the entrance.
The muscles in her legs ached because of the tension and the long

walk up the hill to the garden, and she rubbed them.

More people were coming into the garden and children were running up and down the stone steps, some laughing, one crying after falling because of an untied shoelace. Delia knelt in front of him, then began to comfort him and tie his shoe. She took out a tissue and began to wipe off the little boy's face, then put the tissue in his hand and closed it. *One must always carry a tissue darling You never know when you're going to fall again   It's good to know you can take out that tissue and wipe your own tears*

Delia looked up to find a man standing right beside her, offering his hand to help her get up. On instinct, she took it, recognizing immediately afterwards the touch of Roger's hand. She waited for her heart to step up its pace, for her mouth to dry up, her hand to tremble as it reached toward the one offered by the man she had made love to so many times in her fantasies. But all she could feel now was a sudden desire to lie down on the cool ground next to him and sleep.

"Let me help you up." Roger was smiling. "That's how I've remembered you," he said. "A rose, praying."

"My sins have been great," Delia said, and her response surprised her. Her eyelids felt heavy and she breathed in deeply in an effort to fight off her sudden fatigue. She looked directly at him.

"Disappointed?" Roger held on to her hand.

"No, not disappointed." She paused. "A bit awed."

She was going to continue, but felt something pulling the leg of her pants, and looked down. The little boy she had comforted a moment ago was handing her the tissue she had given him. "I don't need it anymore, thank you," he said and ran off to join his mother waiting for him a short distance away. Delia waved at them, and put the tissue into her pocket.

"Are you hungry?" he asked and Delia nodded. "A small place in San Francisco, but the food is very good. Would you like to go there?"

Delia nodded again. How easy it was to say yes to him, to go anywhere he wanted to take her, to trust him so implicitly, she thought as they walked to his car.

I should be thinking   But I'm not thinking   I'm not thinking   No flowers   No trees   Not a sound Only the bright sky   Endless sand   Think Think

A voice inside her warned about some danger, but by the time she deciphered its cryptic message, she was sitting beside him and the car was heading down the street, toward the campus.

Chapter 12

Ocean   Clouds   Sun   A blinding light to the naked eye   Truth   Burning away iris cornea and lens The past   How then should we look at it   From a slanted angle   Perhaps   Through a darkened crystal Obscuring the star so that we may see the crown   Its majestic flares Hundreds of thousands of miles above the spinning mass Gathering plasma   Atom by atom   Moving swiftly through the darkness of space   The darkness in our souls The solar wind   The star dims   Lights on The tears long dried A white spot on the skin   Where once a scar was Crimson at the edges   The moon is rising Yellow crescent moon There was no moon that night   A few stars only James Joyce The evening star opposite the moon Hard to say goodbye to a dream   A fantasy   An old pain we've lived with for so long   We'd do anything not to feel it   Sit this way Eat only that   Don't think Don't feel Don't breathe Don't   Don't   Icy cold moon   Anything not to bring it back   One day we eat the wrong thing   We wait for the pain to come   It doesn't   It doesn't We feel sad   We mourn its passing The old enemy is no longer there to pit ourselves against Icy cold Venus No one to tell us we're still alive   What do we do then Look for another pain   Perhaps another passion It follows the other   Icy cold passion on the evening sky Reflections of the sun   I would have been a reflection Only that It's absolute summer   Absolute summer   Cruel The words Absolute summer   The moon is rising Joyce This man called James Joyce Once he wiped my tears Understood my sorrow   My fears   My loneliness He knew me like no one had before A dream to dream on loveless nights A dream of passion There isn't a cloud in the sky   No fog tonight Hard to do what we must do   Say what we must say Feel passion stirring in you   And say no   Such an absolute word So many stars out tonight   Or stay silent Silence This double sharp edged blade that wounds two hearts at once   A tiny star so close to the moon   Caught in her halo It's easier to bear the pain than inflict it   An optical illusion   Tiny star Probably bigger than the sun   I should go inside   The last chapter   Clean the floor Cook a meal   Anything but write that final chapter What's so important about this story   Bigger than the earth All the souls in it   A huge ball of fire Spinning spinning in the cold darkness of space   Eternal fire   It's dangerous to think this way   Nothing is eternal   What'll I do then Stars also die   Publish it   Find another pain No Mattie I'll publish it   Yes I'll do that   For me and for you Will he understand Jeff He must   He will What if he doesn't Fellow traveler   This is my story   My song I was born to be Delia in the world   To seek the elusive pair Perhaps the tiny star went nova years ago   Nova Love and truth Its light still there   Through the meandering creeks of feelings And the winding hard roads of reason   To hunt the light Fellow traveler if by chance   Nova   The wind whispers this song in your ear   Nueva   Know that I still love   New   And want to be loved Novela In the end   Rising from the ashes of the past When all is said and done   Old star   Only that truth can save us New star   Only that truth can save us The new old story

Delia was lying flat on her back, eyes closed, arms stretched above her head and knees raised to ease the pain on her lower back when she heard the doorbell ring. It was eight o'clock in the morning on her last day of vacation. She had been writing all night long; now the last chapter of her novel was finished and been added to the end of the 500-odd pages on her desk. *One year's work Was it worth telling   Yes   Now what Put it in the drawer   Forget about it   At least it's done Whatever happens   It's done*

For two days before finally sitting down to write the last pages, she had allowed every conceivable task to interfere with doing it, until the night before, when she could no longer fight the urgency to end the story.

"Delia," she heard her aunt Marta say outside the door of her room. "Are you up? Jeff's here."

"Thanks, Auntie. I'll be right there," Delia answered, lowered her knees and, still on the floor, stretched her whole body a few times. She felt weak while getting up and had to sit on her bed until the feeling went away. She breathed in deeply a few times, walked to her desk, picked up the manuscript and headed for the kitchen.

Jeff was upset, she thought, as she entered and deposited the heap of papers on the table. *Why shouldn't he be* She managed a weak smile. In the past two weeks, she had seen him only once, on the evening she returned from Berkeley.

"Did Berkeley get you down?" he had asked and looked into her eyes as if wanting to be reassured that she was the same as when she had left. He smiled when he saw the cooler she was carrying. "You brought it—Bott's ice cream." Delia put it down. He opened it, then the cartons of ice cream, scooped some out with his fingers. He gave Delia a taste, then had one himself. "Sourdough and a book of poems, too."

Delia sat down and listened to him read some of the poems aloud.

"He's good." He flipped the book over to look at the name on the cover. "Gary Soto. Are there any other books of his at the library?"

"No, but there will be soon. You know how difficult they get when it comes to Chicano literature." Delia got her notebook out and copied the name of the publisher.

Jeff moved toward her, but changed his mind and sat on the chair opposite her. Every time Delia returned from a trip, there was a moment of hesitation between them, an interval they filled talking about things other than their personal feelings. They circled around each other, closing in little by little; but this time it was different.

"It's getting late," Delia said and got up. "I better be getting home."

What's the rush? Jeff wanted to say, but didn't. This time Delia would have to make the first move, talk to him as she had promised before she had left to Berkeley.

"I'll call you tomorrow." She drove off.

For a week he waited for her call, and when it did not come, he called her, but Marta told him the same thing every time. *"No puede venir al teléfono.* I'll tell her to call you." Now he had her in front of him and could not begin to ask for an explanation.

Marta excused herself as soon as she saw Delia enter with the manuscript in her hands. Delia seemed calm and collected when she returned from her visit with Mattie, but spent every waking hour typing away in her room, eating little and hardly getting any sleep. When Marta inquired about it, Delia handed her the incomplete manuscript to read, but not before asking her not to show it to anyone or make any comments until the final chapters were written.

Marta read it avidly, and tears silently rolled down her cheeks during those passages in the novel that spoke about Sebastián and Ricardo, and about Delia's ambivalent feelings toward her parents and her life in Los Angeles. Marta felt like a fool, because she found herself crying as well when Delia described her happy summers with her in Monterey. There was nothing sentimental in Delia's writing, and Marta attributed her tears to her own sentimentalism and the feelings of pride and joy she felt at discovering her niece and herself anew.

She read and re-read the section Delia had titled "The Lean Years," that spoke about the Third World Strike. She cursed the university officials, then cursed the other students for the unfair treatment Jeff had received at their hands, and finally felt guilty for not being there for her niece during the hardest time of her life.

Like most parents and relatives of those students, she had worried about the reprisals against them. She had been afraid they would lose their opportunity to graduate from such a prestigious university, thus canceling out their chances for a life different from her own, a better life, she had thought. She wanted Delia to stand upright instead of stooping over in the fields to put food on someone else's table, to fill the pockets of the rich growers. It had been difficult for Marta to understand that Delia and the other striking students were fighting for the same ideals their families held in high esteem.

"They would have accomplished so much more," Marta told Cloti, "if only we had been there to support them."

"It's never too late," Cloti answered. "It's never too late. Look, Marta, this idea Delia has about organizing Chicano mothers against war . . ."

"What about it?"

"I think it's a good idea. Part and parcel of all this. This is our chance to help," Cloti answered and Marta agreed, but told her friend to wait until Delia finished writing her novel.

Every morning, after Jack left for work, Marta prepared breakfast for Delia and sat in her own room reading the next installment. "Good for you!" Marta said aloud when she read about the episode where Delia hit Fernando with the Spanish dictionary.

One night, after reading about Delia's nightmares and the events of that early November evening when Delia met Roger, Marta woke suddenly. "What will Jeff think of all this?" she said under her breath, but thought that Delia knew better and would never show it to him.

One of those days Delia had been away in Berkeley, before Marta read the manuscript, Jeff had stopped by to ask for her advice.

"I guess you know I'd like to ask Delia to marry me," he said. "As soon as I finish repairing the house."

"I think you should," Marta said. "Nothing would make us happier than seeing you two married." She looked at Jeff, who was absent-mindedly spinning the empty glass of lemonade. "Is there something stopping you?"

"Her. She's stopping me." Jeff was quiet for a while. Marta had never seen him depressed, but she did not say anything. "Every time I try to approach the subject, she . . . Maybe I should just say it clearly, openly." He sighed. "I don't know what to make of it."

Marta thought carefully about her answer. "Delia is afraid. For good reasons, too. We've expected so much from her. She's had to be three people. Don't you see?"

"I *do* see, Aunt Marta," Jeff said. "And I understand. That's why I've never pressed her for an answer, but I think there's more to this." He looked at Marta. "Do you know what it is?"

Marta was going to look away but did not, not wanting Jeff to suspect that indeed there was something else that Delia had not told him. She knew that Delia intended to see Roger again. "Give her time. She's desperately trying to pull her life together, to find out what it is that she wants in life." Marta patted Jeff's hand. "I do know she's been happy with you. She's been happy, perhaps for the first time in her life." Marta smiled. "I don't mean to sound melodramatic. You see? She has not been able to see all the good in her life yet."

Marta had meant every word she had said to Jeff, and felt confident that Delia would come back from Berkeley with renewed feelings for him. She was not sure about that any more, because Delia had mentioned in passing she had seen Roger in Berkeley. Now, Jeff was there, all tied up in knots, and Delia was about to give him the manuscript to read. Delia wanted to go to him, ease his pain and kiss away his anger, but she held off. She sat down.

"You've been back two weeks!" Jeff was quite upset. "You don't answer my phone calls." He looked at Delia sitting at the table, pale and drawn, a dazed look in her eyes. His anger began to turn into worry. "Are you sick?"

"I'm sorry," Delia managed to say, smiling at him. "Please, sit down." She pointed at the manuscript. "I want you to take this home and read it as soon as you can." She saw the puzzled look in Jeff's face, got up and walked over to where he was. She rested her head on his chest and put her arms around his neck. "We'll talk about it after you read it."

"I don't understand." He held her at arm's length. "What is it?"

I don't have to do this   No   I want to do it
I love you   I "I love you." Delia said the words softly, then louder and smiled at him. She walked over to the table, picked up the manuscript and handed it to him. "I'm sorry I couldn't find a box to put it in. It's the story of my life. It's not well-written, but it's not bad reading."

Jeff looked at the manuscript, then at Delia and began to move toward the door without saying a word. He had expected, feared the worst, and now he did not know what to think. He turned around, still puzzled, to look at Delia, but she was smiling, a happy smile. He went back and bent over to kiss her.

"Careful," she said, "You're carrying my life in your hands." She laughed. "I'll come to see you, tomorrow, after work. We'll talk about it then." She opened the kitchen door for him, then went with him to the car door.

"Tomorrow," he said and put the manuscript on the car seat, next to him.

Delia waited at the door until the humming of the engine became indistinguishable from all the others. She headed back to the kitchen followed by Marta, whose hands were shaking. "Darling. Are you all right?"

Delia smiled at her aunt. "I'm all right, Auntie." She saw that her aunt was quite distressed and pale, pulled a chair closer to Marta and made her sit down.

Delia knelt in front of her aunt. "I know you're worried," Delia said and she hugged Marta. "It'll be all right. Everything is going to be all right. You'll see." She said it with such assurance that Marta smiled and the color returned to her cheeks.

"He'll forgive you, I'm sure," Marta said when she felt like herself again.

Delia got up and pulled another chair to sit in front of her aunt. "It's not forgiveness I want from him. I haven't done anything wrong. There's nothing to forgive."

Marta looked confused. "I thought. Well. You saw Roger in Berkeley and I thought . . . I don't know what I thought. What is it then?"

"I want him to understand and accept me as I am. As I've been." Delia got up and served a cup of coffee for her aunt and another for herself and put them on the table. "Jeff is still in love with the girl I was when we met. I'm not like her any more." She sighed. "Yes, I saw Roger. I spent a day with him. Perhaps I could have fallen in love with Roger, but I already loved Jeff." *The purloined letter*   *Contemptuously staring at us from the card rack*   *Crumpled*   *Simple*   *Ordinary I searched for happiness hard and long*   *It was everywhere I went*

"I don't understand," Marta said. "I thought you were trying to tell Jeff that you're going to marry Joyce."

"Oh, Auntie. I'm sorry. I should have explained. I'm sorry." Delia passed her hand over her aunt's head. "How can I marry a dream, a fantasy? Just now, you called him Joyce. Don't you see? He'll always be Joyce. In my head and in my heart he's Joyce. A dream."

"So you decided not to marry him."

"I don't think I ever wanted to, but I had to find out what my feelings were, what I wanted." Delia lowered her eyes. "I was using every excuse not to commit myself to anything, go on blaming others for my own lack of courage. Joyce was only an excuse not to accept my love for Jeff." She smiled. "It was a comforting dream while it lasted. It's over now."

Marta smiled, too. "You know? Just now, when you smiled, you looked so much like Asunción your great grandmother."

"The storyteller." *The weaver of words   The weaver of silver threads   The writer   The silversmith*

"Yes, a storyteller, like you." Marta opened her eyes wide, as if she had just remembered something. "Do you have a copy of your novel?" Her enthusiasm was obvious.

"Not of the last three chapters. Why?" Delia was surprised but delighted by her aunt's interest in her work. "Did you like it?"

"Like it? I love it. I've been waiting for you to finish it." She snorted. "I've been dragging Jack to bed early every night so you would have peace and quiet to write. He probably thinks I've finally flipped, but I didn't want to tell him why. I kept my promise. I didn't tell anyone." A white lie, Marta thought, but one that would not hurt anyone. "*Dios mío*, you don't think Jeff would . . ."

"Destroy it?" Delia completed Marta's question. "No." *Would he   No   Probably trample on it with the horse No He wouldn't   He's a poet   But he's a man first No He wouldn't   I don't think I can sleep   I'm so tired A walk   I need to clear my head*

The sun was beginning to set when Delia came back from her walk by Cannery Row. She had lain down for a while hoping to get some rest, but the thought of Jeff sitting somewhere at the ranch, reading her manuscript, had kept her from relaxing enough to fall asleep.

As the day wore on, she was tempted to take out the copy of the incomplete manuscript she had and go over it, just to figure out how long it would take him to read it. *Why am I worried Everything in it happened before we met again   Except for Roger   In Berkeley   He'll be angry because I didn't trust him   How could I   He'll have to understand I'll make him understand   How many pages can one read in six hours* A futile task, she thought, as she put the copy back into the drawer of her desk. There was nothing she could do but wait.

Walking always helped her think clearly. As long as she was moving, no matter how many people were around her, she felt she could concentrate on a problem and, if not solve it, at least look at it calmly.

Mattie was that way, too. Over the years, they had attempted answers to questions about the Chicano movement, the nuclear arms race and the meaning, or lack of it, of the American short story, while walking down the long pier at the marina in Berkeley.

Berkeley, Delia thought, how far away it seemed to her at that moment; yet, she had been there only two weeks before, walking down that same pier with Roger.

"I don't want to go to San Francisco," Delia had told him as the car approached the overpass at the end of University Avenue, and the freeway sign came into view. "Do you mind if we go to Spenger's instead?" *Is that you   Saying that   In that tone of voice   What's the matter with you   No I don't want to go to San Francisco   Why are you punishing him I'm not   You called him   Yes I did   I did*

Delia had sat next to him, in silence, looking straight at the road. Then suddenly, she was not only speaking but requesting a change of plans, in a polite but tense tone of voice.

She would relax after a while, Roger was certain, once they had shared a meal and the awkwardness of meeting again after such a long time had subsided. "Why not? Just tell me how to get there."

Delia did not relax, not before or during their meal. As soon as they sat at their table, her stomach began to hurt, and she looked at the menu trying to find something that would not make the ache worse. She ordered clam chowder, fish a la carte and mineral water, but ate little.

Roger ordered a salad with asparagus and artichoke hearts, a hamburger and iced tea. Delia was surprised at his selection. She expected him to order oysters on the half shell, perhaps filet of sole with a delightfully light lemon butter, as the menu said. She found the irony amusing.

"I study them; I don't eat them," Roger said when catching Delia's amused look. "You have a very nice smile, a very inviting smile."

Cue   Cue   The game has begun   Joyce
Take your places ladies and gentlemen   Wouldn't have said
that He wouldn't   Forget that   Why am I here Easy
Joyce   He's   changed   No   I've   changed   No
We There's no we   No trees   No flowers   End-
less   sand   Scorching   sand   Sleep   Sleep
Don't wake up   Don't

"Thank you," Delia said and looked away. She was glad when the meal was over and they were walking back to the car.

At least the ache is going away   His is just beginning
Why am I fighting this   Am I   Next   I ate too
much   he'll   say   Why   am   I   so   cold   I'm   tired
Why did I call him   He won't say what he thinks   I
won't say what I think   What's he thinking

"Would you like to walk to the marina?" Delia asked him and looked at him directly for the first time since they had left the garden.

She was staring at him and Roger, aware of it, lowered his eyes and nodded. The evanescent image of the man she had made love to, in the mist, on that early November night, flashed in her memory and swiftly vanished. She shuddered and swallowed hard.

Roger raised his eyes and turned to look at her. "I'm not what you expected, am I?" he asked so suddenly that Delia swore for a moment he had read her mind.

"I think you are what I expected." *Suspected* "Suspected." Delia did not know exactly why she had corrected herself, and was surprised when she did not feel uneasy about her behavior. The same thing had happened to her while talking with Mattie the night before—an urgency to articulate what was in her mind at the moment, so that words that began as thoughts would finish in speech.

Roger laughed. "I like that. Let's walk." He took her hand. Delia liked the touch of his hand.

> *Rough palm   Soft back   Distinct   Rough hand Soft hand   One hand Joyce   Roger   It's so hard So hard   It's the same man   The same hands The same walk   The kind eyes   Hamburger Iced tea This is ridiculous   Ironic   Ridiculously ironic*

Delia was beginning to feel better when they reached the long pier at the marina, but her legs and feet still ached. "Would you mind if we sit down for a while?"

"I thought you'd never ask," Roger said, looked around for a bench, then saw the rocks at the bayshore and pointed in their direction. "They'll have to do."

"That's fine." Delia let go of his hand, walked ahead and sat down. Roger stood next to her for a while, putting his hand over his eyes to look at the city of San Francisco, across the bay. "Do you like living in the city?" Delia asked.

"I do. Very much." He sat next to her. "Do you still live in Berkeley? Mattie didn't tell me."

> *A   connection   Finally   Mattie's friend Mattie's friend* "No. I left Berkeley about a year and a half ago. I live in Monterey now."

"Why Monterey?" Roger stretched his legs, then got up, found another rock to sit on so that he could look at her better.

"Why San Francisco?" Delia asked facetiously.

Roger laughed, and Delia remembered the first time she had asked him who he was, on the evening of Mattie's Day of Dead party. He had laughed in the same way as now, but then he had been James Joyce and she, Saint Theresa.

> *You're there   Trapped in that other mind   I see you Then you're gone again   If I put my arms around you If I drew you to me   Would you stay   Would you For a year and a half* "I thought of you many times." *There it is again   I'm like a child   Speaking my mind You're going to get in trouble I'm going to tell on you   No Delia Don't tell Mom She's going to get mad   Mom Ricardo*

got your scissors   Now you've done it

Roger had reached down to turn over a small rock where he had seen a tiny crab hide, when Delia said that. He looked at her, then down, but the crab had slipped away. He put the rock back in place carefully before looking up again.

Crabs will do that to you every time   Now you see them now you don't Delia was going to get up, but Roger held her down.

"I've thought of you, too." He stood up and held his hand out to her, but Delia got up on her own. She stood in front of him, looking into his eyes. She breathed in deeply, in an effort to slow down the accelerated beating of her heart. Then, a coldness spread all over her body.

Roger wanted to take her in his arms, kiss her, as he had done on that November night when they had met, but something in the way she was looking at him made him change his mind. He was feeling like a school boy who had just been told he had failed a test.

"Let's walk down the pier," he suggested, grasping at hope, trying not to think about the futility of his enterprise. Delia turned around and headed toward the pier.

They had walked a short distance, when Delia touched Roger's arm and motioned him to a place by the guardrail. "I owe you an explanation," she said and put her fingers on his mouth when he tried to say it was not necessary.

Roger leaned on the guardrail and looked down. Delia looked at his profile, his eyes fixed on the water below, and for a moment the words failed her. The coldness of the emotions she had experienced by the rocks was slowly growing into a feeling of tenderness that tempered her words when she finally spoke again.

"I thought of you often, about meeting you again, making love as we did that night, in the mist, in the dark. I wanted to have again that feeling of peacefulness I'd had in the arms of the man who called himself James Joyce. I wanted him to soothe the pain, to wipe away the tears and the sorrow, but something in me always stopped me from calling him." Delia looked at Roger, who had raised his head and was now looking straight ahead, but would not look at her. "I think I suspected my reasons for not calling you all along. You see? When James Joyce came along that night I grabbed onto him, and later to his memory, because . . ."

"Because you needed something to look forward to, something that would ease the pain inside, make you forget what you had lost," Roger said and turned around to look at her. "I had hoped that wasn't the case." "

"You knew about it?" *This man knows what I'm going to say even before I know myself*

"How arrogant young people can be," he said teasingly. "When my wife died I also looked for something that would ease the pain and make my sorrow at losing her go away." He pointed toward the Golden Gate Bridge. "I found the sea." He turned to Delia. "But then one day I met you, and I hoped."

"I'm sorry." Delia could hardly say the words; tears were rolling down her cheeks, and she took out the tissue the little boy had given her back at the rose garden and wiped her face with it. "I really am sorry." The tissue was beginning to fall apart.

He took his handkerchief out and finished wiping her tears. "You can't take this one," he said putting it back in his pocket. "You don't need it."

Delia smiled amidst sighs.

"Spend the rest of the day with me." Roger leaned on the guardrail and looked up at the sky. "Until midnight. Then I'll take you home." He turned to look at Delia. "Will you?"

"What did you have in mind?" Delia took a few short breaths and passed her fingers under her eyes, to wipe away the remaining tears. *The proverbial moth playing with the open flame What if   Isn't that what I came to find out*

"The city is full of things to do. We can go to a concert in Golden Gate Park, stroll, go to see a play at the Magic Theater, or go sailing and have dinner at Greens in Fort Mason." He smiled at her. Delia was hesitant. "I promise to behave. It'll be difficult, but I'll try."

Delia had never been on a boat and the idea of spending such a beautiful afternoon sailing was exciting to her. "Sailing, then. Do you have a boat?" Roger nodded.

She was happy, looking at San Francisco and Berkeley at the distance, passing under the Golden Gate Bridge for the first time, then gazing into the ocean to fathom its depth, feeling the tingling in her stomach when the boat swerved to head back to the bay. *How*

*does that poem go   Neruda   The seafarer
One night he lies with death at the bottom of the sea   El
fondo del mar   Sounds better in Spanish   Endless
ocean Liquid dunes   Loneliness is king   I wanted
him that night   And he was there for me   Understood
my sorrow my loneliness   I gave myself to him without hesitation   For the first time   For the first time*

"I see now why you love the sea," she said to Roger when they docked at the Marina. "Mattie read to me what you said about diving." *Sweet   Liquid death   Freedom   At last*

"That." He laughed. "I'm not very good with words."

"That sounded pretty good to me." She took off her life jacket, handed it to Roger and climbed out onto the dock after him. She stopped to look at the western sky, the golden light of the dying sun, now a huge ball sinking slowly into the ocean. "There won't be fog tonight," she said under her breath.

"No, there won't be fog tonight." She heard Roger repeat very close to her ear, then felt his fingers on the back of her neck, then her face. She shuddered and pulled gently away from him. *I can't   Please don't ask me   You see I've been such a fool*

"There's someone else in your life, isn't there?" he asked and Delia turned around to see him. *I wish I could   Spend the rest of this day with you   I would be gone in the morning You see   I love him   I couldn't say that before tonight Jeff   His name is Jeff*

"Are you a mind reader or something?" she teased, trying to ease herself out of giving any explanation. *That Mattie* "Did Mattie tell you?" Delia realized she was again saying whatever was in her mind at the moment. She could not help laughing, feeling like an adult enjoying the candor of a child.

"No, she didn't. I'm just a wise old man."

"Now you're being facetious. An old man. Really."

"In some cultures, a man my age is already a sage," he said. "Is he good to you?"

Delia was puzzled.

"The man you love." He took her by the arm and they began

187

to walk back to the car.

"He is. I've been a fool. Even if I stayed with you tonight, I would be gone in the morning." She answered spontaneously and realized that she was speaking to him without any hesitation. "You must have been a very good doctor; you're a caring person. I realized that the very first time we . . . you talked to me. I think I could tell you my darkest secrets . . ."

He threw his head back and laughed. "People usually do." He looked at her. "I already know your secrets. I learned them that night." He smiled when he saw her blushing. "Artemis. The one from Delos. That's what your name means."

"Yes, that's what it means." *Faithful to the essence of the name given me at birth*

Roger let go of her arm and put his arm around her shoulders. "I'm sorry I didn't try to find you sooner. Delia, the beautiful huntress. You should have dressed like her, like Artemis, that night. Why Saint Theresa?"

"I admire Saint Theresa." *A lot of the huntress in her too The passionate quest for a love beyond mortal love* Delia smiled. "Why James Joyce?"

"Same reason as yours. *Ulysses* is a difficult work to read, but very rewarding in the end. Joyce was able to find the extraordinary in the most ordinary things a man does." He laughed. "Don't get me started on that." He looked around.

"What is it? What are you looking for?"

"A telephone. I just realized Greens, that restaurant I told you about, might not be open on Sundays." He shook his head. "We'll get in the car and look for one. Maybe just go directly there."

"It doesn't matter. I'm hungry enough to eat anything," Delia reassured him. *Even a hamburger   Artichokes and asparagus   And iced tea* "Do you like being a marine biologist?" *He must think I'm crazy   Asking questions like that out of the blue* "I was thinking about my reaction to your liking hamburgers," she explained when he looked baffled.

"I see. Yes to both. I like hamburgers and I like being a marine biologist." He paused. "I loved medicine. Once. Why did I quit then, right?" He pointed at the car across the street. "Mattie says it's time I forgive myself for not being God. Maybe she's right." He chuckled.

"Are you thinking of going with her to Honduras?" Delia asked, looking in both directions as they crossed the street. "Now you're being the mind-reader." He laughed again and pressed her against him. She put her arm around his waist. "Yes, I'm giving it serious consideration. Medical doctors are definitely needed there."

"Would you treat someone who might be fighting against the Sandinistas?" she asked, making Roger stop in the middle of the street and look at her.

"I hope I never have to find out what the answer to that question is."

A cool breeze was beginning to blow, so they stepped up their pace, reached the car and drove away toward the Union Street area and stopped at the Cafe Cantata to eat.

They moved from the subject of literature to music and poetry. Roger told her about his frequent trips to the Sea of Cortez, his friendship with the old Mexican diver who had given him his first lessons, and their search for sunken treasure.

They strolled down Union Street, looked in store windows on their way to the car, then drove back to Berkeley, passing by the Rose Garden on their way up to Mattie's house. Delia told him about the episode earlier that day, which she had already titled "A Poodle in Paradise." Soon after, Roger stopped the car in front of Mattie's house.

"Are you coming in?" Delia asked, after looking at the house to check that Mattie was still awake.

Roger did not answer right away. "No. You give her the news." He tilted his head and looked at her. "Goodbye, Saint Theresa." He leaned forward and held her in his arms.

"Goodbye, Roger," she whispered in his ear, opened the door and ran toward the house.

On her last evening in Berkeley, Delia went with Mattie to San Francisco for dinner and afterwards to a concert at Davies Hall. Back at the house, Mattie started a fire regardless of it being a warm evening, and they had to open the windows not to suffocate. They sat around talking, drinking brandy and listening to all their favorite records well into the night.

Delia told her about her encounter with Roger, her face glowing with the certainty that she had finally found the answers she had been looking for.

"Little Delia has become a woman. What now?" Mattie said and ruffled Delia's hair.

"Make peace with my mother. Begin that group. Finish my novel." A new set of dreams, Delia thought, but now she was sure she could attain them. "Show it to Jeff. Take it from there." She opened her mouth, took a deep breath and let it out slowly. "Then I'll probably rewrite the whole thing. Confession time is over."

"Why show it to Jeff now? Why not when you've rewritten it? Is there anything in it that he shouldn't read?" A feeling of concern was nagging at Mattie, but she could not quite express it.

"Everything. Almost everything," Delia said under her breath. "Who I am. What I am. All there, in black and white."

"Why do you feel you have to do that now?"

"Because he'll find out eventually. Because I can't go on telling half-truths to myself and to those I love." Delia looked at Mattie who seemed suddenly upset. "What's the matter?"

"Boy. The Catholic Church did quite a job on you. This need to confess. *Coño*! *Carajo*!"

Delia laughed. "And the Panamanians did you a good one, too. Swearing, and in Spanish."

"They did, didn't they?" Mattie sat down and began to laugh, too. "Now, seriously. Why do you want Jeff to read this?"

"Because I want my life. I'm tired of being what someone else wants me to be. I want to stop living my nightmares, being afraid of myself, always asking for forgiveness." Delia was getting tired of having to explain the reasons that, as far as she was concerned, required no further clarification. *She's just worried about me   Why shouldn't she be   I've hesitated for so long I've changed   Have I   Really   Maybe I'll weaken again   Go back to the old ways   Silence No I can't go back to that   I guess it'll take time for people to see me with different eyes   I'll have to be patient* "Anyway," she added. "No matter how much I change things, names, in the rewriting, Jeff will know, my parents will know. Nothing can be the same after that."

Mattie put her hand on Delia's. "You're right." She could not help worrying about what Jeff might do. How would Delia take it if he ended their relationship? "What do you think he'll do?"

"I don't know, Mattie." Delia picked up a piece of lint from the carpet and began to roll it between her fingers. "I think he will understand." She threw the ball of lint away. "It might hurt some, but he will. I'll make him understand." She bit her lower lip. "I do love him very much. I do want to spend the rest of my life with him."

"And you're still willing to risk it?" Mattie smiled.

"Do I have a choice? Does any woman really, if she wants to be true to herself?" Delia stood up.

"I usually don't pray, but this time I'll make an exception." Mattie winked at Delia. "I'll pray for both of us, since I'm going to follow your example and try to publish my articles. Let's have another brandy. I think we deserve it."

The next afternoon, Delia stopped at the market and bought a cooler, two bags of ice and two loaves of sourdough bread; she picked up a half gallon of strawberry ice cream for Jeff and a half gallon of blueberry cheese cake for herself from Bott's on College Avenue. She arranged everything in the cooler, using the bag of books of Soto's poetry she had bought for Jeff to hold the lid in place.

She crossed the Bay Bridge with her precious cargo and from far above it she saw the fog moving in waves toward the city, the three columns of the Sutro Tower emerging from it like Neptune's trident from the ocean. It would be over the East Bay at about the same time she reached Monterey. It would wrap like cotton candy around the pine tree at Mattie's house, where she had once stood half-crazed and frightened on a Day of the Dead, in a city called Berkeley, a place lost in the fog.

> *To this desolate place*
> *where flowers bloom in darkness*
> *and birds die singing at dawn*
> *with bow and arrow I've come*
> *to the precincts of this day*
> *to hunt the light.*